HARD UNDERWRITING

Non-fiction books by Philippe Espinasse
IPO: A Global Guide (Hong Kong University Press, 2011, 2014)
IPO Banks: Pitch, Selection and Mandate (Palgrave Macmillan, 2014)

As joint author:
Study Manual for the IPO Sponsor Examinations in Hong Kong
(Hong Kong Securities and Investment Institute, 2013)

As co-author:
The IPO Guide 2012 (LexisNexis, 2012)
The Hong Kong IPO Guide 2013 (LexisNexis, 2012)

HARD UNDERWRITING

a novel by

Philippe Espinasse

P&C BOOKS

Hard Underwriting

ISBN 978-988-14272-0-5 (paperback)
ISBN 978-988-14272-1-2 (Kindle)

© 2015 Philippe Espinasse
Published by P&C Books, a division of P&C Ventures Limited
10/F Central Building
1 Pedder Street, Central, Hong Kong

Edited and typeset by Alan Sargent
Cover design by Damonza

Contents

For Rodney Ward

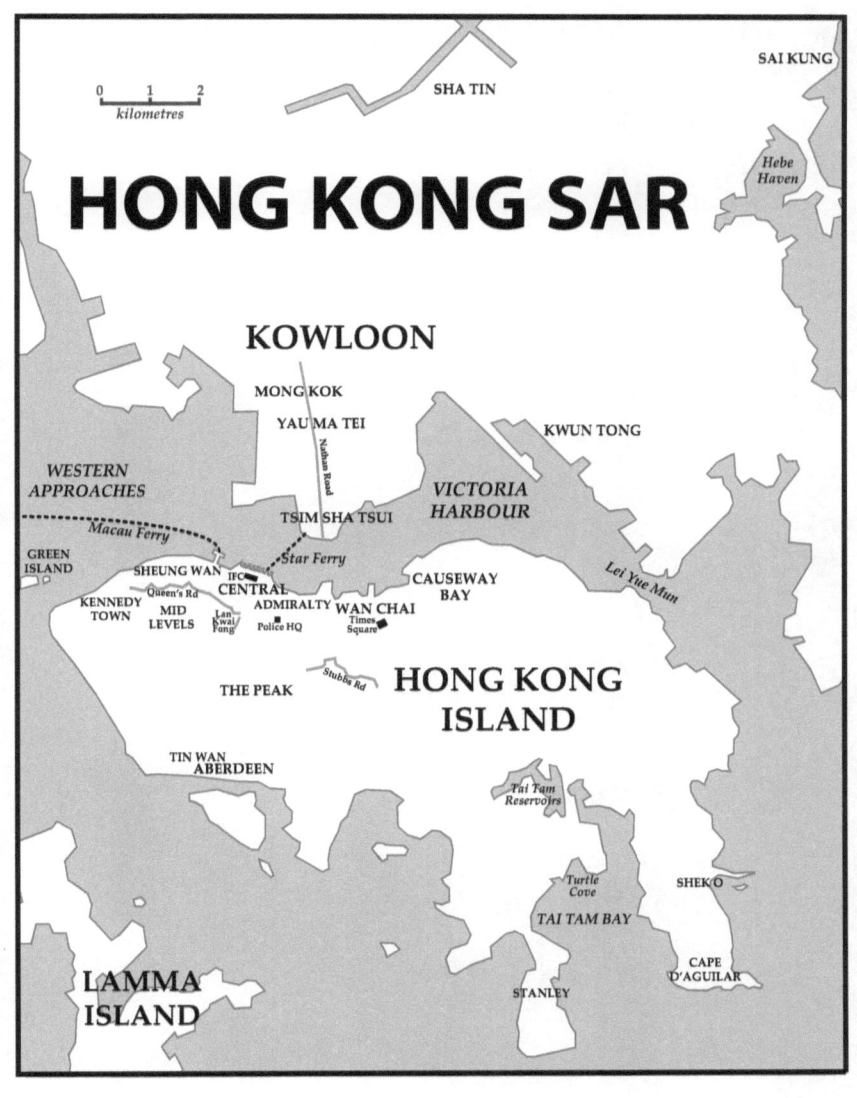

Part I
STEEL

CHAPTER 1

0:58 am, Central, Hong Kong, 29 September 2017

A REFRESHING, LATE SUMMER SHOWER fell on the city as a group of giggling girls crossed the street. They hopped over puddles and the rivulets making their way down the gutters and sought refuge from the rain in a nearby bar. It was almost one in the morning but the area was still busy, even though it was only a Thursday. Music blared from one venue to the next in a raucous cacophony. Lan Kwai Fong was one of two main clubbing and entertainment districts on Hong Kong Island. Created in the 1980s, it continually reinvented itself over the years. It had seen endless changes in bars and restaurants, but a handful of longstanding favourites were still going strong. They never ceased to channel a steady flow of patrons.

Visitors and foreign residents made up much of the clientele and many of those who came there did so as respite from the punishing hours they had to work. Conversely, the money was good, even if the generous packages of the past had largely been discontinued, and the tax regime was one of the world's sweetest. Overall, it was a satisfying life, especially when compared to one in a Western world depressingly stuck in deflation and unemployment. Bar the odd typhoon, the weather was also much nicer.

The rain finally stopped. Andrew Short, a tall, fair-haired Australian in his late thirties finished his beer and tossed the empty bottle of Beck's into a street bin. He followed D'Aguilar Street and then Wellington Street towards his home in the nearby district of Sheung Wan. It had, yet again, been a boozy evening and by now, he had really had enough. Things had started with late afternoon drinks at the Captain's Bar in the Mandarin Oriental Hotel, with fellow bankers. A team dinner at a private kitchen had followed. It had ended far too late. Against his best judgement, his senses already dulled by the alcohol, he had gone to Lan Kwai Fong with some of his colleagues for a nightcap.

Andrew passed the Kee Club, a members' only nightclub, whose premises were located above a Chinese restaurant. Glossy roasted geese hung in rows in the kitchen window, almost a mirror image of the queue of people trying to get in. He walked up towards Lyndhurst Terrace and crossed the street, now within spitting distance of the Mid Levels escalator. At that time the moving walkway was still and silent. It would start again at 6 am, when it would ferry commuters for the best part of a kilometre, down to the business district of Central. Later, it would switch directions, heading back up to the high-density blocks of condos. Andrew passed the concrete staircase that led up to the escalator and followed Gage Street. It was badly lit and quiet, a marked contrast to the noisy daytime scene with hawkers selling everything from mangoes and orchids to razor clams. The air was damp, with a faint smell of rotting food. Above, a signboard with Chinese characters advertising a noodle shop creaked, swaying in the light breeze, water dripping from its metal bars.

Andrew's apartment was nearby. He had bought it at a depressed price at the height of the SARS crisis, after relocating to Hong Kong in 2003. He was now sitting on a substantial paper profit, which he looked forward to cashing in one day as a tax-free capital gain.

He was almost home when a silhouette behind an arcade pillar caught his attention. The man was of average height. He was dressed in dark colours, blending in with the shadows. He wore a surgical mask, a common sight in the city. For some reason, even partly hidden, the face looked familiar. What was most unusual, however, was that the stranger was standing completely motionless, looking straight at Andrew with a strange intensity.

The banker did not worry unduly and stopped paying attention. Hong Kong was one of the safest places in Asia, if not the world, certainly compared to New York and some of the other cities he had lived in. Perhaps the man was drunk, not an unreasonable assumption at this late hour. Or maybe he was high on drugs. Either way, it would be best to just ignore him. Sheung Wan was simply not an area in which to fret about mugging, even at night. Andrew searched with his right hand in his trouser pocket to retrieve his keys. He sensed the stranger had now moved and positioned himself just behind him. Maybe there was more to it than he had first thought.

He slowly turned his head to investigate and heard a high-pitched scream. All he saw next was a flash of metal. He felt a punch to his gut. His knees buckled and he collapsed on the floor, banging his head hard on the pavement. Dizzy and now lying in a puddle, he brought his trembling hand to his lower abdomen. He felt a warm liquid and a wet, gelatinous mass trickle down his fingers. The rain had started falling again. The man was gone. Andrew's vision started to play tricks, blurring surrounding objects in a growing vortex of flashing lights. It suddenly dawned on him, without a shadow of a doubt, that he was going to die, alone in this dank alleyway. Terror filled his mind. Then sounds started to fade away. He was cold. He could not feel his feet and fingers any more. He kept blinking, fast, his breathing increasingly laboured. Finally, darkness took over and everything went black.

CHAPTER 2

Sha Tin, New Territories, 18 August 2006

ETHAN HAD THE DREAM again. He woke, panting and sweating, holding on to the sheets as if for dear life.

It was at the end of his second year in the Special Duties Unit, an elite paramilitary detachment of the Hong Kong Police Force, better known locally as the 'Flying Tigers'. It had only about 100 members, compared to the 28,000 police officers serving in the city. In its forty years of existence, fewer than 390 people had made the cut. Much to Ethan's surprise, he was one of the twenty-five per cent who completed the eleven-day initial selection course. The following nine months of counter-terrorism tactics, hostage-rescue drills and physical-endurance exercises pushed his body and stamina to their limits. Upon graduation, he could shoot a target the size of a clementine from a distance of 100 metres with a 9 mm Heckler & Koch MP5 submachine gun.

When the call had come, Ethan was one of those on duty. There was no uniform. A quick reaction time was key and SDU members turned up wearing whatever they had on at the time. That day, he wore a pair of jeans and a grey polo shirt. He and his fellow officers from the Action Group's 'B' Assault Team had each donned some twenty kilogrammes of gear. His own equipment included, in addition to his MP5 with a telescopic sight, a bulletproof armoured vest, protective earphones, night vision goggles, and an SIO NBC respirator. He also carried his Glock 17 semi-automatic pistol with spare magazines in a holster on his right thigh.

Their pre-mission briefing had made the target look straightforward. On the eleventh floor of a decaying residential block in Sha Tin, in the New Territories, a desperate man had taken his family hostage. He had threatened to kill his wife and toddler, and then himself. It was a dramatic end to an everyday drama that had first seen the man lose his job and gradually fall into alcoholism and, later, drug abuse. It was not even clear exactly what he was trying to achieve. Ethan reckoned he was perhaps simply craving attention, after having been ignored by the rest of society for too long.

The negotiator had done his very best but, after a few hours, it was clear the man could not be brought to reason. It had then been decided by the powers-that-be to send in the SDU to neutralise him. The idea was not to shoot him: that would be done as a last resort, only to immobilise him. There had been no chance to explore the inside of the premises with a spy camera, but the team had studied blueprints of the flat. It was a small dwelling of not more than 325 square feet. There would not be much of an opportunity for the man to hide inside. Security bars prevented entry through the windows, so the SDU could not rappel down from the roof. They would go in through the front door with a battering ram, throw in a couple of flash-bang stun grenades and rescue the wife and kid. End of story. Nothing they had not all done or trained for many times before. The whole operation was expected to be over within a few seconds.

There was an unnerving silence as they arrived on the eleventh floor lift lobby. The smell of steamed rice hung in the air. A two-man team prepared to break the front door down. Ethan and his partner Steven, working as a pair, stood behind them, ready to burst into the flat. Ethan whispered a count-down, so that they could synchronise their moves.

'Three, two, one, go!'

The lock gave way under the heavy mass of metal. Ethan kicked in the door, threw in a couple of stun grenades, and stepped into the apartment. His line of fire focused on the left, Steven's on the opposite side.

Everything started to go horribly wrong. Two more armed men were waiting for them, in addition to the disgruntled father. Instead of the expected meat cleaver, they now faced two AK-74s. Each weapon was capable of continuously shooting thirty 5.45 mm cartridges. As the SDU officers battled the two men who shot at them from behind a makeshift barricade of cheap furniture, Ethan heard the child's cry. He turned his head and saw the father. The man glared back and shot his four year-old daughter at point blank range with a pistol.

After this, the shoot-out continued uninterrupted for several seconds. In the end, all of the flat's occupants, including the mother, were killed. Steven was also a casualty. Ethan himself took a round in the upper arm, but the injury was light and would be of no consequence. A subsequent enquiry described the entire operation as an unmitigated disaster, flawed with intelligence failures.

What never went away, however, was the dream. In it, Ethan first always heard the girl's desperate cry for help. Before he could react, he felt the loud crack of the shot. Then his point of view switched to that of the bullet, moving in slow motion through the air, sliding through hair and cranial bones then piercing connective tissue and fibrous membranes. As it dove deeper, it inflicted fatal damage on a scale equivalent to several times the round's diameter, before exploding outwards again, in a red, white, pink and grey shower of bone chips. It was always the same. Elation and a rush of adrenaline at first, followed by foreboding and, finally, horror.

A ringing snapped him from the past back to his room. Drenched in sweat, Ethan opened his eyes and saw the flashing light of his mobile. His hand grabbed the handset and he answered the call.

CHAPTER 3

6:30 am, Sheung Wan, Hong Kong, 29 September 2017

CHIEF INSPECTOR OF POLICE Ethan Blake parked his car, a battered grey Toyota, on Lyndhurst Terrace. It was already hot, over thirty degrees Celsius. He wore plain clothes, rather than his uniform with the rank badge featuring three diamonds. As second in charge of his unit in the Department of Crime and Security, also known as the 'B' Department, he was stationed at the Arsenal House police headquarters in Wan Chai. More than ten years earlier, the botched mission in Sha Tin had been the SDU's first-ever failure, out of more than 150 operations. He had left the 'Flying Tigers' and joined another unit in the wake of the incident. It had taken time for him to get over the shame, but he had since steadily risen through the officer ranks. In his mid-thirties, he was now well on his way to making superintendent, perhaps in another year's time.

Ethan was a bit of an oddity in the force. Born of a British father and Chinese mother, his name made others assume he was an expatriate police officer. Only 120 of these remained in the city, as compared to nine times that number when the crown colony had been returned to Beijing. But there was no mistaking his Chinese features. And his Cantonese, a requirement for serving in the police since the mid-1990s, was as fluent as his English. With jet-black hair, he was of medium height – 174 cm – and build. He was no longer required to follow the gruelling training regime imposed by the SDU, but was still in excellent physical shape.

Violent crime was uncommon in Hong Kong. Just over sixty cases of murder and manslaughter had been recorded in the past year. But even that had been a bit of a record. Many of these took place in the New Territories, or in the marine region, which covered the port and the outer waters. For Hong Kong Island itself, the numbers were down to single digits, and at a forty-year low. It was not a bad result for a territory of 7.2 million. Maybe Hong Kong was a world-class city after all, as the government liked to remind everyone, on all occasions. The murder that had been perpetrated the previous night was therefore sufficiently rare to justify the presence of a chief inspector at the crime scene.

Unlike most Hongkongers, Ethan was not a tea drinker. The Pacific Coffee branch at the corner of Hollywood Road would still be closed at this hour, but he was badly in need of caffeine to jumpstart his system. Cursing, he walked down Gage Street and saw a closed tea house on his left. On the way, he passed a small market stall. Three elderly women were already busy showcasing their wares, as they did every single day. They wore traditional *Hakka* hats, with fringes on the brim shaped like miniature curtains. All three were wrinkled and bent.

'Good morning, aunties,' he greeted them jovially.

Police tape was already restricting access to the street. He flashed his warrant card to a couple of beat-patrol officers on guard duty and walked towards the small crowd that had assembled near the junction with Graham Street. The crime-scene team had started taking pictures and combing the area for clues. Among them, he recognised Suki Lam. In her mid-twenties, with shoulder-length hair tied back in a ponytail, she had recently been assigned to his unit as its most junior inspector, after completing the standard criminal investigation course, as well as a short stint in a crime post. It was she who had called him earlier. She too was wearing plain clothes today, with a pair of blue jeans, a beige blouse and low-cut hiking shoes.

'Hello. Have you eaten yet?' asked Ethan.

She nodded curtly in answer to the traditional Cantonese greeting.

'What's the story?' he asked.

'*Gweilo*. Late thirties. Never seen anything like it. Almost cut in half.'

Ethan looked down at a tall, blond man. Around him, investigators were busy swabbing and collecting tissue samples. There was a nasty bruise on the right side of the man's head. What had been a well-cut, navy-blue suit and an impeccable, white tailored shirt were now completely ripped from one side to the other. They were soaked in blood and what looked like dribbling internal organs. Some of the liquid had oozed towards a pair of once immaculately polished black shoes. A small pool had formed where one of the feet, at an angle, stopped the nauseating liquid from flowing further down. The smell was revolting.

'What a mess,' he said.

'The owner of the flower stall found him earlier. Around 5:45. She said she didn't touch anything and called us immediately,' said Suki.

Ethan took a closer look at the body.

'It's a very clean cut. What do you think did it?'

'It doesn't look like it was a meat cleaver,' she said, 'so it's unlikely to be triad killing. And they don't target expatriates. I'd say he was killed by a machete, or some sort of long knife, maybe even a sword?'

'Perhaps. Do we have an estimate for the time of death?' asked Ethan.

'The doc said some time between midnight and two o'clock. Looking at the eyelids, neck and jaw, *rigor mortis* has only just set in. Personally, I'd say closer to two is more likely. Otherwise, he would probably have been discovered earlier. Some of the restaurants close very late around here.'

'Yep. All makes sense to me. But let's leave that to the coroner for now. Who's our man anyway?'

'Andrew Short. Australian. Permanent resident. We found his Hong Kong ID, as well as business cards in a silver holder. It looks like he was an investment banker. Not a mugging. His wallet is still there, together with a thick wad of cash. And also his watch.'

She looked down at her notes, which she held with a pair of surgical gloves.

'Italian made, Panerai. He also had a BlackBerry and an iPhone on him,' she said.

'Any idea what he was doing there?'

'There was a telephone bill in one of his pockets. He lived here. We also found some keys. They match the front door lock. There was a credit card slip from the Captain's Bar, at the old Mandarin Hotel, and also one from a private kitchen in D'Aguilar Street, both from last night. They had quite a bit to drink, too. Corkage alone was close to two thousand dollars.'

Ethan made a quick mental calculation and sighed at the number of bottles they would have consumed.

'Let's get a few constables to check out the neighbouring buildings. Maybe someone wasn't sleeping and saw something out of the ordinary,' he said.

'Will do.'

Suki sipped a yellow liquid from a clear water bottle, in which green tea leaves gently floated.

'Look for CCTV camera tapes. Although frankly in this area, it's mostly older blocks. There can't be that many. If he came from Lan Kwai Fong, then he would have arrived the same way I did, so let's extend the search to the eastern end of Wellington Street. Also the opposite way, right down to Gough Street, and back up to Hollywood Road. Whoever killed him might have come from there.'

Suki jotted in her notepad. Ethan could be patronising at times, but she had learnt a lot since joining his team. She was becoming increasingly proficient, not only at processing large amounts of data, but also at seeing the wood for the trees.

'We should also notify his consulate, and his employer,' he added.

'That would be Morgan Roberts Securities. He was a managing director there and ...' again, Suki looked down at her notes, '... also head of equity syndicate for Asia, whatever that means.'

'Okay. Ask them for next of kin. We'll need a meeting with Morgan Roberts, as soon as possible. HR department. And we should visit the Captain's Bar and the private kitchen when they open for business, later today. We need to find out more about this guy. Who he was with, what he said, whether he got into an argument or fight with someone.'

'Sure.'

'I'll ask Andy what he can glean from his mobiles. Especially anything Short might have sent or received over the last twelve hours. We'll have a catch-up with the team in the afternoon to compare notes. Can you tell the others?'

Suki nodded.

'That's where he lived, right?'

'Yes. Just there, the blue door.'

'Okay. If he lived alone, make sure no one accesses his flat. Check the keys for fingerprints, in case someone visited afterwards. Personally, I doubt it. Whoever did this probably wouldn't have stayed for long.'

A crowd of curious onlookers had already started to assemble, just behind the police tape. The media would also turn up soon, as always, for their daily dose of human misery. Homicides involving expatriates were extremely rare and this one had all the hallmarks of a high-profile case. The ACP, the Assistant Commissioner of Police (Crime), himself, one of the top two honchos and directors of 'B' Department, would clearly keep tabs on it personally. The press would be all over the story too. Ethan felt like he had picked the short straw.

He checked his watch. For the first time that morning he allowed himself a faint smile. The coffee shop would be open by now.

CHAPTER 4

THE MEETING WITH Morgan Roberts had been arranged that same morning. The bank had provided the police with the contact details of Andrew Short's mother, in Melbourne. She in turn, had been informed of the demise of her son. Short also had a brother, who lived in Singapore. He was already on a flight and would be able to identify the body, hopefully later in the afternoon. Not that there was much doubt about the identity of the deceased, but one had to follow procedure.

Morgan Roberts' offices were on Central's waterfront in IFC Two, one of the twin office towers at opposite ends of the International Finance Centre shopping mall, one of the largest in the city. The tower's address is Number 8 Finance Street and, true to form, a variety of investment banks, brokers and hedge funds populate its eighty-eight floors. Eighty-eight is a particularly auspicious number, as the word 'eight' sounds like 'prosperity' in Chinese. Some 15,000 people work in the building, an impressive glass and metal anthill of busy executives; pretty much all of them exclusively devoted to the making of money.

The venerable firm of Morgan Roberts, a leading American investment bank, occupied several of the higher floors. Ethan registered at a desk on the ground floor and was issued a pass granting him access to the building. After changing lifts at one of the transfer lobbies on the thirty-fifth floor, he finally arrived at the bank's reception. There, a spectacular cascading fountain and a water pond with *koi* carp greeted him. In *feng shui,* water signifies wealth, and there was no mistaking what Morgan Roberts was all about. Three uniformed female receptionists sat behind a massive white marble desk that must have weighed several tons. Ethan introduced himself and showed his warrant card. He then asked for Miranda Lai, the firm's head of human resources. One of the receptionists quietly ushered him into a large meeting room. The rooms were named after cities, all major financial centres. Modern artwork graced the walls. The furniture looked expensive, but, at the same time, it was functional.

The views encompassed the harbour and entire panorama of Kowloon. According to folklore, the rolling hills beyond were the backs of the 'nine dragons' that, in Cantonese, gave the peninsula its name. The hills faded into thin clouds in the distance. Facing him, another gleaming skyscraper had recently emerged. Together with IFC Two, it created a giant gateway for the cruise and container ships that criss-crossed what was still one of the busiest waterways in the world. At 108 floors, the International Commerce Centre, was, for now, the tallest building in Hong Kong.

More often than not, these days, the view was shrouded in mist and smog, by-products of the increasing pollution both in Hong Kong and across the border in mainland China. That day, however, the sky was a blue palette. For once, the scintillating skyscrapers showed all of their crisp edges. After knocking at the door, a tea lady brought Ethan the cup of espresso he had requested when shown in. Miranda Lai finally arrived.

She introduced her colleagues, after handing out her name card with both hands, as was customary. First was a towering Englishman in his fifties with a loud voice, named Rodney Simmons. He was the firm's head of regional investment banking. Next came an amiable Indian, Ashok Patel, who introduced himself as head of equity capital markets. A diminutive, but severe-looking Chinese lady called Karen Wong was last, and the head of legal and compliance.

The bankers all moved to one side of a polished teak table, facing Ethan.

'Thank you for seeing me at such short notice,' he said, 'I'm very sorry for your loss.'

'What do we know at this stage? What happened?' asked Miranda Lai.

'Mr Short's body was discovered after dawn, just outside the building in which he lived. We're still investigating, but it looks like he was stabbed there last night.'

Karen Wong sighed and covered her mouth with her hand. She quickly added, 'Forgive me, we're all very shocked.'

'Could you tell me about Andrew Short, please? We don't know too much about him,' asked Ethan.

Simmons nodded, 'He joined us about six years ago, from Credit Suisse in Hong Kong. He had also spent a few months with them in London and Dubai.' He looked briefly at a small notepad placed in front of him, and added, 'Prior to 2001, he was with Goldman Sachs in New York. That's where he started his career. He was a very safe pair of hands, well liked by everyone. Just a great guy.'

'What was his role exactly?'

'Andrew headed our syndicate desk for the region, within our equity capital markets department. He reported to Ashok,' said Simmons.

'Syndicate?'

Ashok Patel took over at this point.

'His responsibilities included liaising with his counterparts at other firms, and also the marketing phase of transactions, across twelve countries. Basically the whole of Asia, excluding Japan and Australia.'

Ethan nodded.

'His title was managing director, as I see some of you also are. How many are there at your firm?'

'We have a fifty-one MDs in Asia, excluding Japan, out of 2,000 employees in the region. It's our most senior rank,' snapped Miranda Lai, who was not one of them, at the same time nervously kicking a heel against a chair leg.

'I see. And how well did Mr Short perform?'

Patel answered again.

'As Rodney has alluded, he was very good at what he did – my God! I can't even believe I'm already talking about him in the past tense! He had a lot of experience, across many products and jurisdictions. We promoted him shortly after hiring him. We took great care of him, too. He was particularly well paid, even compared to many of his peers.'

'He had just closed a great block trade for us in the Philippines,' said Simmons. 'We made a killing,' he continued, perhaps a bit too enthusiastically, 'sorry, forgive my unfortunate choice of words.'

Ethan raised his hand to indicate no offence had been taken.

'Do you know anyone who might have had issues with him? A recent dispute?'

'I'm not aware of any. As I said, he was well liked, by his seniors and juniors alike,' said Patel, stroking an immaculate grey worsted suit with the back of his hand. 'But it would perhaps be a good idea to talk to his direct reports,' he added, 'they would have known him better, on a personal level.'

'Listen,' cut in Simmons, 'we're in the business of making money here. More often than not, our gain is someone else's loss, whether it's trading equity, selling a company, competing for IPO business or even hiring a star analyst.'

The compliance lady discreetly shook her head, clearly not liking the speech.

'I can't say investment banks are held in high regard, these days. We've also taken a lot of flak since the sub-prime crisis and the collapse of Lehman Brothers. Clearly, this is a very competitive, an *increasingly competitive industry,*' he continued, 'but, at the end of the day, it's still a small world. We all know one another. There are obviously issues between firms from time to time, but clearly not to the point where we would kill each other. At least, not in this century.'

'He was divorced, I understand?' asked Ethan.

Ashok Patel sighed.

'Ah yes. That's, how shall I put it, a rather . . . complicated story,' he said, pulling at a cuff.

'What do you mean?'

'Well, I believe it was about three or four years ago. His wife, Kylie, got intrigued by regular payments made from one of his accounts to a bank in Thailand. I think it was the Thai Military Bank, one of the largest. She confronted him, and he finally admitted to a long-standing relationship.'

'That Thai girl was an absolute stunner, actually,' said Simmons, keen to add colour to the story.

'The issue, you see, is that he had also fathered a child with her, in Bangkok,' said Patel.

'Oh, I understand.'

'But that wasn't the end of it, far from it. Strangely, Kylie let him be, at first. But, a year later. . . .'

'Yet another woman?'

'I'm afraid so,' acknowledged Patel, 'and in Thailand, as well. Thank God, no baby that time.'

Rodney Simmons repeatedly nodded, his lips pinched, fondly remembering the episode. It had obviously done the rounds many times within the firm.

'So, would you say Andrew Short was a bit of . . . a player, then? Sorry, I'm not sure what the right choice of word would be.'

'Let's just say his personal life was complicated. But as far as his work was concerned, it was first class,' said Patel.

'Could it have been his ex-wife seeking revenge?'

'I wouldn't know, of course, but it's doubtful. She received a large lump sum as part of the divorce, and I believe substantial alimony payments. I can't see why she would have put an end to the arrangement. The divorce goes way back, water under the bridge and all that. And, obviously, the same goes for Porn and Hom.'

'I beg your pardon?' asked Ethan, suddenly taken aback.

'Sorry. The two ladies, in Thailand.'

'Oh, right.'

'When will the family be able to send his casket and personal belongings back to Australia?' asked Miranda Lai.

'In a few days' time, I hope. We still have to conduct an autopsy before the coroner can grant the order to take the body outside Hong Kong. I'm sure you understand. I won't take any more of your time. My colleagues or I will contact you later, if we have further questions. And I suspect we may want to talk to his team members, as was kindly suggested.'

After he had left the building, Ethan's mobile rang. It was Suki.

'All the paperwork's in hand. There were no prints other than his on the keys. But it looks like no one could have gone to the flat last night anyway. You'll understand when we get there. And he lived alone. Shall I meet you there at noon for a look-see? They will expedite the autopsy for us later today. The pathologist will be Alfred Kwok.

CHAPTER 5

11:59 am, Sheung Wan, Hong Kong, 29 September 2017

A S ETHAN RETURNED to the crime scene, the heat was almost unbearable. Suki waited opposite the blue door under a small canopy, in an attempt to shelter from the blistering midday sun. The building was one of only a few in that part of Sheung Wan to have undergone a major makeover. It looked very slick, especially compared to some of the older *tong lau* in the surrounding area, their peeling paint and rusty window frames relics of a distant era. It was a low-rise for Hong Kong, with only six floors, but it had a round-the-clock reception desk. This was manned by an ageing and stiff Nepalese man, who had served in a British Gurkha regiment, prior to the 1997 handover. There was no CCTV outside the building, but the reception and common areas were all under the surveillance of a network of wall-mounted cameras. Some of Ethan's colleagues had already taken the disk that contained the recordings for the previous twenty-four hours. The night-shift guard had been questioned in the morning. He had not seen anything. The entrance door to the building was closed at night and did not offer a view of the street.

The lift, a rarity for a building dating from the 1950s in this part of town, had been replaced fairly recently. Ethan and Suki rode it to Andrew Short's penthouse. On the way up, they saw through its modern glass doors that each floor was comprised of three apartments. The top level, however, was different. It had been extensively remodelled and merged into a single, much larger, flat. The front door was painted black and heavily reinforced, access to it restricted by blue police tape. The caretaker downstairs had told them there was no alarm system. They both donned plastic gloves. Two keys from Short's personal set gave them entry to the property. There were no signs of any untoward visit, lending further credence to the night guard's testimony. It would have taken a considerable amount of time to pick what were obviously high-quality locks and, under the added scrutiny of a security guard on the ground floor and of a camera lens, it sounded implausible.

'As I mentioned on the phone, he lived alone. But an *amah* came twice a week, in the morning, on Mondays and Thursdays. She works for someone else in the building, but she's been away in the Philippines for about a week,' said Suki.

Most of the apartment was open-plan. It had a modern kitchen and a combined living room and dining area. They were set around a circular staircase that led to a roof terrace. Windows on three sides bathed the loft in light, the impression of airiness emphasised by the high ceiling. To the back were two bedrooms, each with a sizeable *en suite* bathroom. Only one looked to have been lived in. There was an extensive collection of wristwatches. Short liked them bulky and flashy. A closet spanning an entire wall was full of custom-made suits and shirts, with a smaller assortment of casual clothes.

Much of the kitchen was taken over by three side-by-side, custom-made, floor-to-ceiling, temperature-controlled wine cabinets with glass doors. There was no mistaking some of the labels, mostly high-end châteaux and domaines from Bordeaux, Burgundy and the Rhône Valley. It was expensive stuff, an investment banker's treasure trove. Andrew Short had obviously been a bit of a wine buff.

'Wow!' said Suki, 'there are two rows of DRC! And cases of Pétrus too! That alone is worth as much as a small flat.'

Ethan opened the door of a large refrigerator in silver metal. In it were an apple, two eggs, and a dozen bottles of beer, from German and Czech breweries. There was also a half-empty bottle of Puligny-Montrachet ier Cru, tightly closed with a vacuum stopper.

Everything was very neat, almost impersonal. There was little artwork, other than a handful of framed posters, and only a few books, the usual well-thumbed best sellers he would perhaps have read on airplanes. No safe. No car keys. The furniture was sparse and mostly contemporary, except for a Chinese opium bed in dark tones recycled as a chic coffee table, and which took up much of the sitting room. On it were piles of auction catalogues and wine and sailing magazines. Ethan made a mental note to check with the Marine Department if Andrew Short owned a boat. Many yacht clubs were dotted around the territory.

Facing a wall was a writing desk, almost bare. On it was a laptop computer. A flashing router on the floor hinted at an active Wi-Fi connection. Next to it, a colour printer was idle, its green stand-by light on. A thick pile of investment banking pitch books stood at its side. Perhaps Short worked from home from time to time? There, he would review presentations drafted by junior bankers, late at night back in the IFC Two tower. In a drawer, they found a tiny plastic bag with a white powder.

'So, it seems our banker had a taste for the high life,' Ethan said.

'It's not all that unusual is it? Especially in the finance industry,' replied Suki. 'But, don't you think it's an almost depressing apartment? I find it very clinical.'

'He probably didn't spend much time at home. Maybe he ate out a lot? He was divorced, by the way, quite a story too. I'll tell you later. Those bankers travel a fair bit, you know.'

'Yes, but he had lived in Hong Kong for more than a dozen years. There's hardly anything personal at all here. Perhaps he simply didn't care?'

'I agree there doesn't seem to be much worth probing. The only thing remotely of interest, other than the cocaine, is probably the computer. Andy should take a look, after he's gone through the mobiles.'

Ethan disconnected the laptop from the mains and placed it in its padded pouch he found lying on the floor.

All that remained to explore was the upper level. The staircase led to a small landing, from which a door opened onto a terrace. It was covered in teak wood, with a small palm tree in one of the corners. There were a few towers around, but most of the nearby buildings weren't all that high. The terrace was quite pleasant, with open views of the city. Waterproof sofas faced each other around a coffee table. Above, a piece of heavy-duty canvas provided protection from the sun. It was canted so that water wouldn't accumulate on the fabric when it rained. In a corner was a large electric barbecue – Short was

Australian after all. It was an intimate area for socialising, away from the busy streets down below.

Short's flat singled him out as a workaholic. But it offered no clues to solving his death. They would need to investigate his past and his work.

CHAPTER 6

3:45 pm, Wan Chai, Hong Kong, 29 September 2017

THE INVESTIGATION TEAM had assembled on the sixteenth floor of the East Wing of Arsenal House. It was one of the four buildings that made up the police headquarters on Arsenal Street, in the district of Wan Chai. The main forty-seven-floor skyscraper included state-of-the-art facilities, with several conference rooms and even an indoor shooting range. Peter Ma, the assistant commissioner and head of the Crime Division, had insisted in meeting with Ethan beforehand. There were high expectations at the most senior levels that the case would be solved in short order, he had said. A brutal homicide of an Australian was the last thing the government needed, Australia being a major trade partner of China. The victim had also been a high-profile financier, and with a good reputation to boot, at least on a professional level. It was bad for the image of the city, especially at a time when renewed calls for democracy had again put the spotlight on the territory. Ethan's instructions were that things needed to be wrapped up sooner rather than later. But at this stage at least, it looked like a completely random killing. It was about as bad as things could get.

'The constables questioned most of the residents in the flats with a view of the crime scene. Because the body was found early, they were able to catch them before they went to work,' said John Mok. He was one of the inspectors assigned to the case, an enthusiastic and bespectacled twenty-six-year-old, with bad skin. 'But, so far,' he added, 'we've drawn a complete blank. No one saw or even heard anything. We're following up with the other neighbours, but I'm not too hopeful. The whole thing happened very late at night and they would already have come forward if they had noticed anything. The night shift caretaker in Short's building could not have seen anything from where he was sitting, so that's a dead end.'

'What about the CCTV cameras?' asked Ethan.

Suki answered this time.

'There were none facing outside on Gage Street itself. Most of the buildings there date from the fifties and sixties, all low-rise. So security is more lax. We're still collating the disks from the cameras in the streets that are further away.'

'Did anything of interest happen at the bar and restaurant?'

'The staff at the Captain's Bar at the Mandarin Oriental remember Short very well,' said Charles Au. He was tall and athletic, and had a reputation within the group as a bit of a ladies' man. 'He was with two others, male colleagues. They had a bottle of champagne, Cristal. There was apparently much toasting going on. They were a bit noisy, but the waiters recalled nothing out of the ordinary. They left after about an hour and paid a good tip. They did not get into any argument with anyone. They were regulars, apparently. Same story at the restaurant,' he added, 'they were joined by four others, three males and one female. Again, it looks like they were all from his office. They were the last customers to leave, well after midnight. They had brought their own wine with them. Nine bottles in total, all top labels. No wonder the staff remembered them well! But I'm afraid there's not much of interest to report either. Some of them hailed taxis in the street outside the private kitchen, but Short and two others walked up towards Lan Kwai Fong.'

'Charles, can you have a word with Short's team at Morgan Roberts, especially those who might have left the restaurant with him? I'll give you a contact name there,' said Ethan. 'And, John,' he added, 'can you check with the Marine Department if Short owned a boat? Suki and I visited his flat earlier. It looks like he was a bit of a sailing enthusiast.'

'Sure thing.'

'One more thing, can we look into his ex-wife? And I understand there are also two Thai women with whom he was in long-distance relationships.'

'Bloody hell!' said Charles.

'One of them even had a child with him.'

'I'll do it,' said Suki, as she played with a pencil.

'I'll have a word with the Organised Crime and Triad Bureau,' continued Ethan, 'it hardly looks like a triad killing, but let's see what their contacts have to say. I'll also put in a call to the Narcotics Bureau. We found a small dose of cocaine in Short's apartment. It was most likely for personal use, but you never know. Andy, anything with the phones?'

Andrew Li was a short, geeky type, and a genius with computers, smartphones and anything related to information technology. He was also the only one of them wearing his uniform.

'All done,' he said. 'The BlackBerry was issued by the bank, Morgan Roberts. There were ninety-seven messages in his inbox, all dated yesterday. Those on prior dates had all been deleted from the handset. I'll need more time to recover these from the bank's server. Pretty much all were work-related, ongoing transactions, pitches, internal issues, that sort of thing. There were also a few messages about last night's drinks and dinner. Charles, I'll give you the names. It should save you quite a bit of time. It looks like they were celebrating a big deal they had just closed in the Philippines. Other than that, nothing, really.'

'And the iPhone?'

'That was his personal phone. I managed to get access too. There wasn't much on it either. We found correspondence with wine merchants and auctioneers, messages about upcoming dinners. There was something about a junk party, but it was an invitation, nothing about a boat he might have owned. There were a few photos too, frankly all pretty uninteresting. But, now that you've mentioned it, some of the pictures must have been of those two women in Thailand. There were a couple of emails to someone there as well. Maybe it was one of them? They're real bombshells by the way, and the kid is quite cute too.'

'Can I see?' asked Charles, suddenly excited.

'Later!' cut in Ethan. 'Andy, can you have a look at his computer? We just recovered it from his flat. Otherwise, let's focus our efforts on his colleagues, any boat he might have owned and review any CCTV footage. Let's catch up here, at 8 am tomorrow. What really bugs me, though, is that we're no closer to identifying a motive. ACP Ma is already breathing down my neck and asking for results. By the way, Suki, did the brother arrive from Singapore?'

'Yes. He's already identified the body at the mortuary. At least we can tick that box. We're going there next, by the way. Short and his brother were not all that close apparently, they had hardly met in years.'

'I see.'

'At Morgan Roberts, Short had named his mother as next of kin, to be contacted in the event of an emergency. His brother had no idea why anything like this would have happened. He's planning to stay, at least until the body can be flown Down Under. I have his details if we need to talk to him again.'

CHAPTER 7

3:10 am, Causeway Bay, Hong Kong, 29 September 2017

MINORU ITO HELD THE silk-wrapped handle with his left hand, the cutting edge facing out, and slowly cleaned the blade with wrinkled *nuguigami* paper. He started from the base of the dull back of the blade, gradually moving up until he reached the tip. The paper was wrapped over his right thumb and forefinger, and he progressed along the flat sides of the blade towards, but never touching, its razor-sharp edge. The slow motion detached the abrasive, low-grade powder he had sprinkled over the metal to remove traces of grease and liquids and to polish the steel. He used a new piece of wiping paper and next applied oil from a small bottle. It soon revealed intricate designs in the metal. He never failed to be amazed by the complex, wavy tempering patterns in the *hamon*. They were different on every single sword and the Japanese language had an almost infinite variety of names to describe them. Some evoked the sea, others mountains, trees, or even mystical elements.

The blade had been forged from high carbon *tamahagane* steel, in the Edo period. He returned the sword to its black lacquered scabbard and secured the handle to the sheath by tying a silk braided cord several times, both above and below the guard. This would prevent it accidentally falling out of the scabbard. He then held the sword horizontally, resting on both hands, level with his eyes. The point faced left, with the cord loop on top. He bowed slightly, paying respect to the *katana,* before wrapping it snugly in a silk bag and placing that in a soft travel bag that lay flat on a wooden stand in a corner of his room. He closed the luggage with a small padlock and pocketed the key. He finally returned the bottle of oil to his wash bag in the bathroom, before flushing the wiping paper down the toilet bowl.

Minoru had come highly recommended. His line of work was unconventional to say the least, but he had been well trained. The killing of the *gaijin* the previous night had happened as planned. It had been easy. No one had stopped him and, it seemed, no one had seen him either. The body was discovered too late for the homicide to be reported in the morning's papers. The web had pictures and extensive descriptions of the crime scene, but no information on possible suspects.

Some of the financial weeklies, such as the *International Financing Review* or *GlobalCapital,* had at first only brief mentions of the death. Their respective websites, however, as well as those of *FinanceAsia,* Bloomberg, Reuters, and the *Wall Street Journal,* now all carried extensive obituaries. News agencies had widely syndicated the information, not just locally, but also in Europe and the US. The murder of an expatriate was sufficiently rare to elicit interest. That of a senior and well-known investment banker would be front-page news.

Minoru did not like Hong Kong. It was a city of extremes. The new rich there advertised their wealth far too prominently for his liking and he loathed their questionable tastes. He also disliked the Cantonese language that often sounded more like it was shouted, rather than spoken. The hordes of Mainlanders who flooded the shopping districts of Causeway Bay and Tsim Sha Tsui had no manners. Meanwhile, in spite of all the glitz and glamour, a quarter of the city lived below the poverty line. Some unskilled and elderly inhabitants even survived in cage-like dwellings not even fit for dogs. Above all, Hong Kong was a place devoid of tradition. There were virtually no historic buildings left. All had been knocked down to erect gleaming towers, above ritzy shopping malls. It was a city that had sold its soul to consumerism. In short, it was a place with no honour.

Tradition and honour were what mattered most to Minoru. He had grown up in Kyoto, the only child of a couple who had continued the family custom of manufacturing handmade rice straw *tatami* mats and bamboo chopsticks. The business slowly dwindled after the war and the American occupation, and the economic boom of the 1960s passed them by. Minoru was an assiduous student, although, in truth, he by far preferred taking *kendo* and *iaido* lessons at the local *dojo* to school. But there was no money to support his attending a prestigious university that would guarantee a lifetime career with one of the larger banks, insurance companies or electronics conglomerates.

Instead, Minoru made the unorthodox choice of a career in the Jieitai, the all-volunteer self-defence forces. His grandfather, who had served in Burma and the Pacific, and had survived to tell the tale, quietly gave him his blessing. Better to live a life of righteousness and discipline than slave as a *salaryman*, he had said. Minoru joined the naval academy at Etajima, in

Hiroshima prefecture, and first studied there for three years, including a fifteen-month special security programme. He then applied for recruitment with the Tokubetsukeibitai, the Special Boarding Unit of the Navy, or SBU. It had been established in 2001 as the equivalent of the US Navy Seal teams and British Special Boat Service squadrons. Noted by his superiors for his stamina, will and endurance, he had passed with flying colours.

Training with the unit, he came to master both unarmed combat techniques, as well as close-quarters shooting with the Heckler & Koch MP5 submachine gun and SIG Sauer P226R semi-automatic pistol. He acquired fluency in several languages, including Korean, Tagalog and Bahasa Indonesia, in addition to English.

With the SBU, Minoru was involved in maritime anti-terrorist duties and saw action in Somalia in 2009, as part of an anti-piracy force aboard the destroyer *Sazanami*. But he became increasingly frustrated by the limitations imposed by the Japanese constitution. Training was all well and good, but he had joined the Special Forces to fight. The Jieitai had more recently been deployed abroad for peacekeeping operations, but most of its duties consisted of assistance with disaster relief or, for his own unit especially, in campaigns against smuggling and illegal immigration, in tandem with the Japanese Coast Guard.

After six years, Minoru decided to quit, much to the surprise and regret of his platoon and unit commander. He had a bright future with the navy, they had argued, but to no avail. He moved to Tokyo and spent a year intensively practising martial arts, surviving on odd security jobs. The skills he had honed in the military, however, did not remain unused for long.

CHAPTER 8

Ueno, Tokyo, 18 April 2011

O NE DAY IN SPRING, a businessman named Hiroshi Takai, whose trading company often acted as a front for the *yakuza*, called on Minoru. Takai-san had obtained his details through a mutual acquaintance, now retired, who had once served in his detachment. One of Takai-san's relations had a problem and was prepared to pay handsomely to see it go away. The problem turned out to be a high-profile, and highly corrupt, politician from Chiba prefecture. The official had, over the years, collected many bribes without delivering promised public infrastructure contracts. He now threatened to dump Takai-san's consociate altogether, to entertain more lucrative offers from the competition. A man with a code, Minoru had at first discarded the thought of getting involved. But money was running out. The body of the politician was later found with a severed spinal cord, floating in Tokyo's Sumida River.

Soon afterwards, Minoru decided to disappear. The best way to do so, he reasoned, was to fake his own death. He lived alone, in a small studio apartment near Ueno Station, in central Tokyo. He had no interaction with his neighbours. Up to now, making a living through short-term jobs, he also had no real work colleagues to speak of. His parents were both long dead. As is the custom in Japan, their remains had been cremated. Minoru had no other living relatives. There would be no DNA to match to the body.

He spent time at night in the Shinjuku entertainment district and soon befriended a man called Akihiko Nobu. The man told him about his life and, through much questioning, Minoru established he was unemployed, with no family and no fixed address. Importantly, he was about the same age and roughly of the same height and weight as Minoru. No one would miss him. There would be no family member or employer contacting the police about his disappearance. Minoru bought him rounds of beers on a regular basis, always taking care to choose a new venue every time. One evening, having plied Nobu with several bottles of *sake,* he took him back to his apartment.

It was 2:30 am and no one saw the two men ride the lift to the sixth floor. The building offered cheap accommodation. There was no security guard on duty. The residents' comings and goings were also not recorded by security cameras, unlike in higher-end developments. Akihiko Nobu was dead drunk after an epic drinking marathon. Minoru pretty much had to carry him all the way to his front door. Once inside the flat, he donned disposable plastic gloves and searched Nobu for anything that might help with his identification. He discarded his wallet and removed its contents. A watch was the only item of jewellery. He replaced it with his own on Nobu's wrist. He also put his own wallet in one of Nobu's trouser pockets. An identity card was not compulsory in Japan. The main purpose of such a document was to match the local government's record of a

46

residential address. With no current fixed abode, Nobu had not had any need for one. The photograph on his driver's licence, however, could readily pass for Minoru. The address it stated, in a distant suburb of Tokyo, was no longer current. Minoru dressed Nobu in his own clothes and discarded the man's garments in a plastic bag, which he would dump at a refuse collection point in another district.

He installed Nobu, by now collapsed and asleep, on a battered mattress. He emptied several bottles of *sake* into the sink and placed them next to Nobu, together with a glass. He wiped down all the hard surfaces in his flat. The apartment was small, and there was not all that much to go through, other than the single window, doorknobs and kitchen panels. He also spent time rubbing a few items of furniture and the ceramic tiles, basin and shower in the tiny bathroom.

Satisfied, he lit a cigarette and placed it between the man's fingers. Sedated by the huge quantity of alcohol he had consumed, Akihiko Nobu never woke up. The burning cigarette ignited the sheets, made of cheap, highly flammable synthetic material. As the flames engulfed the small apartment, Minoru closed the door. The flat neither had a fire alarm nor sprinklers.

Nobu's charred remains were discovered some thirty minutes later, after a panicked neighbour had called the Fire Department. His death had come long before the flames started to melt his skin and flesh. Smoke inhalation and carbon monoxide sent him into an ever-deeper coma. The thermal damage scorched his respiratory system, burning his nose and mouth. The routine enquiry later pointed to singed nostrils hairs and carbonaceous sputum.

The case was clear cut and rapidly closed. His remains were cremated and his ashes mingled with those of the destitute and anonymous dead, after a short Buddhist ceremony. For the Japanese authorities, Minoru, a former serviceman in the Jieitai with no known relatives, had died in a tragic accident that night in Ueno. The blaze was traced to a burning cigarette that had ignited the bedding as the victim lay asleep.

Minoru was now off the grid, forever. He officially became Hakihiko Nobu, one of many subsequent identities, and started a new life. Through Hiroshi Takai and others, more work found its way to him. Over time, he developed a reputation for ruthlessness, reliability and discretion in his newfound career. To his contacts in the underworld, he soon became known simply as Shiryō, the spirit of death.

CHAPTER 9

9:20 am, Causeway Bay, Hong Kong, 29 September 2017

SHIRYŌ LEFT HIS SERVICED APARTMENT and walked randomly for a long time to make sure he was not tailed. His tradecraft, first learnt during the security course at the naval academy, had been honed through years of experience. He made full use of bay windows, underground passages and abrupt U-turns to reveal possible followers. He returned close to where he had first started his walk and entered one of several anonymous Internet cafés he had located over the last few days. They were becoming increasingly rare in an age when almost everyone carried a smartphone. As a result, they tended to be low-end, anonymous places that catered to backpackers on a budget. As often, the venue was not under the surveillance of CCTV cameras. Even if it had been, all it would ever show was a man of average size and build, wearing a grey hoodie, a baseball cap and sunglasses. He paid for thirty minutes at a counter manned by a spotty teenager with a bleached mullet haircut. Hard-rock music played in the background.

He sat down at one of the cubicles and sipped an insipid brown liquid that passed for coffee. The other customers were a mix of local slouched adolescents, hooked on videogames, and American and Australian tourists perusing Facebook and other social networks.

He logged onto a Gmail account and clicked the red 'Compose' box at the top left of the screen. He ignored the addressee and subject lines and typed a single, pre-agreed but inconspicuous word in the main body of the message. Next, he clicked the top right hand cross, automatically saving the message as a draft. No traces of the email would ever be found, since it had not actually been sent. But, by signing in to the same account, its recipient would be able to read it, before deleting it forever. He logged out of the account and browsed newspaper websites for a while, staying on their home pages, never reading specific articles. He finally clicked on the 'History' tab and erased the list of websites he had consulted.

Shiryō returned to his serviced apartment through a new circuitous route. He remained there for the rest of the day. It was now time to plan his next move.

CHAPTER 10

T HE VICTORIA PUBLIC MORTUARY was located at Number 34 on the road of the same name, in Kennedy Town, Western District. The forensic pathologist, Dr Alfred Kwok, had already met Wayne Short, the brother of the deceased. Accompanied by a member of Ethan's team, he had unequivocally identified the body. A tall, blond, surfer-type, his casual appearance indicated a line of work the complete opposite of his brother's. Wayne Short owned several bars and nightclubs in Southeast Asia. One of them was a notorious establishment in Pattaya, Thailand. He had indicated he did not care to retain clothing worn by his brother. The family's wish was for the body to be flown to Australia, where it would be buried as soon as practicable. Other personal belongings could be returned at the same time.

The mortuary was an austere white building, a colour associated with death across much of Asia. It had a row of narrow windows on its first and only floor that faced the China Merchants Wharf and, beyond, Green Island and the Western Approaches. Its flat roof offered an escape from the oppressive atmosphere of a repository for the dead. The mortuary was the only one on Hong Kong Island, and one of four in the city.

Dr Kwok was a genial man in his mid-fifties, with grey hair and a matching moustache. He had, over the years, developed a strong sense of *humour noir*, perhaps as an antidote to the almost daily confrontation with death his job demanded. Ethan, who knew him well, greeted him warmly and introduced Suki. She had only once before attended a *post-mortem* examination. She was not thrilled at the prospect of repeating the experience, especially in connection with what had been a particularly gruesome stabbing. The cause of death was clear, but the coroner still had to go through the motions to legally define it as a homicide.

Ethan and Suki put on green gowns and shoe covers and entered a room at the back of the building that had the unmistakable stench of formaldehyde and bleach. Andrew Short was still in a body bag, although the seals had already been removed to allow his identification. Dr Kwok, who now wore plastic gloves, first photographed the corpse while still inside the bag. At the same time, he described aloud, for the benefit of a digital voice recorder, details of the torn and ripped garments in which the victim was still clothed. He removed the evidence bags in which the hands had been wrapped and cut the fingernails. The clippings joined other samples, including hair and fibres. An overhead UV lamp helped him to locate secretions on uncovered skin and items of clothing. The body was X-rayed as Kwok, Ethan and Suki retreated behind a partition wall. Next, a moody assistant with a bad limp, whom Kwok had earlier simply addressed as Wai, assisted in removing the body bag, as well as undressing and cleaning the body.

Suki steadied herself at the sight of the wounds. It was one thing to look at a fully clothed dead body, but another when the damage was suddenly revealed in the whole horror of its naked reality.

'Are you OK there?' asked Ethan.

'I'll be fine,' she answered, taking in a deep breath.

That was a mistake, given the atmosphere heavily saturated with chemical smells.

'But we're only just starting, Sweetie,' whispered Kwok.

He had a mischievous smile as he donned a clear plastic face shield. He weighed and measured the body. Wai helped Kwok to place it on a canted aluminium table. Its raised contours allowed for drainage of blood and other bodily fluids. Short lay face up on the table. Behind him, a rubber block made the chest protrude forward. It would allow for more precise cuts, as Kwok proceeded with his examination.

Kwok worked steadily and methodically. 'The deceased is a white male, in his late-thirties, with blond hair and . . . blue eyes. No tattoos or birthmarks are apparent. A cut of . . . fifty-one centimetres can be seen, starting from the right lower torso, ending on its upper left. The cut has created extensive damage to the abdomen. Hey, that's a pretty neat cut, Ethan,' he suddenly said, turning off the recorder.

'Any ideas what could have done it?'

'I'd say a machete, or a sword, perhaps? It's almost as clean as a cut made by a scalpel, but obviously it's much wider, deeper and longer.'

The internal examination proper then started. Kwok made a deep, Y-shaped incision, starting first from the left and right shoulders and meeting at the breastbone. It also extended all the way down to the pubic bone, above and below the diagonal cut that straddled Short's abdomen. He peeled back the skin, muscle and soft tissue with a scalpel, and pulled open the chest flap, revealing the ribcage. He cut further down its sides to better access the internal organs.

By now, Suki was very pale, Kwok's debonair demeanour in sharp contrast to her growing unease.

'Suki, if it's too much for you, there's no shame in waiting outside,' suggested Ethan.

'The terrace is actually quite pleasant at this time of year,' encouraged Kwok.

'I'm sorry. Thanks. If you don't mind, I think I'll spend some time up there, and return a bit later,' she said.

'That's my girl,' said the pathologist, 'but, unfortunately, you'll miss the best part.'

Cutting further, Kwok detached the larynx, oesophagus, major arteries and ligaments. He then severed the organs from the spinal cord, bladder and rectum.

'Careful now,' he said.

He pulled out the entrails in one piece and examined them, weighing, dissecting, and taking samples as he went along. The major blood vessels were also dissected. He cut open the stomach, examining and weighing its contents. By now, the smell was almost unbearable.

'Hey Ethan, it looks like our friend had quite a lot to drink. And I'm not talking *cha* here.'

'Yes, our preliminary investigation revealed a rather lively night out on the town yesterday.'

'It must have been quite a party! Now, on to the brain,' he continued.

He removed the rubber block from Short's back and placed it under the neck. He made a wide cut across the forehead, from one ear to the other. He pulled away the scalp and revealed the skull, much like a soft fruit being ripped open. An electric saw cut into the skull and exposed the brain. Kwok severed its connection to the spinal cord and tentorium and carefully lifted it out.

'I'd say we're pretty much done, Ethan,' said Kwok.

At that point, Suki returned to the examination room, feeling much better. The process had taken the best part of an hour and fifteen minutes.

'Ah! Back in time for the *mignardises!*' Kwok teased her. 'We still need to go through the results of the dissection and forensic toxicology report, but I'd say Mr Short died sometime between one and two in the morning.'

'That concurs with statements we've already collected,' said Ethan.

'He was a healthy young man. Quite sporty too, I might add. Not bad looking either, what do you think, darling?'

Suki managed a faint smile.

'While he had a bad concussion on his head, most probably the result of a fall, the cause of death is evidently the very deep abdominal wound. It would have been caused by an extremely sharp long knife, machete or, more likely in my view, a sword. The cut was made starting from the lower abdomen, and ended on the upper part of the torso. By the way, the killer was right handed. There was only one cut. It was obviously fatal. He would have died within a minute or two at most, both from the loss of blood and as his vital organs systematically failed. But he would have passed out within seconds.'

'When can you come back to us with the rest of the report, Doc? The ACP is shaking the tree quite a bit on this one,' asked Ethan.

'As you know, it normally takes up to a few weeks, but you're in luck. We're not that busy at the moment and a couple of laboratories also owe me favours. I'll try to get something back to you by early next week. But if I find something untoward in the meantime, I'll obviously give you a call straight away. Meanwhile, I'll email the rest of my report to you by tomorrow morning.'

Kwok peeled off his plastic gloves and took a quick glance at his watch.

'I'll even rush it for you. Boy, it's eight o'clock already, and I'm hungry like the wolf! My wife will kill me if I'm late for dinner again!'

CHAPTER 11

DEMONSTRATIONS WERE SOMETHING of a rarity in Hong Kong. They were also often held on Sundays. The territory's inhabitants were, for the most part, too focused on making money to allow them to interfere with their weekday business routines. Frequently, the number of constables assigned to keeping an eye on marches and sit-ins was equal to, or even larger than, that of the demonstrators. With renewed claims for democracy within the Special Administrative Region of China that was Hong Kong, the force had been on high alert again for several weeks. Banners popped up repeatedly and everywhere, and especially in front of the government's and chief executive's offices on the waterfront in Admiralty. Ethan had driven past a number of them on his way to police headquarters in the morning. The elections had just been delayed and it was as yet unclear whether the city would experience a resurgence of civil disobedience on the scale of 2014. The pro-democracy activists were increasingly making their voices heard, frustrated at the lack of change on the political front.

Little progress had been made on Andrew Short's murder case. Analysis of the CCTV footage had tracked his return from Lan Kwai Fong to his home address. He had walked on his own and had not had any notable interaction with anyone along the way. No footage of anyone behaving remotely suspiciously in the streets around his apartment had surfaced. Although he was still a member of the Royal Hong Kong Yacht Club, Short had sold his boat, an X-Yachts sailboat, to a corporate buyer, two months prior to his death. The team had found he had recently been looking to purchase a new vessel, but that didn't seem likely to be relevant. His colleagues at Morgan Roberts had confirmed what Ethan's team already knew about the night's events. Two of them had joined him for a nightcap after dinner, but they had parted just after 1 am. At least, it had further narrowed down the time of death. They had all painted the picture of a friendly and experienced colleague, with no known issues. Everyone seemed to like him; this was remarkable in a notoriously cutthroat working environment. It was a meagre harvest of actionable facts.

Kylie, the banker's wife, was in Sydney at the time of his death. She had asked how she was now supposed to make ends meet. The two Thai women, one in Bangkok, and the other who now lived in a small town close to Chiang Mai, in northern Thailand, had been similarly devastated.

Short's home computer and smart phones had not provided further clues, other than the fact that he had spent a fair amount of time, late at night, browsing hardcore porn websites. It had pointed to a vigorous interest in Asian women, but that could hardly be called a breakthrough.

Discreet enquiries with the force's other divisions had similarly drawn a complete blank. Informers did not believe the triads had had anything to do with the killing. Neither his photograph nor his name had been recognised. His death did not appear to be related to narcotics trafficking either, although Ethan had asked his team to probe Short's bank accounts for suspicious transactions. But this was more to close the loop rather than based on the belief he could have been involved in the drug trade. He was clearly an occasional user, but just did not fit the dealer type. In all probability, the search would only uncover his monthly salary of HK$400,000 and payments of bonuses, the latter representing a fat multiple of the former, on an annualised basis. As his manager Ashok Patel had said, he was rather well paid. Expenses would likely consist of mortgage payments, trips abroad, dinners, cases of wine and tailoring bills.

Above all, why had he been killed? Was it a random event, or had it been the man, or even the bank, which had been targeted? The ACP was pressing for answers, but Ethan still had none to give him. His mobile's ringtone interrupted his thoughts. The screen flashed the caller ID. It was Alfred Kwok.

'I wasn't expecting your call so soon,' said Ethan, 'have you found anything?'

'And I wasn't planning to call you over the weekend either. But I've found something all right.'

'Do you mind if I put you on the speakerphone? The team and I were just going over the latest developments. It would save me repeating things again for everyone's benefit.'

Ethan motioned to his colleagues to come closer and laid the iPhone flat on a coffee table.

'As I was just saying,' continued Kwok, 'I've barely started work on the toxicology report. I began with the blood samples.'

'I'm all ears.'

'I'll make it nice and short. Basically, we found minute traces of two foreign agents. After analysis, one was a fine abrasive, commonly used by *iaido* practitioners to clean their blades.'

'*Iaido* is the martial art where people train with swords, right? As in *samurai* swords?'

'Very good! I'm impressed, Ethan. Yes, as in *samurai* swords. Basically, that abrasive is usually found in a small, silk-wrapped ball that is affixed to a wooden or bamboo handle. It's called *uchiko* powder, if you really want to know. The ball is tapped on both sides of the blade from the base to the tip, and then the powder is whisked off with a tissue, or fine polishing paper. It's used to remove traces of old oil, as well moisture, sticky gums and particulates that find their way onto the blade after cutting targets for practice. Mostly, the targets are rolled-up rice-straw *tatami* mats that have been soaked in water to mimic the consistency of human flesh. They're thick and tough, but a skilled practitioner can slice through them like butter.'

'My, my,' said Ethan, 'and the other compound?'

'I found traces of oil of cloves. Its viscosity makes it ideal to clean swords. It's actually also known as sword oil, or *choji* oil. Its purpose is to remove whatever traces remain on the blade, after the *uchiko* powder has been wiped off.'

'So what killed him was a Japanese sword?'

'It was, most definitely. It also fits the profile of the cut to a tee: very clean, very straight, very long and very deep. By the way, Japanese swords come in several sizes. This would be a medium or perhaps even a large one, for sure.'

'Thank you so much, Alfred. Thank God, we now have something tangible on which to focus.'

'You're most welcome. I'll call you again if anything else surfaces but, for now, that's all folks, as they say. The rest of my preliminary report is in your in-box, but I fear there's nothing in there you do not already know. Oh, one more thing, please tell Suki she's welcome back any time. I already miss her.'

Ethan looked at Suki and blinked. For the first time that morning, she flashed a wide smile.

CHAPTER 12

11:58 am, Central, Hong Kong, 30 September 2017

A QUICK CHECK HAD ESTABLISHED there had not been a homicide in Hong Kong perpetrated with a Japanese sword, at least, not since the end of the Second World War. Hong Kong was one of forty-nine jurisdictions in Asia with an Interpol National Central Bureau. A search for similar cases in the region, and beyond, was now ongoing. Ethan placed a call to John da Silva. Da Silva was also Eurasian, of Portuguese descent. He had served in the Hong Kong Police for as long as anyone cared to remember, starting well before the handover of the British colony to China. He was a meticulous man of few words, and his specialties were forensic ballistics and ballistic fingerprinting. The bulk of his work and expertise consisted in analysing firearms, but he had, over the years, also become the force's point person for matters related to all weapons, whether these had shot bullets, stabbed, or pierced their victims. Da Silva suggested, as first port of call, a visit to a shop located at the far end of Queen's Road, Central.

It was just before noon when Ethan climbed to the first floor of an ageing shopping mall, and entered what looked like a

Japanese antique shop. A dusty suit of *samurai* armour greeted visitors, complete with a helmet from which two horns protruded. It also sported a frightening facemask. The main focus of the shop, however, was unmistakably on swords. A number of these were on display, on wall-mounted racks. They were of all sizes, their handles tightly wrapped in colourful silk or cotton and, for some, in leather. Their scabbards exhibited a variety of designs too, ranging from sober, jet-black lacquer to ray-skin patterns and, more surprisingly, bright red and gold paint. It was clearly run by an enthusiast. No customers were browsing. The shopkeeper, a Chinese man in his early forties, read the *Apple Daily*, seated behind a glass counter that showcased sword guards and other paraphernalia. His face partly hidden behind a laptop, he was dressed in faded jeans, with an un-tucked blue check shirt. His black hair was short at the top, but tied in a long ponytail at the back. It framed a smiling and welcoming face.

'*Jo san,*' he said, using one of the Cantonese expressions for 'good morning'. 'Can I help you?'

'Good morning! I'm with the Hong Kong Police,' said Ethan, showing his warrant card, 'we're investigating a murder, which we believe was committed with a Japanese sword. My colleague John da Silva suggested I get in touch with you.'

'Ah, John . . . it's been a long time! I'm Ken Tsui, by the way. Please call me Ken. That would be the killing of that Australian banker, wouldn't it? I just read about it in the paper,' he added, vaguely pointing to the daily with his forefinger.

'Correct.'

'Well, what can I tell you?'

'I'd like to learn about Japanese swords. How and by whom they are used. How to go about buying one, among other things.'

'Listen, I'm just about to wrap things up here, and close the shop. I have a class at two in Kwun Tong. I teach *iaido,* you see. If you have nothing better to do, why don't you come with me? We could talk on the bus, and perhaps grab a quick bite of noodles at a *dai pai dong* there. You could watch the class too. It would probably answer a number of your questions.'

'That would be great. Thank you.'

Ken locked the door to his shop. They both walked down to the street level and caught a Number 101 bus that linked Kennedy Town to Kwun Tong, on the eastern edge of Kowloon. The trip would last for the best part of an hour. They would have plenty of time to talk.

There was no doubt the *iaido* teacher knew a great deal about his subject. He could have spoken for hours. Over the first ten minutes or so, he explained the origins of Japanese swords and briefly mentioned the key periods.

'After the war with Russia in 1905, the Japanese realised they were fighting with inferior, Western-made swords,' he said. 'That's when they decided to revert to the blades they had used prior to the abolition of the *samurai* class. These were widely issued to the army in the 1910s and 1920s. A simplified but deadly fighting style was also developed for the military, at the Toyama Academy near Tokyo. Without going into too much detail, the American occupation at the end of the war nearly put an end to all that. As servicemen returned home many Japanese swords, including extremely valuable antique blades, found their way to the US as souvenirs.'

'But there has since been a revival of sorts, right?'

'Absolutely. There are now a number of fighting schools in Japan, teaching different techniques. It's a very traditional martial art, but it's gaining in popularity again. And not just in Japan, but also in the US and in Europe. Of course, there are also many collectors who do not practise themselves. Some swords are centuries old, and very expensive, worth in some cases US$50,000, sometimes even much more.'

'And in Hong Kong?'

'Oh, it's pretty marginal here. We're probably not more than a hundred practitioners, and spread across a few *dojos* as well.'

'I noticed there are swords of different sizes.'

'Yes. *Samurai* warlords always carried a matching pair. It was called a *daishō*. It literally translates as "long-short". One was a longer sword known as a *katana*, I'm sure you've heard that word before. The shorter version was actually a medium-sized sword called a *wakizashi*. I'll show you some when we get to the *dojo*. In the earlier periods, the longer sword was paired with an even shorter blade called a *tantō*. But it was principally used for stabbing, rather than slicing. For self-defence, women even used their own version of a *tantō*, known as a *kaiken*.'

By now, the bus had reached the other side of the harbour. It drove east, towards Kwun Tong. The district, still largely industrial, was dotted with warehouses, garages and dispatch centres for courier companies.

'And the *wazi* . . . how did you say?'

'*Wakizashi.*'

'Sorry. *Wakizashi.* Is it used in a different way from the *katana*?'

'Yes. The *wakizashi,* since it's shorter, is used single-handedly, whereas the *katana,* most of the time anyway, is used with both hands. And when used with only one hand for certain strikes, it's always held with the right. There's no such thing as a left-handed sword practitioner. In addition, in the past, the *wakizashi* often served to sever arteries, rather than slice through limbs, or even entire body parts. Of course, both weapons can be equally lethal in the right hands.'

'And do you use real swords for training?'

'Generally we do not, except for us *sensei,* teachers, or for experienced practitioners. Most of the time, students use *iaito,* swords that have a blunt edge, but otherwise similar in all respects, size and weight, to real ones. But when we cut targets, obviously, we use *shinken,* real cutting swords. To my knowledge, our club is the only one in Hong Kong where members can practise the actual cutting of targets.'

'I see. And how easy is it to buy a Japanese sword?'

'Well, for one, I sell some at my shop, as you saw, although these are mostly antiques. But even swords that are several hundred years old are perfectly serviceable, if they have been well maintained that is. They can obviously be bought at many places in Japan, although that requires an export permit from the agency of cultural affairs. It's generally not a problem, although the most valuable antiques are considered as national treasures, and cannot be exported at all. In addition, there are many good producers of modern swords, in Japan, of course, but also in the US, Korea and Thailand, among other countries. You can even buy swords over the Internet, generally from America, not that I would recommend it myself. Obviously all of these are much cheaper than custom-made Japanese swords produced in traditional forges, like mine, here.'

Ken tapped a plastic carrying bag of about a metre in length with his hand to emphasise the point. To the uninitiated, it looked like he might have been carrying a small fishing rod.

'In Hong Kong,' he added, 'most of the swords used for cutting practice are actually made in China. They're much cheaper, as you can imagine, but not bad value at all for beginners.'

'Is that so? Well, there isn't much that China doesn't produce nowadays! Listen, I'm sorry to impose this on you, but could I ask you to take a look at this photograph? Mr Short was killed on Thursday night with a single, diagonal cut. As you can see, it started from his right lower torso – to the left on that picture – and it exited his body near the left shoulder. Perhaps you'd be familiar with this?'

Ken looked intensely at the picture. His face suddenly lightened up.

'Of course,' he said, 'it's a *hidari gyaku keisa*, a reverse diagonal cut to the right. It's one of the basic cuts. I teach it all the time. That one looks like it was perfectly executed. The forty-five-degree angle is absolutely faultless.'

CHAPTER 13

THEY HAD EATEN A QUICK LUNCH at a small outdoor stall before reaching the building where the *dojo* was located. Most of the other tenants were industrial businesses. Colourful but incoherent tagging was painted on the front door of the building. They were far from the glitz and luxury of Central, and it showed. Nearby, employees of a courier company feverishly sorted parcels on the pavement. They rode a rickety and slow service lift. It was used, most of the time, to ferry wooden pallets between delivery trucks and the warehouses that populated the upper levels. They finally arrived at their destination on the fourth floor. As the lift's double doors opened, Ethan saw that the open-plan *dojo* occupied an entire podium, spanning more than 4,000 square feet. The premises were punctuated by imposing concrete pillars, but the twelve-foot ceiling gave the place an airy and bright atmosphere. Mirrors were affixed to the entire length of one of the walls.

Ken changed into his uniform. It was similar to that worn by *aikido* fighters, although it was black, rather than the white and grey colours Ethan was more familiar with. It included a pair of pleated baggy trousers, secured by long flat ties. Ken explained that the garment was called a *hakama*. There was also an ample, double-breasted cotton shirt or *gi,* with sleeves that stopped around the elbows. A bright cotton belt, rolled several times around the waist, and split-toe Japanese socks completed the kit.

Ken fetched several swords, which he placed on a dark oak stand. It could accommodate a number of them. He first showed Ethan a *katana,* then a *wakizashi,* and finally a *tantō.* Ethan silently looked at these. His first thought was that walking in the streets of Central with a *katana,* even late at night, would hardly have been inconspicuous. Instead, a *wakizashi* might perhaps have been used. It would have been much easier to hide, perhaps in a rolled up magazine or newspaper, or even a backpack. Ken explained that even *katanas* came in a variety of sizes. The blade length could vary from about sixty-five to eighty-five centimetres, to which should be added the handle, which usually measured between twenty and thirty centimetres. In turn, the longest *wakizashi* could reach a length of up to sixty-five centimetres, actually not all that much shorter than a *katana.* In addition, the cut that had stabbed the banker was primarily associated with a *katana* technique, rather than one performed with a *wakizashi.*

The weapons were perfectly balanced. The wooden handles were wrapped in cotton, silk or leather, over a layer of scratchy ray- or sharkskin to avoid slippage. These wrappers were further tightened by the insertion of small metal charms called *menuki,* to offer a secure and comfortable grip.

A number of members of the club had now arrived. They quickly changed into their respective uniforms. There was a mix of sexes and ages, from teenagers to visibly much older practitioners. In all, about ten people attended that day. They picked up a number of used *tatami* mats, secured in bundles of five or six, and rolled these up in tight tubes, closed by elastic bands. They would be used as targets in forthcoming training sessions, after soaking in water for a few days to attain the desired weight and consistency.

The course started formally, with a bow-in ceremony. Arranged by order of seniority, the participants first bowed to a wall, to which a framed calligraphy had been affixed. They then bowed to their teacher and lastly to their respective swords. Ken had explained there was a particular way to hold a sword when bowing, or indeed when presenting it to anyone else, for the purposes of examination.

In many photographs dating from the war, members of the Imperial Japanese Army could be seen presenting their swords to US servicemen to signify their surrender. To a casual observer, these pictures looked like they recorded an act of submission. However, in many cases, the swords had been offered with their cord loops facing down, rather than up, or their tips, the *kissaki,* pointing to the right, rather than to the left. To those in the know, such gestures were clearly insulting.

The swords, still in their scabbards, were inserted in their owners' cotton belts. A flat cotton or silk tie, a *sageo,* Ken had said, secured the lacquered magnolia wood sheaths to their uniforms. The swords were drawn. Each participant checked that the handle was securely locked onto the blade by one or two simple bamboo pins. They then repeated eight basic cuts in the air ten times, while counting in Japanese.

'*Ichi, ni, san. . . .*'

It was all a bit surreal. *Katas,* or choreographed steps, followed. They started with a series of five simple movements, and then a more complex series of eight, simulating combat against enemies attacking from all directions. Each *kata* concluded with the sword being silently and elegantly returned to the scabbard, without its owner looking. The feet also precisely reverted to their starting positions. After each strike, Ken had said, a sharp-angled move called *chiburi* signified the flipping of an enemy's blood away from the blade. It was macabre but strangely fascinating at the same time. Loud cries accompanied every movement, breaking the otherwise eerie silence that permeated the massive room. The much-anticipated cutting practice came next.

A number of rolled up *tatami* mats had earlier been taken from almost man-size plastic drums, in which they had soaked in water over a few days. They were affixed to heavy target stands by spiking them onto pointed wooden pegs. The stench of decaying straw was unmistakable, and very strong. Taking turns, the members attempted to cut targets with their weapons according to various patterns. They included downward diagonal cuts, horizontal cuts, as well as the distinctive, upward diagonal cut, which Ethan now knew had killed Andrew Short. A few cut their way with difficulty through only a couple of targets. Some of the more senior ranked, however, went through double or treble that number, dispatching the mats with alarming speed and efficiency.

At first glance, cutting targets appeared easy to Ethan until he saw some of the junior trainees fail to even cut through a single mat. They planted their swords in the bundles of rice straw, from which they then had, with much effort, to be extracted. Ken had said it took years of practice to master the various techniques.

Ethan concluded that Short's murder had most certainly not been a random act. It was perhaps the work of a deranged sword fanatic, or long-time practitioner of the martial art, perhaps from this very club. In such a case, he or she would probably be caught soon. Alternatively, it could have been a planned execution by someone who was already a master. Either way, the motive behind the homicide remained a mystery. But there was simply no way someone could have decided on a whim to buy a *katana,* or a *wakizashi,* and wandered at night in Sheung Wan to test it on a passer by. Not with the perfect cut that had opened the banker's body.

At the end of the session, Ken promised to email Ethan the list of the club's members. He would also highlight their respective years of practice. To the list would be added the information requested from Interpol's databases, as well as that yet to be collected from the other *iaido* clubs around the city. At last there was a promising and concrete lead to follow.

CHAPTER 14

3:30 pm, Central, Hong Kong, 3 October 2017

J ASPER JERSIN, JJ TO HIS FRIENDS and colleagues, had just met the head of structured solutions, in one of the rooms adjacent to the trading floor. He was being made redundant, with immediate effect. His licence with the Securities and Futures Commission would expire that same day. After a short meeting with human resources to sign documents and return his security pass and corporate credit card, he would be escorted out of the building by a security guard. His personal belongings would be placed in a cardboard box, the only thing he would be allowed to take away from the office. He had suspected for a while some sort of imminent restructuring within the department, but the news had still come as a complete shock to him.

For seven years, first in New York, and then in Hong Kong, he had helped corporate and institutional clients, and mostly the bank itself, hedge investments through complex derivative trades. These had often involved devising extensive financial models, something his MSc in Physics from MIT had well prepared him for. All the same, his fast-paced career with Rose and Rudd Securities, or R&R, was now at an end. His days as a master of the universe were over, at least for a while.

No real explanation had been given. Under the authority of new 'joint global heads', the department was being restructured. It was, yet again, morphing into another beast. He was just one of the casualties of a change of strategy. He would, of course, continue to be paid his monthly salary for the duration of his gardening leave, a full three months. The bank would also cover the services of a consulting firm and use of a service office, to help him get back on his feet. He should see it as an opportunity, not as a failure, they had said. After the meeting with the skinny bitch from HR, JJ had rushed to the men's room, locked himself in one of the cubicles and snorted a line of cocaine. Now grinning, he exited the firm's regional headquarters for good.

JJ was an American from the Mid-West, in his mid-thirties. He was not vastly overweight, but could easily have shed five, or even ten kilogrammes. He often turned up bleary-eyed. He shaved erratically. Even though he wore expensive suits from some of the city's best-known tailors (although never a tie), his appearance was often that of someone who had spent the night on the streets. And, often, it was indeed the case.

Of course, he had a bit of a drug problem. Many of his fellow traders were also users. You had to, to face the crazy hours and the stress brought about by the huge stakes of their derivative trades. The stuff was readily available everywhere in Hong Kong: cocaine powder, crack cocaine, ketamine, methamphetamine, MDMA, it was all there for the taking. But, for him, the real revelation had been the sex.

He had never really had much of it, neither in high school nor at university. He was not particularly good looking. Some had even called him 'fatso' or 'geek'. After his arrival in Hong Kong. JJ suddenly found himself with far more disposable income than most people of his age. The girls were everywhere. They were everything he was not: slim, sexy and wild. And they were also cheap.

He started visiting prostitutes on Lockhart Road, in the red light district of Wan Chai. They were mostly from Southeast Asia: Filipinas, Indonesian or Vietnamese. He could be violent at times. He did things to them he had never imagined before. But they never complained, too happy to take his dollars. Some were regulars, others one-time encounters. After a while, he became more daring. Soon, he regularly brought several street-walkers at a time to his apartment, for drug-fuelled orgies that lasted through the night. The weekends were even worse. Often, he would hardly leave his bed at all. He started exploring the region too, especially over bank holidays. He became a fixture of Walking Street in Pattaya, Thailand, and a patron of the many brothels and bars in Angeles City in the Philippines. He would take pictures of himself with the girls and post them on Facebook. Among his colleagues at work, he became known as 'The White Hunter' or even 'The President of Vice', a play on his corporate title.

He knew he could never go back to work in the US. He was now addicted to his life of debauchery. Some on his desk even joked he had caught yellow fever. But he was now out of work. Eventually, the money would run out, and he would be forced to leave.

Suddenly depressed, and in need of company, JJ walked at a brisk pace from Central to Wan Chai. It was now close to six in the afternoon.

He arrived outside one of his regular bars. A group of girls, all provocatively dressed and made up, sat on plastic stools on the pavement, calling to passers by. They smoked cigarettes, making small talk, until one or more prospective customers appeared. Two of them recognised and greeted him. They knew very well what he was after, and they were ready to oblige.

Within a minute, JJ walked in through a velvet curtain. It hid a dimly lit interior, all in red tones and in bad need of refurbishment. Psychedelic music from the 1970s played in the background. The whole place felt like one of those depressing bars in which sailors spent their dollars, drunk on cheap booze to forget interminable crossings. In truth, that's what it probably had been a few decades earlier. Once inside, he immediately realised he was the only patron. He could not have cared less. The mama-san greeted him and poured him a drink. The vodka burnt his throat, and he immediately felt better. A girl appeared and sat next to him. Even though she was very young, her experience showed immediately. Her miniskirt was so short he saw her almost non-existent panties, as she eased herself onto the barstool. Her hair was black, long and straight. She started stroking his hand and face and, within minutes, whispered obscenities in his ear, almost licking him as she talked. The barmaid topped up his glass.

CHAPTER 15

I T HAD NOW BEEN A FEW DAYS since Short's body had been discovered. The media frenzy had quietened down. New information had failed to surface and attention had turned back to focus on political issues. The big question was still whether Hong Kong's citizens would be allowed to elect their chief executive under unrestricted universal suffrage, and by when. In 2014, several hundred thousand students and pro-democracy activists had brought entire districts of the city to a standstill, for seventy-nine consecutive days. By any reckoning, it had been one of the most significant developments in the territory since demonstrations protesting the Tiananmen Square massacre in Beijing, in June 1989. Prior to that, the last time people had demonstrated in such a visible way had been in 1967, when communist sympathisers had rioted against the British colonial government.

Shiryō had watched the excitement come and go with satisfaction. He walked randomly for a while in the streets of Causeway Bay to make sure he was not followed and entered a new Internet café, not far from his serviced apartment. He paid upfront for an hour's connection and an espresso, at a reception desk staffed by a Chinese girl with pink spiky hair. She took the money, barely looking at him, and poured the drink from a high-pressure percolator. The coffee was surprisingly decent. Shiryō sat in a quiet corner of the room. As usual, most of the other customers were tourists and spotty teenagers, hooked up in a trance on massively multiplayer online games. They were far too busy killing aliens or navigating fantasy worlds to notice him.

Simple searches with selected key words on Google first unearthed a series of press releases, posted by the company that employed his target. Contact names were listed at the bottom, together with their professional email addresses. It gave him a good feel for the email format the company used, and he ventured a guess at what the target's email address might be. Shiryō used a network tool to validate it. He now knew how to reach his target via electronic mail.

Through an identity he had previously set up, he logged onto Facebook. There, it took him fifteen seconds to find the target's wall, which offered details of friends, posts, photos, and videos, alongside a treasure trove of personal information.

'Unbelievably sloppy,' he thought.

He scanned the wall for a few minutes, and quickly identified the target's main areas of interest. One of them was Ferrari cars and the other was Michelin-starred restaurants. There were a number of photographs of the target, happily posing in front of fast cars, or in the company of famous chefs, all smiles with a glass of wine in hand. Hong Kong had, in a short space of time, become addicted to foreign celebrity chefs who suited its money culture.

He created a simple webpage allowing registration for an 'extravagant, once-in-a-lifetime private dinner' prepared by one of Europe's best-known chefs. The venue would only be revealed to the guests later. The date for the dinner was given as the following Saturday. He reasoned that a weekend would be less likely to conflict with the target's professional travels. The webpage explained that only a few select couples had been invited to the free event to promote the launch of a new restaurant in Hong Kong by the thrice-starred chef when he relocated to the city. To cap it all, Shiryō added a list of wines to be served at the party. The assortment included first-growth Bordeaux, Grand Cru Burgundies, well-known names from the Rhône Valley, and even rare boutique wines from California, all from superlative vintages. It was simply irresistible to any self-respecting foodie.

Shiryō next set up a new email account with an address that suggested an exclusive public relations company. He sipped the last drops of coffee, and ordered another. He then wrote a carefully crafted invitation. The recipient simply needed to click on a link that would take him to the website he had just created. A registration would trigger an email confirmation, but, more importantly, the target would also automatically download malware that would bury itself deep in the servers and operating systems of his employer.

It would create a spy server that only Shiryō could monitor. It would give him real-time access to all of the target's messages and correspondence. The malicious software would delete itself after a week. Implementing the scheme had taken just under fifty minutes. Satisfied, Shiryō dispatched the email message. He finally erased the computer's browsing history before leaving. He wandered in the streets of a nearby district and soon found a nondescript *ramen* place to rest and gather his thoughts over lunch.

It would not take long for the target to fall into the trap. In a few hours' time, he would check in at another Internet café and start his remote surveillance. Within a day or two, at most, he would know where, when and how to strike.

CHAPTER 16

S UKI HAD JUST SPENT THE BEST part of twenty minutes at an apartment in the western Mid Levels, checking the whereabouts and alibi of yet another member of the Kwun Tong *iaido* club. It was the forty-seventh and last on her list. Like most of the other practitioners, the man was soundly at home and in bed at the time of Short's murder. It had been easy enough to confirm with the video recordings held by the reception desk at his residence. What had first looked like a promising lead now appeared to go nowhere. She called Ethan to update him on the latest developments.

'I've now gone through my entire list and haven't been able to identify one who sounds remotely suspicious. Everyone was either in bed, had a rock-solid alibi, or was out of the country.'

'John and Charles looked into the other *iaido* clubs, but basically got the same result. This isn't working,' said Ethan.

'What about Short's bank records?'

'Other than the payments to Thailand, nothing really stands out. He was spending a lot of money, but not on anything that has triggered alarm bells. And incoming funds also look legit.'

'Anything from Interpol?'

'It's also proving much more difficult than I initially thought. Interpol has databases for all sorts of crimes. The main ones relate to firearms, dangerous materials and child abusers. They even have some on international crime networks and maritime piracy. But, oddly enough, there isn't a database of crimes committed with Japanese swords.'

'Did we manage to get anything at all, though?'

'It's really a question of liaising with each of the National Central Bureaus across the region. There are almost fifty of these. And if you add those in other major countries, that's another ninety-seven bureaus in Europe and the Americas alone. For starters, we've already made enquiries on the Mainland. We got no luck there. We have of course also touched based with our correspondents in Japan.'

'And?'

'There've been a number of cases. However, most of them appear to have been related to *yakuza* syndicates, principally the Yamaguchi-gumi, the biggest one, but also the Sumiyoshi-kai and the Inagawa-kai. Local politics also feature highly. There was even a famous case in 1960 where a socialist party leader was killed by a sword in a public hall in Tokyo, while giving a speech. The whole thing was broadcast live on television. Millions of people saw it. I looked at the footage on YouTube, you wouldn't believe how fast the strike was.'

'So back to square one, I guess. Did Andrew Short have anything to do with Japan in his line of work?'

'Good point, and I already checked. He had travelled there a few times, but mostly for holiday trips. According to Morgan Roberts, he looked after Asia excluding Japan and Australia. It's the usual arrangement for global investment banks in Hong

Kong, apparently. He had also never been posted to Japan, neither at Morgan Roberts nor at other houses.'

'Do you think we might be dealing with a killer from Japan?'

'It's a possibility, but it will likely take a long time to investigate. There are almost 25,000 Japanese living in Hong Kong and the number of visitors from Japan topped 1.3 million last year.'

'But clearly not all of them are proficient in *iaido*, right?'

'Clearly not. At the same time, our assassin may not even be Japanese at all. If not a resident, he or she could even have entered Hong Kong under a false passport. In addition, there's a large contingent of sword practitioners in the US. If anything we could probably cross reference lists of qualified practitioners in the major countries with both residents and arrivals in Hong Kong. It could involve a huge pile of paperwork, and it may not even result in an actionable lead in the end. Let me have a word with the ACP to see what he thinks.'

'In the meantime, I'll get contact names at the various *iaido* federations in other countries from Ken Tsui.'

'That would be great, Suki. Clearly, we're not facing someone who just bought a sword and taught himself how to cut. That thing is really, how shall I say, technical, I saw it with my own eyes. But it's also a skill our killer could have acquired anywhere, and a long time ago. Records may not even exist any more.'

'It's late, boss, and you sound like you need a drink.'

'I probably do.'

'I'm offering. Where are you now? I'll come over and pick you up. I think I might need a drink myself.'

CHAPTER 17

8:30 pm, Causeway Bay, Hong Kong, 3 October 2017

T HE TAXI SLOWED DOWN and stopped to pick up Ethan in Wan Chai. On the radio, an enthusiastic voice on RTHK 3, an English-language station, and a surprising choice for a Chinese taxi driver, broadcast yet another nanny-state message on the importance of taking care with scaffolding.

'Employees and their companies within the Special Administrative Region of Hong Kong can now obtain information, and also benefit from advisory services on occupational safety and health,' it said over a background of upbeat music. 'Interested parties should call the hotline or consult the website of the Labour Department at www.labour.gov.hk. Let's all work together for a safe, harmonious and enjoyable working environment in Hong Kong! Watch over your colleagues, as they also watch over you, improve your workplace, and take care of yourself! Be safe and healthy at work!'

A slight evening drizzle had started, as often in this season. Suki wore a man's blue shirt with her trademark jeans and hiking boots. Her black hair was, as usual, styled in a ponytail. She gave directions to the driver.

'So, where are you taking me, Suki?' Ethan asked.

'I thought we might as well keep the theme. A Japanese bar in Causeway Bay.'

'You must be kidding.'

'I'm dead serious. The Japanese make the best cocktails, you know. And the service is from another planet.'

The car stopped in Yiu Wa Street, a narrow, one-way lane in the shadow of the busy Times Square mall. Ethan and Suki were dwarfed by the rows of surrounding skyscrapers. The building, called 'Bartlock Centre', was rather scruffy in appearance. It seemed to host a wide array of offices, bars, video-game parlours, and other assorted businesses. An ageing security guard showed them to the lift. Suki pressed the button for the twenty-seventh floor, next to which a faded sticker read 'b.a.r. Executive Bar'.

They reached the desired floor and he saw a small plaque, affixed on wooden door painted in tan colour. All it said was 'Members Club'.

'Are you a member?'

'Don't worry about that.'

The bar was cosy, and simply decorated with comfortable leather chairs and sofas, and dark wood panelling throughout. The whole place could probably not accommodate more than a dozen customers. On one side, a bar counter ran the entire length of a wall. Behind the bar were literally hundreds of bottles of whisky, not just from Scotland, but also from Japan, Ireland, and other countries.

'I recall you're partial to a good whisky. I thought you'd like this.'

'I like it already.'

A balding and besuited Japanese bartender, who must have been in his fifties, was busy carving an ice ball. Next to him, a younger barmaid carefully measured and poured liquids into a shaker. The list of drinks included whiskies from a seemingly endless number of distilleries, as well as cocktails, which, the barman explained, featured seasonal Japanese fruits. Ethan opted for a vintage Port Ellen, a single cask, peaty single malt from the island of Islay. The distillery had closed years before, but small batches were sometimes released. It was a rare find.

'Single or double?'

'Double, no ice, just a little water please.'

Suki settled for a tequila-based cocktail that included fresh peach purée, among other ingredients.

'Now, you *have* to see this,' she said.

The barman almost performed a feat of acrobatics as he shook the mixture, all while retaining such a serious expression that Ethan could not help but smile. The glass came complete with carved pieces of fruit and a mini paper umbrella. It was all a bit ridiculous, but you had to admire the handiwork. The place was decidedly old style, but quite sophisticated.

'Thank you for this, Suki.'

'You're most welcome, boss. Sometimes you just have to escape the daily grind. Places like this help, don't you think?'

'Indeed. Well, since we're bonding, you never told me how you came to join the police force,' he said.

'Hmm. That's a long story,' she answered, 'as far back as I can remember that's what I wanted to do. I think it started with something I saw when I was a little girl, the suicide of an old man on our housing estate. He had jumped out of his window. It was all very sad, really. I was playing outside and saw everything. The police came very quickly. I remember this officer talking to me, trying to distract me. But of course, I never forgot it. After my BA in law at Hong Kong U, I went through the inspector selection process. I never really thought of doing anything else. I don't think I could have been a lawyer . . . but what about you?'

'Nothing so traumatic. I suppose I wanted to see some action, not be stuck in a desk job. I did a lot of sports, then. The army might have been an option before the handover. Instead, I spent a couple of years with the Flying Tigers.'

'Yes, I'd heard about it. I also heard you'd resigned.'

Ethan looked at his glass, silently, and thought for a few seconds about the little girl in Sha Tin, and the bullet's journey through her brain. The whisky burnt his throat, but in a nice, warming way. The heavy peat aromas led to more complex, tar, salt, and even medicinal flavours. Just what was needed on a day like this. He enjoyed Suki's company. She looked very dedicated and serious at first. But she knew how to let her hair down and could even be great fun. She was ambitious too, but not in a nasty, knife-in-the-back sort of way.

'Do you think we'll ever find him?' she finally asked, breaking a long silence.

'I don't know. We're a bit stuck right now, aren't we? But you said "him". Have you already decided our killer's a man?'

'I think so. It was so gruesome. Cutting someone open like that. As much as I try, I can't see a woman doing it, for some reason.'

'You'd be surprised, Suki. I came across a few female murderers in my time, and they can be just as twisted and nasty as men, believe me. Do you remember Nancy Kissel, the wife of that expatriate banker from Merrill Lynch, a few years ago? She bludgeoned him to death, after feeding him a milkshake laced with sedatives. Then she rolled up his body in a carpet and put it in a storeroom.'

'Yes, of course, how could anyone forget her? At least we got her, and she's locked up for life.'

A small, after-dinner crowd had arrived. Ethan and Suki ordered another round of drinks, enjoying the moment, finding out more about each other. They tried not to talk about work too much, but they kept coming back to the case. Someone had committed a horrible crime and was getting away with it, soundly sleeping it all off, perhaps even only a few blocks away from the welcoming Japanese bar.

Part II
WATER

CHAPTER 18

9:20 am, Central, Hong Kong, 4 October 2017

PIETER DU TOIT was ecstatic. It was not often that a three-fucking-Michelin-star chef visited Hong Kong.

Pieter had visited Redzepi's restaurant for a long weekend in Copenhagen only three months before. It was obviously the reason why his name was on the list. Overjoyed, Pieter, a South African, clicked on the hyperlink and registered for the dinner. The confirmation came, seconds later. He just loved the discreet way the whole thing had been arranged. The time and address for the dinner would only be advised on WhatsApp on the day of the event. That was brilliant! The teaser, however, had already revealed some of the wines that would be served and they were truly spectacular.

Pieter picked up the phone and dialled the syndicate desk at BSA, Bank of Southeast Asia. He asked for his counterpart, Cynthia. That chick had top model looks and the social life to match. He had been in hot pursuit for months, but now was perhaps as good an opportunity as he would ever have.

'Cynthia, baby. Pieter here.'

'Hi Pete. What can I do for you today?'

'Listen. I remember you wanted to try Noma in Copenhagen.'

'Yes, but forget it. They open reservations on first January and by 11 am the place is booked for the whole year.'

Jawelnofine. I know. I went a few months ago. But listen, Sweetie, I have it on good authority that René Redzepi himself is relocating to Hong Kong. For real.'

'Is that right? I didn't even know.'

'And, even better,' he said, pausing for greater effect, 'I've been invited to a preview dinner next Saturday, with none other than the man himself in the kitchen.'

'Are you kidding me?'

'It's a very private dinner, for only thirty people. I have a table for two. And one of those seats is for you.'

'No way! Where is this thing happening?'

'That's the thing, you see. A PR firm is arranging it. The place and time will only be revealed on the day. You won't believe the wine list. Sounds *lekker,* right? Are you in?'

'Of course I'm in. Thanks, Pete. Nice of you to remember.'

'How could I forget? See you *just now.*'

Feeling rather pleased with himself, du Toit turned to his deputy, a podgy Scot in his late twenties. Clifford was busy messaging someone on Bloomberg.

'Bru,' he said, 'tell me the details of that junk cruise on Friday. I need to send a reminder to the investors.'

'I thought the guys in Equities were doing it?'

'Izzit? Nah, better if I do it, so the PMs know whom to thank for their allocations next time. Will you let Sylvia know, so that we don't get our knickers in a twist?'

'Departure is at noon from Pier Nine. It's the one at the corner, just next to IFC Two, behind the Ferris wheel. Lunch and drinks will be served on board.'

'Ag, I bloody well hope so!'

'Then, the plan is to anchor off Turtle Cove Beach for a swim, water skiing, banana boat rides and so forth. And then back to Central. Weather forecast is fine. It should be good fun.'

'Ja, nee, thanks. Hey, Clifford?' he asked.

'Yep?'

'You're staying here, right? In case that block trade finally happens on Friday? The banker upstairs said it might.'

'If you say so, then I guess I am,' answered a grumpy Clifford.

'Sorry. *Bru,* listen, I'll be there for the next one.'

Pieter frenetically drafted a message to confirm the final arrangements for the outing to the small group of portfolio managers. They were all likely to take big positions in forthcoming placements led by Swiss Securities. They needed nurturing, and several colleagues from the trading floor would also join the cruise.

'Hey, I hope that girl from BlackRock goes topless!' chuckled Pieter.

'Take a picture for me.'

Swiss Securities' office occupied half the floors of a mid-size tower in Central. Two kilometres away as the crow flies, Shiryō had just logged in to Pieter du Toit's email account. The South African put the finishing touches to his memo. Once he was done, the bank's disclaimer at the bottom was three times longer than the actual message. Satisfied, he ceremonially pressed the 'send' button.

'Cast off,' he added for good measure.

CHAPTER 19

THAT EVENING, PIETER du Toit went out on the town with a couple of mates. There was nothing in particular to celebrate. It was just an ordinary Wednesday night in Hong Kong. The evening started with a few beers at a pub in Lan Kwai Fong. A cheap Thai dinner in Wan Chai followed. It sole purpose was to soak up the alcohol as they consumed bottles of Australian chardonnay. By 11:30 pm, du Toit was in fine form, and ready for a *karaoke* session that would last until the early hours. The trio entered a decaying building, just off one of the main streets that catered to vice establishments on the island. They took the elevator to one of the higher floors. The old lady on the door instantly recognised him.

'Mister Peter, long time no see,' she said, in heavily accented English.

'Welcome back!' added one of her colleagues, flashing an expectant smile and smelling the money.

'*Ag* mama, it's been a while,' said Pieter, 'now, we need a room, a lot of whisky and some company.'

'No problem. This time, same like before?'

'You read my mind as always, mama.'

They entered a closed, dark room that was about 400 square feet in size. Two sides were occupied by an inviting L-shape couch in faux leather, wrapped around a large coffee table. The room was dimly lit with a number of candles. On one of the walls, a large flat screen TV was switched on. A scrolling list offered a variety of songs to which guests and their partners could sing. A waiter brought a couple of ice buckets, two bottles of whisky, soft drinks, and cigarettes. He picked up one of the remote controls on the table, next to two wireless microphones, and switched on some background music.

A few minutes later, the old woman was back with about a dozen girls in tow. All were young, some perhaps under-aged, scantily clad, and heavily made up. They lined up for Pieter and his friends.

'Tonight, we have plenty of girls from China. All so nice. Also, girls from Vietnam, Myanmar, Indonesia, and the Philippines,' she said.

The girls stared at them, posing and pouting to encourage them in their choices.

'Fuck me, they're ugly,' said a chubby American called Steve, who worked as a portfolio manager for one of the city's largest hedge funds.

'Whadd'ya all think?' he next asked, after taking a sip from a large whisky and coke.

Jo. Steady, *bru,*' answered Pieter, 'I quite like the one on the left, with the blue miniskirt.'

'Ah yes, that one's a looker, I agree,' said Steve, taking a closer look.

'Wanda. Vietnam girl,' encouraged the mama-san.

'*Izzit?* Well, I'll take Wanda,' said Pieter, 'and you know what, I'll also take the Filipina, Tanya, the one in the pink dress. I've had her before and *bru,* you don't know what you're missing' he added for Steve's benefit.

'Well, they don't call you "Mr Multiple" for nothing, Pete,' replied Steve jokingly.

Steve himself picked Lili, a bored but cute Indonesian girl, who was barely above eighteen. Next to her was Mimi, a Chinese girl who forced herself to smile. Ron, a Kiwi who worked in structured finance, finally chose her after she had bent over, showing her non-existent cleavage in a bid to get selected.

'Let the games begin,' said Ron, after waving away the mama-san.

The girls sat next to their respective companions and poured drinks. They made small talk in their limited English. They then scrolled through the list of songs on the TV screen. Tanya had already unbuttoned half of Pieter's shirt and stroked his chest vigorously.

'Cheriii! You strong man! I want you,' she said with a giggle.

'I want you too!' added Wanda for good measure after giving Tanya a long, passionate and very wet kiss, just to put everyone else in the mood.

'At that rate, we're not going to be here for long,' observed Steve, matter-of-factly.

'You're right,' countered Ron, 'let's sing.'

Just as Steve started blaring the lyrics of a Lady Gaga number, the mama-san was back.

'Mister Peter, same like before,' she whispered handing him a small envelope.

'Gentlemen, it's time to chase the dragon,' declared Pieter, solemnly.

He made three parallel lines of coke on the stained glass table. He straightened them as neatly as he could with an American Express Centurion black card. He rolled up a HK$500 note in a small tube and inhaled one of the lines. Ron and Steve were already drawing their wallets, ready to do the same.

'Now, who deserves these 500 dollars?' asked Pieter loudly, waving the banknote in his hand.

His head was already spinning, as the drug took effect. Tanya was the first to react. She unzipped his trousers fly and, after exploring his underwear for a couple of seconds, gently squeezed his genitals.

'Me! Me! Me!' she answered enthusiastically.

Wanda soon joined her there. Massaging him in sync with Tanya, she whispered in his ear, half biting it 'I like to move it, move it!'

Pieter closed his eyes, enjoying the moment, as in a daydream. In the background, he heard Steve shouting incoherently, in a tight embrace with Lili, microphone in hand.

'Oops, I did it again. . . .'

CHAPTER 20

S HIRYŌ WORE A PAIR of acetate glasses with clear lenses as a disguise. He walked from his serviced apartment in Causeway Bay to Hennessy Road, in Wan Chai. The street was full of shops selling bathroom appliances, floorboards, wooden planks, and domestic tools. On its west side, it gave way to girly bars and loud pubs with evocative names, reminiscent of Hong Kong's past as an outpost for the opium trade and stopover port for the US Navy.

A run-down, angled signboard at street level showed the way to a dive shop. Shiryō effortlessly climbed the three floors to its entrance door. A wide array of scuba gear, including masks, fins, snorkels, buoyancy control devices, wetsuits and accessories, such as lamps and camera cases, were spread across three separate rooms. As a former military diver, he was in familiar territory and knew exactly what he needed. He first selected a weight system, a black nylon weight belt that closed with a simple, stainless steel buckle. It could be unlocked with a single hand, as the other controlled the inflator of the buoyancy control jacket. He added two lead blocks of one kilogramme each.

He chose a pair of black open-heel fins. They were shorter than other models, but still offered powerful propulsion. Because they were fitted with soft and flexible silicone straps, rather than standard rubber spring fasteners, they could more easily be put on and removed. He picked a pair of black neoprene boots with a rubber sole that closed with side zips, on the inside of the calf. He checked that they fitted loosely into the fins' open heels, so that he would not get cramps, even after many strokes. He completed his kit with a matching, low-volume mask, a snorkel, and a simple, wrist-mounted compass. He finally purchased a black waterproof bag in which to carry all of his equipment. Shiryō paid in cash and walked back to his apartment to drop the bag.

Still wearing his clear glasses, he rode the MTR to Tsim Sha Tsui on Kowloon side. A short walk from the station took him to another dive shop, located in a high-rise building. There, he selected a Model 300 Spare Air bottle, a redundant scuba system that offered divers enough air to safely reach the surface in an out-of-air emergency. It came with a holster and a safety leash. It could be used hands free, with a built-in, breathe-on-demand regulator. The vendor was only too happy to fill it up for him with compressed air from a scuba tank. He also pointed out that this particular model came with an adaptor that would enable Shiryō to refill it himself from any K-valve cylinder, and in no more than a minute. The mini bottle included three cubic feet of pressured air. It would enable him to take in the equivalent of between fifty and sixty surface breaths. The waters around Hong Kong were shallow, generally not more than five or six metres, and it would be plenty for what he had in mind.

Having again paid cash, Shiryō walked east towards Nathan Road. He entered a camera shop and bought a short waterproof monocular. The 40 mm diameter lens had a magnification of ten times. He paid with a wad of Hong Kong notes, then paused for a snack and a bottle of mineral water at a cheap sidestreet Thai restaurant. There were more upmarket places in many of the surrounding malls and hotels but Shiryō was keen to avoid CCTV cameras as much as possible, especially when not on the move. Besides, the food was delicious and he needed the break. The damp weather would soon break into a powerful shower. Once rested, he timed his return by MTR to his serviced apartment in Causeway Bay to coincide with the early-evening rush hour. An anonymous traveller, he felt safe among the dense crowd of Chinese and expatriate commuters.

CHAPTER 21

T URTLE COVE BEACH was located to the west of Tai Tam Bay, on the south side of Hong Kong Island. It was one of the few beaches on the island with clear water, making it an ideal spot for swimming. Strangely, it was far less popular than those at Shek O or Big Wave Bay further to the east.

Shiryō carried his waterproof bag and left his apartment around 10 am. He followed his usual counter-surveillance routine and started his trip at the Causeway Bay MTR station. The journey was short. It took him only twelve minutes to arrive at Sai Wan Ho Station where he caught a bus. Overall, it took less than forty-five minutes for him to reach his destination. He had plenty of time left before his target would arrive.

Swiss Securities' motor junk was named *Basel III*. She was mostly used to entertain clients, although employees of the bank could charter her for outings with family and friends. She could carry up to forty people. Her deck included a fully equipped kitchen and bar, as well as a canopied outdoor dining area. That day, she would also tow a small motorboat for water skiing and other activities. The junk waited just to the east of the Central ferry pier. The boat, all decked out in varnished teak and flying Swiss and Hong Kong flags, gently bobbed on the water. Next to her were other pleasure craft, their owners keen to take advantage of the beautiful weather to start weekend activities earlier than usual.

Pieter du Toit turned up at 11:50 am, bleary-eyed. He wore a pair of baggy beige shorts and red leather dockside shoes, below a yellow T-shirt that read ALLOCATE ME IN FULL. His face was partially hidden by a pair of gold Ray-Ban aviator sunglasses and a blue baseball cap with the logo of Swiss Securities. The colours clashed shockingly. He also carried a small backpack. A couple of colleagues accompanied him. One was Sylvia Ip, the bank's head of Asian equity sales, an ambitious Chinese girl from Hong Kong, with long, slick black hair. She was in her mid-thirties. Not only was she attractive, but also dressed in revealing beachwear, barely hidden under a see-through *pareo*. The other banker was the firm's head of Asian equity research, Robert Tan. He was a quiet and somewhat formal Singaporean, who had spent his career regularly moving from one house to another on guaranteed remuneration packages. Thanks to them, his annual bonuses were contractually pre-agreed, rather than based on his actual performance. Robert Tan wore a navy suit, but without a tie. Two buttons of his pink shirt were undone. For him, it was a wild and rebellious statement.

The trio boarded the corporate junk and settled into the cushions that lined the deck at the stern. In addition to the captain and boat boy, the crew comprised two other members, in charge of the food and beverage service. All were Chinese and wore smart white uniforms, with the bank's logo on their chests.

Pieter, Sylvia and Robert were offered glasses of champagne. Tan declined, preferring instead some mineral water. Canapés were brought on a silver tray. Shortly after noon, their guests started arriving. There were half a dozen in total, important clients of the firm's equities division, and portfolio managers at major institutional fund management companies and hedge funds. They were well known to the trio, who now hoped to reinforce their business relationships. Once the guests had arrived, the boat cast off and the captain headed east, in the direction of Lei Yue Mun. The sound system played Duran Duran at full volume.

'Guys, help yourselves! There's plenty to drink and eat, in that order! It will take us a while to get to the beach, so have a *jol!'* invited du Toit cheerily.

On the upper deck, two female investors, one from a long-only fund that specialised in North Asian stocks, and the other, who headed a US$3 billion regional hedge fund, were busy anointing each other with coconut oil. Beside them, a bottle of vintage Krug Clos du Mesnil lay in an ice bucket. Pieter climbed up a wobbly ladder to join them and pour himself a drink.

'Ag. This beats the office any time,' he observed.

He dialled Clifford on his mobile, safely clinging to the handrail with his other hand.

'Bru? Just checking,' he said, before abruptly hanging up.

CHAPTER 22

10:59 am, Turtle Cove, Hong Kong, 7 October 2017

THE BEACH WAS ONLY about seventy metres wide. It was framed by rocks and trees and, further up in the distance, by low-rise buildings on both sides. A few metres offshore was a small floating pontoon, on which kids often played and from which they jumped into the water. Barbecue pits offered visitors a chance to cook skewers on the spot, after a morning or day of swimming in the South China Sea.

Shiryō walked down the steep steps that led from the road to the beach. He then turned right, towards the west side of the cove, where he could drop his bag in an area well sheltered by the tree line. There, he could sit unobserved and scan the horizon with his monocular for signs of the bank's vessel. The climb was not particularly arduous and he reached his vantage point in just a few minutes. It was almost noon. He was glad for the shade offered by the pine trees.

Once in place, he changed into his swimsuit and put on his neoprene boots. They would offer protection from cuts on the rocky terrain. Shiryō ate a few biscuits and sipped water, waiting for his target to arrive. His mask, snorkel, fins, compass and air cylinder were all ready.

It was a glorious day. The cicadas sang non-stop in the trees above him. Down on the beach, a mother played with her infant child. An ageing couple took in the sights, well shaded under a beach umbrella. Anyone sensible would probably soon take shelter from the scorching sun and retreat to an air-conditioned environment. The heat, however, did not unduly bother Shiryō. Earlier in his career he had spent hours scanning the sea for pirates through the scope of his M24, a heavy bolt-action rifle that could propel a 0.338 Lapua Magnum bullet to up to 1,500 metres. That had been aboard the *Sazanami* destroyer, off the coast of Somalia, a country that probably had one of the driest and hottest climates on the planet. He could wait for hours without getting bored, totally focused on the task at hand. From the sky above him, seagulls plunged for juvenile needlefish or squid.

The departure of the junk from Central had been scheduled at noon. She would probably anchor off the beach around 2:15 pm. Sunset was at 6:19 pm. They would likely plan to depart at 4 pm at the latest, to arrive back in Central before dusk. That would allow a few hours of fun in the water after a long lunch. Shiryō intended to strike as late in the day as possible. All hell would break lose after his assault, although probably not immediately. The Marine Police would turn up quickly. *Basel III* was a corporate junk. There would be clear and well-rehearsed procedures in the event of an accident on board, even if Shiryō anticipated an initial phase of panic and confusion.

The arrival of a motor junk suddenly caught his attention. She was headed for the beach in the distance. He could not see her name with his monocular yet, but it was probably too early for her to be *Basel III*. The boat, now closer, slowly turned to starboard before idling. A member of the crew moved to the bow to help with anchoring. After dropping the anchor, the captain revved the boat's engine, slowly steering the vessel backwards. The boat aligned with the prevailing wind, enabling Shiryō to quickly confirm she was not *Basel III*. He was silently pleased. The presence of other craft would add to the confusion. After thirty minutes, another junk anchored in the same area. Shiryō glanced at his watch. It would not be long, now. He emptied a water bottle on his face and neck to fight the heat and expectantly scanned the horizon again.

CHAPTER 23

2:16 pm, Turtle Cove, Hong Kong, 7 October 2017

B*ASEL III* HAD SAILED past the Shau Kei Wan typhoon shelter, exiting Victoria Harbour through the Lei Yue Mun passage. After rounding the Shek O Peninsula, she sailed into Tai Tam Bay.

The portfolio managers were having a good time and Pieter and his colleagues spared no effort to ensure that they did. Finger food was replaced by an assortment of main courses, both Asian and Western. Champagne and wine flowed liberally as music blared on the audio system. A cigar box containing a selection of Cuba's finest was also produced.

Shiryō saw, and then heard, the vessel in the distance. Soon, she was directly in front of him and hove to just off the American Club. She anchored away from the other boats that had assembled near the beach, earlier in the day. Shiryō identified Pieter du Toit through the lens of his monocular. He had come out of the cabin, wearing a pair of green, baggy swimming trunks. After a few minutes of posing and walking around the deck, du Toit climbed onto the roof of the junk and bomb-dived into the water with a big scream. He was soon joined by other passengers, as the impassive crew lowered inflatable toys into the water. The activities would next include wakeboarding and waterskiing, using the small tender that *Basel III* had towed from Central.

Shiryō donned the rest of his equipment and slipped into the water. He was largely hidden from view of the junk by a cluster of granite rocks. The water was fairly warm, but Shiryō felt refreshed after having sat idle for hours at the hottest time of the day. His opportunity soon came. Two female passengers and Robert Tan had had enough swimming and climbed into the speedboat to try a spot of wakeboarding. With the engine roaring, she sped out to sea at great speed. Du Toit, now alone, decided to investigate the other junks anchored in the bay. It was only 3 pm. Shiryō would ideally have liked to wait for longer, but a better occasion might not present itself later. He also could not allow du Toit to get too close to the other boats.

Shiryō aligned the needle and bezel of his wrist compass to follow du Toit's heading, and silently disappeared below the surface. It was difficult to see much beyond a few metres. But, by following the heading on his compass and making regular, even strokes with his fins, Shiryō would soon reach his target. As part of his combat diver training, he had been required to swim underwater for fifty metres on a single breath. He was confident he would use far less than the contents of the Spare Air cylinder to complete his task. Unlike a closed-circuit re-breather, the Spare Air would shoot air bubbles to the surface, but he was sure that no one would notice.

Shiryō knew a fair bit about drowning. Another drill at the Special Boarding Unit had been drown-proofing. It was derived from the selection process for the US Navy Seals. With his legs bound together by Velcro straps and his hands similarly tied behind his back, he had been required to bob up and down in some three metres of water, for a minimum of five minutes. It was meant to test self-control and the ability of the recruit to establish a regular, confident rhythm. To achieve this, one could only take controlled breaths when breaking the surface. Taking too big a breath resulted in an increased buoyancy and difficulty in reaching the bottom of the pool, in turn leading, over time, to an out-of-air situation. Conversely, pushing up too forcefully on the pool's floor, often a sign of panic, led to the straps breaking loose, another cause for disqualification. Shiryō had passed with flying colours, even enjoying what had, for many, been a gruelling ordeal.

He followed the compass heading, swimming near the seabed, and soon saw a pair of green trunks and legs flapping above him. The water was about five metres deep. Shiryō decided to approach du Toit from behind. The first reaction of someone who fears drowning is generally to cling to a nearby swimmer. Subduing du Toit would therefore be much easier if Shiryō did not face him head on. He rose from the deep, placed his hands on du Toit's shoulders, and pushed his knee hard against the South African's back. At the same time, he let go of all the air contained in his lungs. They disappeared below the surface together.

Du Toit exhaled much of his air supply, in a panic perhaps compounded by a fuzzy mind. He had consumed a lot of alcohol in the preceding hours. Shiryō wrapped his legs around du Toit's torso, blocking his arms as they both fell towards the bottom of the sea. Du Toit's head was now desperately shaking, left and right. His legs were also all over the place, forcing Shiryō to control their bodies with his own breathing to achieve neutral buoyancy in mid-water. Soon, du Toit was forced to inhale. Water entered his airway, oxygen depletion and carbon dioxide retention soon followed. As du Toit gasped, he started to hyperventilate, leading to further hypoxemia, meanwhile Shiryō tightened his grip; taking care not to sink too far so that du Toit could not push on the seabed in an effort to escape.

After a few seconds, asphyxia led to a relaxation of the banker's airway and his lungs took in more water. This, in turn, within minutes triggered multiple organ failure. Cardiac arrest and a central nervous system ischemia soon followed. As du Toit went limp in his arms, Shiryō saw an old car tyre covered with coral and algae just below him. He held on to du Toit's body with one hand, reached for the tyre and slipped one of the South African's arms through it, all the way to his shoulder. He then bent the arm at the elbow to make a hook. It would keep du Toit in position for a while, until the feeble current ultimately freed him.

Shiryō knew from experience it could take anywhere from twelve to thirty-six hours for a submerged body to return to the surface. Any search for du Toit would likely involve divers from the Marine Police and, perhaps, volunteers from local diving clubs. Satisfied that the body would remain in place for the time being, Shiryō looked at his compass then followed the reverse bearing back to the rocky shore. His eyes just above the water, he confirmed that no alarm had been raised. The speedboat still towed a skier a few hundred metres away, amid much screaming by the other passengers. Music still blared on *Basel III,* where one of the crewmembers had just opened another bottle of champagne. The other boats did not exhibit any untoward activity. Shiryō climbed out of the water and quickly removed his equipment. He had only consumed forty per cent of the air supply. He dried himself with a small towel and put his day clothes and shoes back on. He donned a plain baseball cap and sunglasses. His waterproof bag on his shoulder, he walked across the beach at a normal pace. He climbed the stairs to the road, just in time to board a Number 14 bus.

CHAPTER 24

12:40 pm, Central, Hong Kong, 10 October 2017

ASSISTANT COMMISSIONER OF POLICE Peter Ma had instructed Ethan to turn up at 12:45 pm sharp, at the Red Room restaurant of the Hong Kong Club. The club, originally established in 1846, was now located in a modern tower to which it had given its name on Jackson Road, in Central, where it faced the grass patch on which the cenotaph stood. Initially, membership had included senior government officials and the heads of Hong Kong's major trading firms or *hongs*. And, to a large extent, that was still true today. Probably the most prestigious club – and, certainly, the most difficult to join – in the city, it still hosted the great and the good of the territory. The dress code was famously conservative and, even in this day and age, it continued to prohibit electronic communications devices in most areas. Giving interviews to journalists was forbidden within its premises.

Ethan wore plain clothes, a navy suit and a red tie, over a white cotton shirt with a cutaway collar. Five minutes before due time, he arrived on the second floor. In addition to bars and restaurants, the club included a library, a barbershop, a fitness centre, and even a bowling alley. The Red Room was on his left. ACP Ma was already there, seated at a table for three, near a window that overlooked the harbour and nearby buildings. He too was dressed in civilian clothes. As the name suggested, the Red Room was decorated in scarlet fabric. Red was an auspicious colour for the Chinese. On the walls, classical paintings depicted views of the English countryside. It was almost a caricature of what a gentleman's club should look like, although, nowadays, membership was also open to women.

The third person to join them, and at whose initiative the lunch was arranged, was none other than the commissioner of police himself, Mortimer Tse. He was the most senior official in the force, presiding over the careers of some 28,000 officers. Peter Ma and Ethan briefly stood to attention as the CP walked towards them. A man in his late fifties with conservative tastes, he wore a sharply tailored grey suit, with a blue tie. Once they had sat, he briefly explained the reason for hosting the lunch at the club.

'I'm meeting with Tung Chee Hwa here at two. So I thought we might as well meet over lunch at the club. The food is rather good, you know.'

Tung Chee Hwa had been the first chief executive of the territory, appointed following the return of the city to the Chinese motherland.

Ethan had met Tse a few times, although always in a formal setting, and never for more than a few minutes. Waiters dressed in immaculate white uniforms with the club's logo on their chests silently hovered around them.

All opted for one of the day's fish courses, steamed garoupa, with wild garlic, rice, *choi sum* and *bok choi*. They skipped the offer of a starter and asked for *pu-erh* tea, a strong but healthy choice. Ethan, the most junior at the table, poured the tea once it had infused, as Tse and Ma gently tapped their forefingers on the table next to their cups, as etiquette dictated.

'I wanted to talk to you both in relation to this boating accident of a few days ago,' Tse said.

'That man who drowned while on a junk trip, sir?' asked Ethan.

'Precisely. At around 4 pm on Friday, Marine Headquarters in Sai Wan Ho received a distress call signalling that one of the vessel's passengers had gone missing, off Turtle Bay Beach. As it happened, he was actually one of the organisers of the outing. Divers from the Outer Waters district turned out in force in inflatable hull vessels. They quickly searched the area in a grid pattern, as per procedure, but it still took a while before they found his body, at a depth of about five metres, just before sunset.'

'A most unfortunate accident,' commented Ethan, philosophically.

'It wasn't an accident,' snapped Tse.

'What do you mean, Sir?' asked Ethan.

'As you know, Ethan,' said Tse in a fatherly tone, 'it can be difficult to tell whether a man has drowned on his own, or as a result of foul play. However, the autopsy revealed traces of bruises to the upper and lower back of the victim. They couldn't easily be explained and also couldn't be matched to the seabed, which was predominantly sandy. Even though the man had drunk a fair amount of alcohol before getting into the water, the pathologist, Dr Kwok, whom I believe you know rather well, is adamant his demise would have been aided, so to speak.'

'That's quite extraordinary,' said Ethan.

'Indeed. Now, the deceased was an investment banker, one Pieter du Toit, South African. He was also a permanent resident. It looks like he was a bit of a big shot with Swiss Securities. It obviously recalls the killing of that Australian banker, more than a week ago. I don't like it, not at all. I fear we could soon have a major problem on our hands.'

'Someone out there is targeting bankers?' asked Ethan.

'Well, the coincidence is certainly troubling. Now, I don't need to remind you both of the importance of the financial sector to this city. For now, this has been classified as an accident. But rumours will soon come out. We can't afford a major panic spreading out among the employees of securities firms.'

'Indeed not,' acknowledged the ACP gravely.

'Moreover, with all that agitation about universal suffrage and the revival of the Occupy Central movement, the finance sector is already under considerable strain. We need to have this sorted out, sooner rather than later. I've already spoken to colleagues from the Marine region. I want you, Ethan, to take over this investigation, while continuing with the Morgan Roberts homicide.'

'Yes, sir, thank you, sir. I must say, however, that we haven't made much headway with the death of the Australian. We're looking at a possible lead concerning the manner in which he was killed, which we are now certain involved a Japanese sword. But it may still take time to unravel.'

'Time, unfortunately, is not something we've got, right now. Beijing will have my ass for breakfast, unless we find out who did this soon. And shit rolls downhill as we all know,' he added mischievously. 'You can have all the resources you require, within reason,' he continued, 'and you have my full backing.

If anyone makes any difficulties, send them my way. Drop everything else. We'll all be in trouble if another banker gets hit.'

'Are you suggesting. . . .' started Ma.

'I certainly can't discount the possibility, unfortunately. Now, if you'll excuse me, gentlemen,' he said after looking at his watch, 'I need to attend to our former chief executive, who, I hope, is not the bearer of more bad news.'

He waved his hand to signal to one of the waiters and asked to sign the chit.

CHAPTER 25

5:58 am, Central Mid Levels, Hong Kong, 11 October 2017

ETHAN WOKE UP BEFORE SIX that morning. As he did most days, he drove to Bowen Road in the Mid Levels. He parked his Toyota at the western end of the road, near a cluster of low-rise residences. Bowen Road was mainly pedestrianised. It stretched across the entire Mid Levels, overlooking the adjoining districts of Central, Admiralty, Wan Chai and Happy Valley, of which it offered, on a clear day, almost picture-perfect postcard views. It was a largely flat road that bisected an otherwise hilly terrain. It was popular with joggers and dog walkers. Running to the end of the road and back totalled almost nine kilometres. It made for a pleasant start to the day, especially before sunrise when the temperature was cool.

Bowen Road, largely deserted so early in the morning, was home to relatively very few buildings. It was mostly framed by a lush tropical wilderness, a green oasis above the concrete jungle that was the northern coastline of Hong Kong Island. The morning run helped Ethan clear his mind. Along the road was a purpose-built fitness trail, but he ignored the various exercise stations, preferring simply to concentrate on his running. He completed the circuit in less than forty-five minutes and returned home in the western Mid Levels for a shower. He then drove to police headquarters in time for the 8 am meeting.

But first, he needed a coffee. With some of his team members, he had bought a high-pressure Italian percolator. The coffee it made was head and shoulders above the insipid mixture offered by the office's vending machines. A number of tea drinkers among those who worked for him had already been converted to the call of espresso in the morning. The aroma stimulated his brain as he entered the meeting room.

'Where shall we start? Suki?' he called, once he had sat.

'I've made some progress cross-checking records of *iaido* practitioners and visitors to Hong Kong, although, to be frank, I'm not sure it will amount to much in the end. Most of the info is slow coming. We're trying to narrow it down, but it involves a lot of liaising overseas and it's hardly a priority for many of our correspondents. Everyone is focused on terrorism threats, Islamic State militants and the like, right now.'

'I see. The CP said we could have as much help as needed, so let's take you off that. I'll get another team to focus on it. I agree it looks tedious. I'd rather have you working on something that you can be more productive with. Charles, what do we know about that South African guy and about what happened on the junk trip?'

'It was an outing arranged by three people from Swiss Securities, including the deceased. The others were the regional heads of equity research and equity sales. A number of portfolio managers, all investor clients of the bank, were invited for the afternoon on a junk owned by the bank. She's very plush, with a bar, music system, and all the trimmings. And, would you believe it, she's called *Basel III!*' said Charles.

'And?' asked John Mok, clearly not getting it.

'The Basel Accords, now in their third round, are guidelines for the supervision of banks. They're agreed by central banks, under the supervision of the Bank of International Settlements,' said Ethan, as if reading from an article in the *Financial Times*.

'Ha ha! That's hilarious,' replied John, in a deadpan voice.

'More pertinently, have we got a handle on the sequence of events?' asked Ethan.

'Yes. The vessel departed Pier Nine in Central, shortly after noon. She then headed east around Hong Kong Island, to anchor near the American Club just off Turtle Cove Beach.'

Charles consulted his notes.

'The junk arrived around 2:15 pm. Lunch was served on board, on the way. It looks like they all had a fair amount to drink. There were enough empty bottles of Krug to build a floating raft! Anyway, around 2:30 pm, some of the party went in for a swim. Most of them either returned on board after approximately twenty minutes or went wakeboarding. There was a speedboat in addition to the junk. The victim, Pieter du Toit, continued to swim, alone.'

'When did they realise he was no longer about?' asked Ethan.

'Between 3:30 pm and 3:45 pm. They could not be more precise. They had a good look around, but could not locate him. He wasn't on any of the nearby boats either. That's when the captain decided to call Marine Headquarters, around 4:10 pm. It was obviously logged, so that checks.'

'And who was Pieter du Toit, exactly?'

'Everyone said he was a pretty good swimmer. He had no known medical conditions. He was a managing director with Swiss Securities. He had lived in Hong Kong for eight years, so he was a PR. He had previously worked for Merrill Lynch, and also Nomura. Where it becomes really interesting is that his job was as head of regional equity syndicate, like that of Andrew Short, from Morgan Roberts.'

'Now, that's quite remarkable.'

'Isn't it just? Du Toit was a bit of a loudmouth. He clearly wasn't everyone's cup of tea, but professionally he was well regarded. He had a lot of experience.'

'What does a head of syndicate actually do, by the way?' asked Suki.

'Basically, equity capital markets, or ECM for short, are departments within investment banks in which people spend most of their time pitching to equity issuers, such as corporates or private equity firms,' explained Ethan. 'They provide product expertise on equity offerings. In practice, they often work with other teams, like those that specialise in a particular country or industry sector. And, quite often, ECM mandates are handed out jointly to several banks, especially when the deal is sizeable, say from several hundred million US dollars or more. Are you with me so far?' he asked.

'So far, so good,' said Suki.

'One of the guys at Morgan Roberts was quite helpful in explaining things to me. Now,' he continued, 'once a mandate has been won, it must be executed. This can take quite a bit of time. Up to several months, or even longer if it's an IPO. Some of the work is to do with documentation, prospectuses, agreements, and the like. Some of it deals with valuation and positioning. And another aspect covers marketing to investors.'

'Right.'

'Equity syndicate desks are more particularly focused on marketing. They liaise among each other to ensure consistency of messages to investors, to market the offer in an organised manner. They coordinate with the equity sales force and the bank's research analysts, and also approach major investors at an early stage. They then oversee what is called investor education, which is when investors are first told about the deal and company, through equity research reports. At the end of that stage, the feedback enables the banks to set up a price range.

'Then, investors can place orders for shares within the range. Based on the amount and quality of investor demand, the deal is priced and the number of shares each investor receives as an allocation is determined, before listing and trading can start on the exchange.'

'What do you mean by "quality of investor demand"?' asked Suki.

'Well, as I understand it, it's to do with the behaviour of each investor after trading has started. Some are known as long-term holders. Others often sell very quickly, as soon as there's a capital gain or drop in price. In an ideal world, deals should be anchored with a core group of some of the larger accounts. Many of these steps are under the responsibility of the head of syndicate.'

'Crystal clear,' said Suki.

'Thank you. I can't believe it's already been two weeks since I discussed this with Ashok Patel.'

'So, it's likely that du Toit would have known Andrew Short, then,' observed Suki, not missing a beat.

'Oh, they knew each other all right,' answered Charles. 'All these syndicate guys know each other. It's part of their job, actually.'

'What else did they have in common?' asked Ethan.

'As far as I can see, that's pretty much it, other than the fact they were both expats, of course. But then, so are 600,000 other people in this city. It's apparently not rare for senior investment bankers to be foreigners, especially at the US, European, Japanese and Australian banks, less so with the Chinese ones, obviously. They were both PRs too. But they did not have the same nationality. They had never worked for the same bank. I checked. They did not go to the same universities. As far as I know, they did not date the same partners, either. Both were heterosexual, but I'd hardly call that a breakthrough.'

'What more could you find about du Toit in particular?' asked Ethan.

'He was a restaurant freak. And he liked Ferraris.'

'What do you mean by "restaurant freak"?'

'He had this thing about Michelin star restaurants. He loved to get his picture taken with top chefs. His Facebook wall was full of them. Boy, he must have tried the whole bloody guide! He had boasted about going to a private dinner with a three-star chef last Saturday.'

'What about the way he was killed? John, you met our good friend Alfred Kwok, didn't you?'

'Yes. The good doctor put me off eating last night, it has to be said. Anyway, the way he sees it is that du Toit was probably quietly swimming when he was grabbed, likely from behind, and pulled below the surface. He was found at a depth of about five metres. Midway down, his aggressor would have immobilised him by wrapping his legs around his body, to prevent du Toit from freeing himself. The scenario is consistent with the bruises identified during the autopsy. In addition, there were traces of scraping, probably by bits of coral, on one of his arms. They were matched to an old tyre lying on the bottom, where he was actually found. Whoever did this tried to stash the body there. It was definitely not an accident,' John Mok concluded.

'Du Toit was quite a big guy, wasn't he?'

'Oh yes, 185 cm. Blond hair. Big teeth. He looked like a lifeguard on *Baywatch!* Kwok reckons it's unlikely the killer would have been a woman, to be able to immobilise him underwater. We're probably looking for a man, and a rather fit one at that.'

'Well, at least it's something. It looks like your hunch was correct, Suki. Just thinking aloud, the killer would have worn full scuba gear then, wouldn't he?'

'Actually, not necessarily,' said Suki.

'What do you mean?'

'Well, as you know, I teach diving in my spare time. To stay underwater for a fair amount of time, there are alternatives to a full-blown cylinder and regulator, especially at such a low depth. They could certainly provide enough air to grab and kill someone unobserved from the surface.'

'Tell us more,' invited Ethan.

CHAPTER 26

MARILAG WAS INTRIGUED by the text message she had just received. It was signed 'JJ'. She was still half asleep. She thought for a few seconds and suddenly remembered. It was that chubby, creepy American, Jasper. Marilag was from Panay, in the western part of the Visayas Islands, in the Philippines. Her name meant 'beautiful' in Tagalog. Not that she was much of a looker, but she tried hard to make herself attractive, wearing a lot of makeup and as few clothes as she could get away with. She had come to Hong Kong on a tourist visa. Only a few days remained until she would overstay its validity.

Visiting Hong Kong was actually the last thing on Marilag's mind. Unlike most Filipinas in the city, who worked as domestic helpers, Marilag had come to sell her body. So far, she was not doing too badly. She plied her trade out of a small bar in Wan Chai. The men would come in, hesitant at first, and would order a drink. They would buy her one too, soon followed by more, and strike up a conversation. After a while, once they had spent enough money for small talk, they would pay the barmaid a bar fine, and take Marilag to a nearby hotel that charged by the hour.

Marilag offered them a simple choice, short time or long time, and would announce a price accordingly. She would keep all of what she earned that way. Most of her clients only wanted her for an hour, or even less. But some men would buy her for an entire night, sometimes even taking her to their own apartments. Marilag was always careful. When they were new clients, she would always text the address to someone at the bar. At least they knew where she had gone, in case she failed to reappear. In that event the bar would send in a couple of 49ers, hard men, fighting members of the triad the mama-san paid protection to. Most of the johns, however, were not violent. They were merely lonely men. Many had no other way of sleeping with a woman, mostly because they were shy. Others simply preferred the anonymity and brevity of an uncomplicated commercial encounter.

JJ was different. He was a regular at the bar, but he sometimes bypassed the matchmaking services of the mama-san altogether. He would call or simply text the girls, asking for sex at all hours. They always went to his flat. It was better that way. The mama-san did not need to know, and would have found out if they had used one of the nearby short-time hotels. She would have asked for a cut, and perhaps sent a Red Pole, a triad enforcer, to teach them a lesson. It was also rumoured that some of the girls had been invited on long weekends with JJ in Macau or Thailand. Now, that must have been something.

JJ was a strange man. He had unusual preferences and sometimes even disgusting requests. Although he did not have a violent nature, he sometimes liked to hurt some of the girls, and on occasion rather hard. He was also well known for having several girls in his bed at the same time. At least, it was probably safer that way, they could watch over each other. A good thing was that he paid well, more than most other clients. And so, they never complained, as he subjected them to perverse humiliations. The money was always handed out in advance, of course. He would offer them drugs too. It helped to dull their senses.

Marilag had only been twice to where JJ lived. It was in Causeway Bay, some sort of hotel, she thought. It was not a particularly high-end place. Nothing like the stories she had heard from some of the girls, who had managed to hook insanely rich guys for an entire night, or longer. Marilag sighed: she had not been so lucky, yet. Perhaps JJ simply did not care about where he lived. He sounded like he made good money, though. Some had even said he was a banker. The place was cosy enough, however, and he would let Marilag use the shower afterwards. The location was convenient too. She could always find a taxi within minutes after leaving, even late at night. Then she would return to the bar and engage with another man. If it were too late, she would instead go straight to the filthy room she shared for an extortionate rent, just above the bar with four others girls, and collapse until late morning. There, they slept in cheap bunk beds. There was no bathroom, only a tap with cold water, at the end of a dark and damp corridor. When she woke up, the cycle started again. The first clients usually arrived just after lunchtime, but most of them came at night.

JJ's text had flashed on her phone early in the morning. The time, in itself, was quite unusual. All it said was 'All night long. Tonight. 10 pm. JJ.' Marilag smiled. All night meant a lot of money. Even better, she might find the time to squeeze in a few other johns, before she joined him after dinner.

CHAPTER 27

'MY POINT IS, if du Toit was killed by someone with full-blown scuba gear, it would have hardly been inconspicuous,' Suki said. 'We're talking of an eighteen-litre tank with a buoyancy-control device, among other pieces of equipment. He would also have needed a boat from which to dive or, if he had swum from the shore, someone would likely have noticed him. With a full tank, that's about twenty kilos of gear, or even more. Of course, a tank could have been hidden near the beach earlier, but you'd still need to retrieve it at some point. Or it could have been left in the water, either before or after the attack. It's not that difficult to don and take off an entire kit underwater, if you have enough experience. But it would have been much easier to use a pony bottle.'

'What is that?' asked Charles.

'When you dive, you generally have about 2,900 psi of compressed air in your tank. After you've consumed three quarters of this, after an hour or so, depending on the profile of your dive, it's time to return to the surface. The overriding principle is that you always have some air left, as a precaution.'

'Understood.'

'But, sometimes, you may not have paid enough attention to your air supply, or there could be a defect with your gauge. You may even run out of air altogether. If that happens, you must share someone else's supply to surface. That's why tanks are always mounted with a back up regulator. But when people dive on their own, of if they are extra-cautious, they can use what is called a pony bottle. It's a smaller tank with a built-in regulator, and provides you with enough air to reach the surface in an emergency. If you're not diving too deep that is.'

'I see. And it would be much easier to conceal, right?' asked Charles.

'Absolutely. They come in various sizes, but are generally no bigger than a bottle of mineral water. They're not designed to dive at depth for a long time. If I had to drown someone in Hong Kong waters, which are basically shallow pretty much everywhere, it's probably what I'd use to make a silent approach underwater.'

'But it's not something you'd be allowed to carry on a plane, isn't it?' asked Ethan. 'So, assuming your theory is right, we could be looking at a resident rather than at a visitor.'

'You're right, even if empty it's unlikely you'd be able to fly with one. The regulator valve would need to be completely disconnected and removed from the cylinder, and it would probably still trigger an inspection. Not the best way to slip through unnoticed at an airport. But it's pretty easy to buy at a dive shop in Hong Kong. Probably somewhere between HK$2,500 and HK$3,000 for one of the larger models.'

'Okay. Definitely something we should look into,' concluded Ethan. 'First, I'll get the team looking at *iaido* practitioners to cross-check names with lists of certified divers. There must be a PADI database, and the equivalent for other certifying agencies. It should help narrow down the profile. Second, John, can you establish, for *Basel III* and the other boats that were in the vicinity, which passengers were in the water between 3 pm and 4 pm? And check if any are certified as divers too. Lastly, we should comb the seabed in Turtle Cove Bay for any diving equipment. And also check the tree line on both sides of the beach for any suspect traces, or even abandoned scuba gear.'

'Sure. I'll liaise with Marine Headquarters. That shouldn't be too difficult.'

'Charles, the killer had to get to the crime scene, either on a boat, driving a vehicle, by taxi, or using public transport. Can you ask if anyone was seen arriving on the beach that afternoon, especially carrying a large bag, and also leaving either side of 4 pm? I assume Marine Headquarters will have the names of possible witnesses. And, if you find anything, can you try to get a facial composite? If he used public transport, he might show up on the bus's onboard video cameras,' said Ethan.

'I'll get onto it right now.'

'And, Suki, since you're our resident diving expert, call the dive shops in Hong Kong to see if anyone bought one of those pony bottles recently. They might even have credit card details.'

'No problem. It's probably not an item they sell that often. It's really specialised equipment, not part of the basic kit.'

'I'll also update the ACP on where we stand. Good work! More coffee, anyone?' asked Ethan, as the meeting ended.

CHAPTER 28

11:01 am, Tsim Sha Tsui, Kowloon, 11 October 2017

S UKI HAD ALREADY RUNG three dive shops. They either did
not carry pony bottles, or had not sold any for a number
of months. She finally got lucky. She informed Ethan and took
a police car to Tsim Sha Tsui. The driver had to make a
significant detour. The demonstrations for democracy and
universal suffrage had now started in earnest again.

The previous night had seen pitched battles between the
police and students, allied to demonstrators from the Occupy
Central movement that spearheaded the demands for political
change. They had spread across several districts, including
Central, Admiralty and Causeway Bay on Hong Kong, and
Mong Kok in Kowloon. The riot police had used tear gas and
pepper spray. In 2014 that had attracted wide-ranging criticism,
both locally and internationally. This time around, no one
seemed to have cared much, but it increasingly looked like it
might have been counter-productive: the number of protesters
swelled by the hour.

A number of streets were already blocked with barricades,
onto which yellow umbrellas, the symbol of the 2014 revolution,

had been affixed. A campaign on Twitter with the hashtag #IamHongKong was also in full swing and had attracted massive levels of support, both within the territory and internationally. Celebrities the world over had started endorsing the protests, some wearing pins or badges that proclaimed 'Je suis Hong Kong'.

The dive shop was located in a high-rise building in a street that ran parallel to the main commercial thoroughfare of Nathan Road. The building dated from the late seventies, and it showed. A cramped, uncomfortable, and smelly lift ride took Suki to the sixteenth floor. There were three shops, including one dedicated to diving equipment. She showed her warrant card and introduced herself to a teenager, whose blue and white T-shirt read ENJOY NARCOSIS. He sat behind a glass counter that showcased a variety of watches and dive computers.

'Good afternoon! I'm Inspector Suki Lam, Hong Kong Police. Are you Nelson?'

He nodded.

'We spoke earlier, about a pony bottle you recently sold,' she said.

'Ah yes, of course! I remember it well because the buyer asked me to fill it up for him from a cylinder. It's unusual, you see. They normally do it themselves from their own tanks, just before diving.'

'Yes. I know. I'm a diver myself. What else do you remember? Did he pay by credit card?'

'I looked it up after we spoke on the phone and, no, he paid cash, HK$2,450. He did not leave a name for the receipt.'

'And do you recall what he looked like?'

'Hmm, he had an average height. Sporty-type guy. Definitely Asian. Maybe Japanese. He spoke English well, without any accent.'

'Possibly Japanese, you said?'

'That's right. I can't remember exactly what it was. Maybe something he said. He also bowed slightly on the way out.'

'You're quite sharp-eyed! Or what he wore, perhaps?'

'No. That was pretty ordinary. I think he had a hoodie and jeans on. Nothing fancy, for sure. He wore plastic or tortoiseshell glasses, maybe black or brown, I can't say. And also a baseball cap.'

'I wish everyone was as observant as you are! Do you have a security camera?'

'Oh yes! Completely forgot about that! The camera's pretty well hidden. Look, here,' he added, pointing to an inconspicuous dark circle above the sales counter, 'there should be a pretty clear picture of him. Follow me, I'll show you.'

The backroom was not much bigger than a large cupboard, and also messy and dusty. Aside from piles of paperwork and assorted catalogues, there was a small TV monitor. It was connected to a simple digital video player, from which a clutter of electric cables emerged.

'So, that sale would have been last Tuesday afternoon.'

He briefly looked at a carbon copy of an invoice. 'Around 1:15.'

He searched through a pile of DVDs and retrieved one, which he fed into the player. He pressed the 'play' and 'fast forward' buttons, and soon reached the desired time, which was shown at the bottom of the screen.

'There you go, we should see him any time, now,' he said.

Suki concentrated intensely on the grainy image. She next called Ethan to convey what she had discovered.

'We're in luck. Well, sort of. They had a video camera.'

'So did we get a picture of him?'

'That's the thing. First of, the quality of the recording is pretty poor. The lens of that camera must have last been wiped clean ten years ago. But perhaps Andy can enhance the image. Worse, he never once looked up at the camera. He wore a hoodie, glasses, and a baseball cap. His head was always at an angle, it's basically impossible to see his face well.'

'Dammit!'

'All we have to go on is that he's of average height and build, and also quite fit. We know that he's Asian, maybe Japanese. If it's really him, he sounds like a pro.'

'Okay. If he were Japanese, that would tie in with the sword. Can you bring that disk back to the office? And call the other dive shops if any are still on your list. It could be a false alarm, so let's not get too excited just yet.'

'There are a couple I still need to call, but I really think this is our man.'

CHAPTER 29

S HIRYŌ HAD MADE IT BACK undisturbed to Causeway Bay. The Number 14 bus had stopped at Stanley Market, a major attraction for tourists on the south side of Hong Kong Island. There, vendors sold assorted trinkets and items of clothing. After alighting, Shiryō had hailed a taxi and instructed the driver to drop him in Central. He had walked back to his apartment, via Admiralty and Wan Chai. There was, of course, always the possibility that the onboard camera of the bus might have captured his face. He always took great care not to look directly at them, but he could not always spot the lenses. But his face would have been largely hidden. The ride from Turtle Cove Beach to Stanley Market had also been short, with only six stops.

He had now disposed of his diving equipment. He had pre-packed it in separate refuse bags prior to leaving the beach, and dropped them in several trash bins along the way. However, he retained the monocular. It was small enough and he might have further use for it.

He had rented the studio flat using an Indonesian passport. Indonesians and Filipinos were the largest foreign nationalities in Hong Kong. Each group numbering about 140,000 people. Most of them were domestic helpers. The British came a distant third, a quarter the number. Indonesians, other than maids seeking employment, did not require a visa to enter the Special Administrative Region. They were entitled to a stay of up to thirty days, more than twice the length of time available to Filipinos. The Hong Kong government still held a grudge against the Philippines following the botched bus rescue in Manila by the local police in 2010. Twenty Hong Kong tourists and their tour guide had been taken hostage and eight had ended up dead. Years after the event, Hong Kong's Security Bureau still had a travel alert on trips to the country. The level of risk could hardly be said to have been the same, yet the Philippines had been bundled with Pakistan and Syria, pending an apology and offer of compensation by Manila. Strangely, many countries experiencing civil war or terrorist unrest did not even feature on the advisory list.

If, by any chance, the police suspected Shiryō of being Japanese, the search would hit a dead end. His apartment was of a middle-of-the-range variety. It was cleaned several times a week and, while the building had a management office for emergencies, it did not feature a reception desk. The magnetic card to enter the building and his unit had been made available from a wall-mounted machine in the street. It read the tenants' credit cards, and Shiryō had previously registered over the Internet. His credit card matched the name on his passport and had been issued, a couple of years before, by a bank in Jakarta. He took care of all of his other expenses through cash payments. Shiryō had arrived in Hong Kong on a direct Garuda flight from Soekarno-Hatta International Airport, in the Indonesian capital. He also carried other documents that matched and led credence to his fake identity. Importantly, he was also fluent in Bahasa Indonesia, should anyone become suspicious. However, every now and then, he liked to hint at being from other countries when interacting with people, to further muddy the waters.

Having again saved a draft message with a pre-agreed code word on his Gmail account, Shiryō left yet another Internet café, checking as usual for signs of a possible tail. He walked past the Sogo department store on Hennessy Road, in Causeway Bay. Over the last forty-eight hours, a number of barricades, spiked with open umbrellas to repel tear gas, had been erected in the area. It now teemed with protesters, all calling for universal suffrage. At this stage, the demonstrations looked reasonably peaceful. Tens of thousands of people occupied several areas in the city. The crowds swelled in the evening, when Hongkongers joined the campaign after work. A massive rally had taken place on 1st October, China's National Day. While the main issue was the city's political system, many were also angry at the increasing inequalities between the wealthy minority and those who lived below the poverty line. The former included the chosen few who elected the leader of the government, with Beijing's backing. The latter now numbered twenty per cent of the population. For those in between, it could take decades to earn the deposit for a squalid studio flat.

Shiryō did not care much about Hong Kong's political system. To many, the protesters' demands were legitimate. They were also expressed in a largely non-violent manner, although that might change as time went by. Those sitting in the streets packed their rubbish and avoided stepping on the grass around public monuments. Cars and bay windows were left untouched.

Shiryō was viscerally anti-communist, but he also believed a country cannot function without a strong central authority. It had been ingrained in his mind as part of his military training. There was no denying that China had, for a number of years now, embraced its own version of capitalism. That, however, did not extend to granting its citizens meaningful voting rights, and it was still far from being a democracy.

For now, the police had their hands full dealing with the protests. The resources available to unravel the bankers' homicides would continue to be strained. In addition, entire areas of the district in which Shiryō had chosen to base himself were blocked to traffic. It would only help him to remain unnoticed if the streets descended into chaos. The thought brought a smile to his face. He bought an espresso at a nearby Starbucks, sat at one of the café's tables, and reviewed the plan for his next hit. He relished the prospect of another perfect kill in a foreign city.

CHAPTER 30

7:30 pm, Western Mid Levels, Hong Kong, 11 October 2017

E THAN WENT HOME EARLY that evening. So far, all they had
to go on was a grainy picture of a man, whose face no one
could really see. It possibly matched that of a passenger on the
Number 14 bus from Sai Wan Ho, several hours before the
latest homicide. He had carried a large bag but, again, had not
directly faced the camera. At least, they now knew how he had
probably got to the crime scene. The combing of databases
continued, so far with minimal results. The passengers on the
boats that had been in the vicinity of Turtle Cove had clearly
not been directly involved in that day's drama. The killer's use
of public transport seemed to rule it out anyway. Witnesses on
the beach had not recalled anything out of the ordinary either.
They would have been too busy, sunning themselves on what
had been a particularly bright day, to notice the arrival of the
killer. The seabed and forested areas near the beach had been
searched but, again, to no avail.

As a new initiative, checks were now being made on all
Japanese male residents and visitors aged between twenty-five
and fifty. It was a mammoth task. But the bulk of the police

force was increasingly busy monitoring and, to the extent possible, taming the flow of protesters in the city. The number of officers promised by the CP to assist with the investigation had trickled down to single digits. The political events had just made what was already difficult work in the best of circumstances turn into mission impossible.

Ethan lived in a 1,000 square foot apartment, just off the western end of Park Road, in a high-rise building typical of Mid Levels. It was comfortable enough for a bachelor and offered decent views of the city, as well as of the South China Sea beyond it. It was sparsely furnished, but with an attractive mix of East and West furniture that echoed his personal cultural heritage. The location was convenient. The area still retained some of the 'old Hong Kong' businesses that were now fast disappearing as gentrification crept in with the extension of the MTR network. Property prices went up, as did rents, sometimes doubling or trebling when due for renewal. Printing presses, stationery and homeware stores were gradually replaced by higher-end shops that sold watches or branded clothes. But, for now, a few mom and pop outlets survived. Even entire streets retained a traditional charm and atmosphere.

Ethan poured himself a large measure of ten-year old Ardberg, to which he added a small splash of water. It clouded the alcohol, a telltale sign it had not been chill-filtered. He savoured the burning sensation in his throat brought by the single malt whisky. He liked his drink peaty and was therefore partial to distilleries from Islay, an island off the rugged western coast of Scotland, whose whiskies sometimes exhibited salty aromas of sea spray. He sat on a battered, but comfortable leather sofa and turned on the television for the evening news. The police had now revealed that the death of Pieter du Toit was being treated with suspicion, an initial step towards the full admission of a homicide. At this stage, the media had only marginally picked up on the information. The broadcasters' efforts were focused on the protests that were now spreading fast across city. National Day, 1st October, and the ensuing bank holiday had seen the number of people in the streets swell to about 250,000. There seemed to be no way out of the crisis.

Ethan could not really see the government backing down. In 2014, it had refused to backtrack on the decision made by the Standing Committee of the National People's Congress. It had decreed that the chief executive elections would only include two to three candidates, all vetted by Beijing. Backing down now would be a major loss of face. For the PRC, the risks of allowing true universal suffrage in Hong Kong were real. It simply would not allow such political contagion to reach the Mainland. Meanwhile, Hong Kong was grinding to a halt. A number of trade unions already supported the movement initiated by student federations. Some of the participants in the demonstrations of 2014 had since been prosecuted, but it had clearly not tamed the people's enthusiasm to join the protests on the city's streets.

At least, Hong Kong had a free press and the events there were being widely reported around the world, unlike what happened north of the border. On the Mainland, censors blanked out reports by the likes of CNN or the BBC. The Chinese state-run television had shown some of the street gatherings, but had not hesitated to paint these as rallies in favour of the motherland. Since 1st July, Hong Kong's Establishment Day, the incumbent chief executive had been arbitrarily maintained in his post, in a worrying *status quo*. The date for new elections had not yet been announced, and there had been no new developments regarding the manner in which they would be conducted. This had contributed in a major way to fanning the flames of revolt.

Like many in the police force, Ethan was torn between a genuine concern for the city and its future, and his duty as a representative of the rule of law and order. Hong Kong had changed much since its retrocession to China by the British. It had, for sure, benefitted from the influx of visitors from a rising middle class on the Mainland. Many had spent their newfound wealth in the territory, fuelling growth and employment, but also leading to much price inflation. The real estate sector in particular had been a major recipient of such outgoings, with the result that many in the city could now no longer afford to buy a home. Meanwhile, decision-making had firmly shifted to Beijing. Nowadays, the civil service pretty much took all of its orders from there, while continuing to favour Hong Kong's big businesses. Most of the tycoons who had prospered under the British had now made strategic allegiances to the new political masters.

Outside Ethan's flat, giant neon displays advertising Chinese brands atop skyscrapers bathed the city in a futuristic, eerie light. But the spectacle could not distract him from the fact that a ruthless killer was still at large and, so far, they were failing in their efforts to catch him. As he went to bed that night, he already knew there would be no escaping the dream, the scream, the bullet, and the little girl.

CHAPTER 31

10:00 pm, Causeway Bay, Hong Kong, 11 October 2017

MARILAG ARRIVED AT JJ's apartment, on the dot of 10 pm, as she had been instructed. She could not remember his flat number and called his mobile, for him to buzz her in. There was a mirror in the lift and she touched up her makeup on the way to the sixth floor. So far, it had been a quiet day. She had only had two clients in the afternoon: a balding British accountant in his fifties, whose wife preferred to live in Milton Keynes, and an over-excited student, barely out of his teens. In both cases, the session had lasted for less than twenty minutes. She had found a credible excuse and the mama-san had agreed to let her leave early. She rang the bell and waited a few seconds for JJ to open the door to his unit. As usual, he was unshaved. His shirt was un-tucked over a filthy pair of jeans, and his breath smelled of alcohol. He was barefoot. As she entered the small apartment, she saw a half empty bottle of Grey Goose on the coffee table. JJ had a strange expression, as well as bloodshot eyes. Immediately, she knew he had taken drugs again. It was not all that unusual. Many people she knew did.

'Sweetie,' he said with a smile, 'come in. Make yourself comfortable.'

Marilag dropped her tote bag on the floor and sat on a cream sofa in the living room.

'Vodka?' he asked, matter-of-factly.

She accepted the drink and quickly downed the shot. JJ liked his booze neat. The alcohol burned her chest and she soon felt rather hot. She took off her jeans jacket. Underneath, she wore a tight, almost transparent leotard above a mini-skirt, and black and red cowboy boots.

'You're very sexy tonight,' he said encouragingly, 'I'm really excited. I think you and I will have a great time. You know what? Why don't we take a bath first?' he suggested.

It was quite unlike him. She welcomed the proposition, not that she had much of a choice. With JJ, it was always better to go along with what he had in mind, even if, ultimately, it might hurt. In the end, she knew he would always be generous. The money was, after all, what it all came down to. But he generally was not this gentle. Perhaps he had had a rough day. Some of her clients sometimes wanted a chat, as well as sexual intercourse. Many of her johns felt insecure. They needed reassurance, although JJ was hardly the type. He disappeared in the bathroom for a few seconds. When he returned, she heard the tap running. She started undressing, which never really took long, and asked him for the night's payment, HK$3,500. JJ gave her nine HK$500 bills and told her to keep it all. Marilag flashed him a wide smile. Things were looking up.

They frolicked on the sofa for a few minutes before retreating to the bathroom. The lights were off but JJ had lit a few candles. Their flames, reflected in the mirror above the sink, added a romantic atmosphere to what was an otherwise drab and dull room. He got into the bathtub first. She went in next, her back to his chest, squeezing her petite body between his hairy legs, arousing him again. Tonight might even be fun after all, she thought. She caressed him expertly for a few minutes with her hands behind her back. He grunted with pleasure, his hands soon all over her. Next, JJ blew the candles. It was now completely dark. The smell of smoke felt strange at first, but it soon dissipated. His hands now stroked her breasts, slowly moving up towards her shoulders.

'Baby, you'll never forget tonight . . . and neither will I,' he whispered in her ear, softly biting her earlobes.

The next thing she felt were JJ's hands around her neck and throat. He started squeezing, gently at first. She knew some people enjoyed doing it, as a sexual game. The pressure of his hands gradually became stronger. She soon felt uneasy, the darkness adding to the feeling of panic that increasingly took hold of her.

'JJ . . .' she whispered, 'stop. It's too tight, baby. I can't breathe.'

JJ ignored her plea. He compressed her airway with renewed strength, cutting the supply of blood to her neck. She was now breathless, the dyspnea inducing ever more violent struggling. She started kicking, splashing water everywhere, but there was no escaping JJ's grip. After about a minute, she simply passed out. JJ felt a few convulsive seizures but, soon, Marilag stopped moving altogether. He was now in a state of extreme excitation. For about ten minutes, he remained in the bathtub, motionless, his hands still locked on her throat as in a strange embrace, slowly catching his breath. The sensation of power the brief struggle had given him was simply incredible. After a while, he felt cold. He climbed out of the tub and wrapped a towel around his waist. He turned the lights back on. Marilag's lifeless, tiny frame had almost completely slipped under the water. Above the surface was a floating mass of black hair, like the tentacles of a strange marine animal coming up for air.

The elation soon gave rise to panic. JJ had not really planned anything as far as her body was concerned. He frantically scanned his apartment for a hiding place. He needed to get rid of her, fast. The sight of her flabby corpse gave him the creeps. Everything would be better once she was out of view. He downed a large shot of vodka. The alcohol rushed through his system, stimulating his senses. He finally found a suitcase in one of the built-in cupboards. It was a large Tumi model with wheels. The black ballistic nylon frame could be expanded with a wraparound zip. As in a daydream, he went to the kitchen and fetched a pack of 100-litre rubbish bags from a cupboard under the sink. Then he pulled the bath plug. The water slowly drained, revealing Marilag's limp and curled body. Her tense face looked like a ceremonial mask of a primitive tribe. Cursing, he lifted her out of the bathtub. Her arms and legs dangled, impeding his movements, but she was not all that heavy. He dried her as best he could before squeezing, with much effort, her skinny frame into one of the bin bags. Her head and shoulders could not go all the way in and he slipped on another bag above her upper body. Next, he sealed the macabre package with duct tape.

He felt much better when he could no longer see the woman's face. He dragged the trussed-up body to the suitcase. He struggled to make it fit in but, by pushing and bending the legs and neck, he managed to jam it in. He then zipped the luggage closed and wheeled it to the balcony, wedging it against the glass balustrade. Satisfied, he closed the sliding window and turned the air conditioning to high. JJ was exhausted. He looked into Marilag's bag and retrieved her mobile. He removed the battery and threw the handset against one of the walls, where it shattered into several pieces. She had deserved to die, he thought. She and her kind were responsible for corrupting him. He had not been like that before. Had he not fallen prey to their temptations, he might still have a job. Now, the devil had taken custody of him.

He briefly toyed with the idea of jumping off the balcony. All sorts of thoughts raced through his brain, but he just could not decide what to do next. He suddenly felt very tired. He collapsed on the sofa and fell asleep, completely oblivious to the siren of a passing police car in the street below.

Part III
EARTH

CHAPTER 32

AMBROSE WALLACE-PHILLIMORE was very upset. His long-standing partner, Oliver, a talented photographer and owner of an art gallery on lower Hollywood Road, had just called. Abruptly, he had announced he was breaking up. They had first met at DYMK, a high-end gay bar, long since closed. It stood for 'Does Your Mother Know?' and was named after a song by ABBA. The entrance was discreetly placed in an alleyway off Arbuthnot Road in Central. It had been love at first sight. They had instantly cozied in one of the purple booths. They had drunk cocktails with outrageous names underneath a huge lampshade of black ostrich feathers. But that had been years ago. Oliver had had enough of Hong Kong's crazy life. He wanted to return to London. He had just been offered the opportunity to join, as a partner, a new and much larger gallery. There was no way their relationship could continue as a long-distance one. Though sorry to see it end, Oliver had passed on the brutal news without any warning.

Ambrose, a British expatriate, flicked back his hair with his right hand. He abruptly left his desk on the trading floor to drown his sorrows in the Starbucks downstairs. Tall and handsome, with thick black hair and chestnut eyes, Ambrose took great care of his body. He visited a fitness centre four times per week and boasted a perfect tan. It owed as much to Hong Kong's beauty institutes as to regular weekend escapes to Bangkok's Sukhothai Hotel, where he liked to lounge by the swimming pool as he recovered from the many nighttime pleasures the Thai capital had to offer. He unfastened the top button of his white shirt, and removed his necktie. Today, the vibrant pink and bright green made a splash, over what was a sharply tailored, grey super-100 single-breasted suit. Ambrose was famous for his loud ties.

He had lived in Hong Kong for six years. He now headed the equity syndicate desk at Eurocredit. Before that there had been stints in London, Sydney and Singapore. A short spell with UBS in Hong Kong, a couple of years before, had propelled him to the coveted rank of managing director. He was just one year short of qualifying for permanent residency, for which he had intended to apply. But now, he did not really know any more. The news from Oliver might change everything, although he sensed there was probably more to his partner's decision than just a professional opportunity back in Europe.

Hong Kong offered a conservative environment at times. However, unlike some of the other major cities in Asia, people with his sexual orientation faced no obvious discrimination. The nightlife, the weather, the beaches and myriad islands more than made up for some of the inconveniences of living in the territory. Hong Kong was also only a few hours away from some of the most beautiful countries on the planet. Thailand, Malaysia, Indonesia, Sri Lanka and even the Maldives were virtually on its doorstep.

He sipped a double macchiato with a dash of hazelnut syrup and decided to pull himself together. Primary equity issuance had pretty much come to a halt in the city, amid the standoff between pro-democracy protesters and the government. Business, however, continued uninterrupted in other markets across the region. Eurocredit was just about to launch a US$700 million block trade on behalf of Temasek Holdings, a major sovereign wealth fund in Singapore. The client was keen to offload some of its higher-yielding and value investments. They had sharply risen, as growth stocks had plummeted. It had been a hotly contested mandate on behalf of one of the most prestigious clients an investment bank could work for in the region. It was also one for which there could be recurring business. As ever, the fees had been badly trimmed, but the league table credit to be gained from executing the deal, especially in a sole book-runner role, would more than make up for it.

Ambrose swiftly gulped what was left of his coffee, stood up, and returned to the lift lobby on the ground floor of Citibank Tower in Central. He did not notice the man who had carefully followed his every move. Once Ambrose had reached the eleventh floor, he stepped out of the lift, swiped his access card on the reader, opened the glass door, and walked across the open-plan trading floor. It was humming with the busy atmosphere of feverish trading. The Hong Kong market was in free fall. There was money to be made, shorting financial and property stocks, as well as the Hang Seng Index. Some institutions were also busy, buying equities on weakness or implementing hedging strategies to protect themselves against further drops in share prices.

Ambrose checked with Mario, a Swiss-Italian vice president in his team, who had prepared the crib sheets for the sales force.

'The briefing notes are ready. We have a sales meeting just after the close of market in Singapore, at 5:05 pm. We'll launch right after that. The research analyst is all prepped up,' said the VP.

'Where do we stand on soundings, Mario?'

'We're already sixty per cent covered, with commitments from four hedge funds and a couple of insurance companies. Prudential is even in for US$100 million and so is Och Ziff. So we're good to go. Initial coverage is already in excess of what the underwriting committee had requested. This thing is definitely going ahead.'

'And where is the stock trading, right now?'

'Has moved sideways all afternoon. Hopefully, it'll close there too. We're still going with a three-to-one per cent discount, which is where we have demand.'

Ambrose quickly glanced at his watch. It was a huge black ceramic limited edition King Power, from Hublot.

'Okay. Another ten minutes to go, then. Let's start rallying the troops.'

Ambrose enjoyed the adrenaline rush that came with executing a sizeable deal. He was certain, now, that he would get over Oliver's betrayal. The more he thought of it, the keener he was to remain in Hong Kong. Once the investor allocations were done and dusted in the evening, he might perhaps even go for a late night dinner at Azure, with Orlando. For a while, he had had his eyes on that cute Filipino, who worked for Citi on one of the upper floors. And then, why not, maybe they might go together for a snuggly weekend at the Amanpuri Hotel, in Phuket. Things were definitely on the up. He turned to the desk's assistant, and asked crisply, 'Queenie darling, can you please get me that little shit, Wai Ping, on the line? *Right now.* We start the fun and games in just a few minutes.'

CHAPTER 33

4:41 pm, Central, Hong Kong, 11 October 2017

SHIRYŌ WAS FAMILIAR WITH Wallace-Phillimore's routine. The banker would not be so easy to corner. He lived in a high-rise complex of three towers on Old Peak Road, in the upper Mid Levels. It housed a variety of one- to three-bedroom apartments, all duplexes. They ranged from 2,050 to 3,800 square feet and were spread, two per floor, over more than thirty levels. Security was tight, not only to enter the development, but also within the individual buildings. There were cameras everywhere, including in the lifts, and throughout the common areas. They included a spa, swimming pool, gym, cigar divan, and even a golf simulator. He had a live-in *amah*. She prepared his breakfasts and evening meals, and looked after his apartment. Every morning, as he was about to leave, she called the lift and kept its door open until he was ready, much to the annoyance of the other residents also on their way to work.

Wallace-Phillimore also had a driver. Antonio, a Filipino, took him to his office in a silver-grey s-500 Mercedes. Opportunities to target the banker on the move would be limited, as they would be in the vicinity of his office, which was similarly heavily guarded and patrolled. But four times a week, from Tuesdays to Fridays, Antonio took him to Sure Fitness, a gym in the Kinwick Centre on Hollywood Road, where he liked to work out and tone his body. On Mondays, Ambrose could not leave his desk. He had to attend a variety of meetings and calls, both with regional management in Hong Kong, as well as, later in the day, his global bosses in London.

On weekends, he enjoyed visiting a high-end spa that catered to male patrons only, but it looked like a small place. Shiryō reasoned instead that the fitness centre would probably be his best option. Sure Fitness was laid out over six floors and totalled 31,000 square feet. It was constantly busy with young professionals of both sexes, who came in at all hours for yoga, Pilates or other fitness classes. It included a cardio section with over seventy machines, a climbing area, an indoor cycling studio with capacity for fifty bikes, and separate zones dedicated to powerlifting, free weights, and resistance. It also had a restaurant and a trendy juice bar.

Shiryō entered a coffee shop at the upper end of Lyndhurst Terrace, a stone's throw from the gym. He ordered an espresso and sat at one of the complimentary desktop computers. There, he accessed a local forum and clicked on the tab for 'Classifieds'. A sub-menu dropped down, from which he selected 'Debentures & Memberships'. Eleven offers were listed. A number of them were advertised as 'Sure Fitness membership transfer'. He selected one that sold a pre-paid membership. It allowed access to all branches of Sure Fitness in Hong Kong, Taiwan and Singapore. It was valid for both yoga and fitness activities, and allowed its owner to book any group classes. Seven months remained on the membership, for which the seller asked the reasonable sum of HK$7,000.

Shiryō inserted a new pre-paid SIM card in a simple 2G cell phone and called the vendor.

The vendor was named Gary Lee. He was constantly travelling across Asia for an IT company and now had little time to train at the gym. Accordingly, he decided to get rid of his membership, which he had barely used. Shiryō introduced himself as John, from Sydney. He was in luck. Gary was in Hong Kong that day and his office was actually close by. They agreed to meet just outside the lobby of the building. Within minutes, Shiryō had paid cash and walked away with the membership card.

He returned to his apartment to pick up some training gear. A short taxi ride then took him to the Kinwick Centre for a reconnaissance tour. Shiryō already knew Wallace-Phillimore always exercised between noon and 1:30 pm. It would have been more difficult for him to do so later in the afternoon, or in the evenings. Equity transactions, such as block trades, were often unpredictable, and generally launched after the market had closed. Allocations of IPOs and other marketed transactions were similarly conducted as daytime came to an end. As head of equity syndicate, he would need to communicate these to the sales force by no later than the following morning. Wallace-Phillimore always exited the club spick and span, in a well-pressed suit, carrying a monogrammed Louis Vuitton bag for his sports gear.

Shiryō rode the lift to the reception on the third floor. The membership card granted him access without a hitch. The facility was open from 6 am to midnight, from Mondays to Saturdays. On Sundays and public holidays, the opening hours were almost the same. Shiryō bought a padlock at the in-house boutique. It mostly sold branded sports gear at inflated prices.

The club's moneyed clientele liked the logo. He entered the locker room and put on his training clothes. The changing area housed a number of shower cubicles, a sauna, a steam room and vanity stations. Some workout gear, towels and toiletries were complimentary. There were also charging stations for iPads, laptops and mobile telephones. It was not all that busy at that time of the day, but Shiryō reasoned it would probably become so in the evening. Even then, a few areas would still offer a good level of privacy.

He went for a tour of the various floors, passing through a fully equipped zone for gymnastics, an athletics training turf, for speed, agility and quickness exercises, as well as an area for stretching and recovery. There were also a number of dedicated rooms for various classes. A wall-mounted notice board listed almost fifty, which catered to beginner, intermediate and advanced levels.

To Shiryō, Sure Fitness was an absurdity. There was loud music all around and the cardio-equipment screens offered a selection of movies and TV programmes. By contrast, he liked to train in the open, on a forest path or in the sea. It also allowed him to prepare for real-life situations. He only had contempt for these temples where human sweat was worshiped. He could not understand why one would want to subject oneself to such a chaotic environment: Hong Kong was already a particularly stressful city. Shiryō ran for an hour on one of the treadmills, looking through the gym's windows at the high-rise buildings that towered over the narrow streets below. He drank three quarters of a bottle of mineral water and returned to the changing room. He showered and left. He would need to be quick, and it would take some planning, but he looked forward to the challenge of operating in such a confined and busy environment.

Shiryō still had about ten days before his Hong Kong entry permit expired. It would be wiser, he thought, to now leave the city and immediately return. It would automatically re-set the validity of his visa to thirty days, and provide him with the flexibility he might need. The easiest way was to make a short trip to Macau. Indonesian citizens were among the seventy nationalities that did not require a visa to enter the former Portuguese colony. It had returned to the People's Republic of China in 1999, two years after the Hong Kong handover.

To avoid roads blocked by demonstrators, Shiryō walked in a northerly direction, towards the Shun Tak Centre. It was a large but ageing commercial and office complex to the west of Central. Most of the ferries and hydrofoils that made the hour-long trip to Macau departed from there. Like hundreds of anonymous tourists, many from China's mainland, he paid cash for a package that included an economy-class open return ticket with the Cotai Water Jet ferry, as well as an overnight room at one of the casino hotels. The Venetian was a fantasy, mock-Italian Renaissance plasterboard monstrosity, but it included no fewer than 3,000 suites. As a guest, Shiryō would be largely invisible, hidden among the many thousands of gamblers and shoppers who visited it every day of the week. There, some took mini-cruises in replica gondolas, complete with Chinese gondoliers. They would glide on the shallow canals that meandered through a giant shopping mall and treat themselves to luxury watches or Western-branded clothes. It was all done in the worst possible taste, although the experience obviously appealed to the masses.

Shiryō was not keen on gambling, but would probably have a few drinks at a bar in Cotai. The trip to Macau would provide the perfect excuse to unwind before he returned to take care of Ambrose Wallace-Phillimore.

CHAPTER 34

7:00 am, Causeway Bay, Hong Kong, 12 October 2017

J J WOKE UP EARLY. He had a stomping headache and his apartment was a mess. He slowly recalled Marilag's struggle in the bathtub, but his memory was fuzzy and he could not remember all the details. He stood up, walked towards the kitchen to prepare a coffee and immediately saw the suitcase on the balcony. It was a strange sight, but there was nothing to betray the fact that it contained the slain body of a prostitute. Until someone decided to open it that is. There was scant chance of that happening soon: JJ had securely locked the zip with a padlock. He had read that corpses became rigid after a few hours, although he had no wish to check. In any event, he could not remember what he had done with the key. As far as he was concerned, she would remain there, all curled up in the luggage, behind the sliding windows. He would think of what to do later. There was no hurry.

He had done the right thing, he reassured himself. For sure, she had deserved what she got. Surprisingly, he had enjoyed doing it too. It had been so easy taking a life. It had made him feel powerful and in control. The aftermath of the killing had been less pleasant, admittedly, but he had managed it. He downed a cup of extra strength espresso. The warm liquid soon made his heart beat faster. He was now more alert. He soon realised someone would come to clean the flat at some point. He had to erase traces of the night's events. He discarded the empty bottle of vodka, Marilag's tote bag and her clothes in the kitchen bin, first wrapping the latter two in a garbage bag. He also tossed in her cowboy boots and her broken mobile phone. He tidied up the rest of the apartment as best he could. The puddles of water in the bathroom had dried up. He removed the candles and placed them in one of the cupboards. Soon, the flat was presentable again.

He flicked on the television and watched the news but there was nothing of interest. He snorted a line of coke and thought about what he might do next. He had not really planned any of what had happened and his deranged mind refused to provide him with the answers he sought. Slumped on the couch, he started playing with his smartphone. The names of the girls he knew were all listed there, like goods on offer in a superstore. It was almost like a game. He only had to click to satisfy his cravings. Within a few hours they would appear and make him feel good. He remained there, slouched, browsing through the list. Soon, his demons would catch up with him again.

CHAPTER 35

9:30 am, Wan Chai, Hong Kong, 12 October 2017

SUKI SAT AT HER DESK, deep in thought. Her left hand unconsciously played with a small green jade charm, which she wore around her neck. It was a little Buddha, mounted on a thin gold chain. Simultaneously, her right hand was busy, spinning a ball pen between her thumb and forefinger, a skill she had acquired during boring lessons in primary school. She achieved impressively quick rotations, which never ceased to amaze some of her colleagues. She kept thinking about possible connections between the deaths of Andrew Short and Pieter du Toit. She abruptly left her desk, on which a clutter of paper constantly threatened to bury her laptop computer, and walked around the corner to Ethan's office. The chief inspector was on the phone. It sounded like an important conversation being conducted in Cantonese.

'Can I have a word?' she mouthed silently.

Ethan answered with a hand gesture, inviting her to sit on a nearby sofa. The call was seemingly with the ACP again. The director was getting impatient with the lack of progress on the bankers' cases, as they were now known in the force. Ethan finally ended the call.

'Hi. Sorry,' he said, 'I have to keep the ACP in the loop, I'm afraid. You look all excited. Got a new idea?'

Suki's face brightened up, 'Actually, yes! Well . . . perhaps. I've been trying to connect the dots between the two murders,' she added.

'And?'

'I mean . . . it's clear someone out there doesn't like bankers. But I don't think that's necessarily the motive.'

'And why wouldn't that be the case?'

'In such a case, the media would have been contacted. Or we would have received some sort of claim. I mean, if you kill bankers because of what they are, or what they represent, surely you'd want the world to know, wouldn't you? Just like terrorists do in Iraq and Syria. They issue videos, send messages and the like. They're angry and they want the whole world to know it. And here, in both cases, we've had complete radio silence on the part of the killer.'

'Good point. Go on,' he encouraged.

'Another thing is that the victims had similar titles and played a similar role at their respective firms. I think it has to be related to something they both worked on.'

'You mean a transaction that turned sour?'

'Exactly. Or, maybe something they had both worked on in the past.'

'It's a good idea. Now, they were both longstanding permanent residents. They had worked for these banks for a while too. In all that time, they would have been involved in dozens, if not hundreds of deals. And there are many capacities in which you can work on these too. It'll probably take a while to look into it. But I agree that if you were able to narrow this down enough, then you might find a lead.'

'Maybe I should have a word with some of their colleagues, to try to come up with a list. There must be an easy way of doing this.'

'I agree. But to temper your enthusiasm, I recall the head of equity capital markets at Morgan Roberts saying that issuers are increasingly using larger syndicates for their offerings. So, over the last few years, you'll probably find that the major houses were all basically in on the same deals, at the very least for the biggest ones. In any event, motive is the key. One that will explain why these two firms and bankers, and not others, were targeted.'

'Yes, unless the number of victims continues to increase . . . maybe there will be more,' she suggested.

'You're not being very encouraging, are you?'

'Listen, why don't I try to dig in that direction? We've nothing to lose and it all sounds quite plausible, after all. It's not like we've been making much progress otherwise!'

'Go for it. Why don't you try that chap, Ashok Patel, at Morgan Roberts, in the first instance? It looks like he's been in the business for a long time. He may have some ideas. He was also rather helpful when I last visited them.'

'Will do. I'll call immediately.'

'And when you see him, please ask about his tailor. That guy dresses sharply like you wouldn't believe,' added Ethan with a wink. 'If it's not too expensive, I might even get a suit or two made. I could do with upgrading my wardrobe.'

CHAPTER 36

S HIRYŌ'S SHORT TRIP TO MACAU had been largely uneventful. He had exited and re-entered Hong Kong unbothered, using his Indonesian passport. There had been no issues either with the immigration authorities in the former Portuguese colony. His new entry permit now allowed him to stay in the territory for another thirty days. It was more than enough for what he had to accomplish. As he had planned, he had sipped a couple of glasses of Japanese whisky in one of the Cotai complex's bars. There, it had taken no more than ten minutes for him to strike up an informal conversation. She had been blonde, with clear blue eyes and a flattering red dress that was also particularly revealing. She had introduced herself as Oksana, in a heavy Slavic accent. She had meant business, quite literally, and after several flutes of Krug, she had joined him in his room.

Seemingly tipsy, although it clearly had been an act, she had tiptoed barefoot in the hotel corridor, her high heel shoes in one hand, the other grasping a silver clutch, embroidered with Swarovski crystals. Taking someone back to his room was a security breach he normally would not have allowed, but he had not detected any threats in her demeanour. Her purpose had been of the simplest variety: sex for cash, and that had suited Shiryō just fine. He had not needed to focus on anything in particular that night and decided to allow himself some downtime after what had been a few tense weeks in Hong Kong.

Oksana's performance had more than matched the promise of her good looks. She had left Shiryō several thousand Hong Kong dollars poorer. She had not asked for payment in Macau patacas: no one used the local currency except the accountants who worked for the strip's casinos. After two and a half hours of wild riot in his hotel suite, Shiryō was exhausted but well pleasured. He had slept uninterrupted for the first time in a while.

The following day, he woke up at dawn to catch one of the earlier Cotai Water Jet ferries bound for Hong Kong. It was a Thursday. On Friday, unless he had to travel abroad, which happened from time to time, Ambrose Wallace-Phillimore would as usual turn up at the fitness centre for his regular training session. Shiryō returned to his apartment and walked to Hennessy Road. There, he made a purchase in a shop that sold display signs for catering businesses and offices. He relaxed for the rest of the day.

On the Friday, he placed a morning call to Eurocredit, using a new SIM card on his mobile and asked for Ambrose Wallace-Phillimore. When the banker answered, he pressed the off button. He now knew he most likely would be in town in the hours that followed. He discarded the SIM card.

At about a quarter past eleven, Shiryō checked in at Sure Fitness. He walked straight to the changing room and donned a pair of grey cotton shorts, with a matching T-shirt, and a pair of Asics trainers. He grabbed a towel and bottle of mineral water, and exercised moderately in a quiet corner of the weight training area.

At noon on the dot, Ambrose Wallace-Phillimore entered. A personal trainer soon arrived and greeted him in a familiar way. They started with a range of weight training exercises, culminating in a short powerlifting session. Ambrose sweated profusely, but he had stamina and seemed to enjoy every minute of the workout. After the trainer had left, Shiryō smiled at Ambrose, making small talk: 'It's hard work isn't it?'

'Oh boy! You could say that.'

'I'm Malcolm, by the way, from Taiwan,' said Shiryō.

'Ambrose.'

'Sorry I can't shake your hand. I'm covered in sweat all over,' continued Shiryō with a smile.

'Oh, I can see that, all right!' answered the banker, already flirtatious.

They moved to the cardio section, where they both exercised on a variety of machines for about forty-five minutes. They finally called it a day and returned together to the changing room. It was now past 1:15 pm. A number of people had already left the gym to grab a late lunch before returning to their offices. There were two other men in the locker area, both now almost fully dressed. Shiryō and Ambrose were soon alone. A long row of showers extended at the back of the room. Ambrose, now stark naked, strutted his way towards one of the first cubicles, whistling a popular tune.

'I wouldn't go into that one if I were you,' warned Shiryō, 'I saw someone getting sick in it when I arrived. Something he must have eaten, I suppose.'

'Oh dear! That's totally disgusting!' said Ambrose, pulling a face. He swiftly walked to another shower cubicle, towards the back of the locker room.

He turned on the taps and was soon engulfed in a cloud of steam. The rain shower washed away the sweat of the training session, as he generously lathered his body with shower gel. Shiryō stripped down too and put on a pair of disposable plastic gloves, which he took from his locker. Except for the cascading noise of falling water in Wallace-Phillimore's shower, the changing room was quiet. Shiryō discreetly looked outside the door, to confirm no one was coming. He placed a wicker basket full of used towels just behind the door. He walked towards Wallace-Phillimore's cubicle, pushed the door ajar and silently joined him under the shower.

'Hey, Malcolm, what's going on? I'm not. . . .'

He could not finish his sentence. Shiryō slapped him on both ears, cupping his hands to cause more damage. It completely disorientated the banker. Wallace-Phillimore jerked to one side, in great pain, his vision blurred. His head spun and he looked completely lost. Shiryō quickly steadied himself under the shower. Then, with the palm of his hand, he hit the banker hard with a flat strike on the base of the nose. He violently pushed upwards as his lower arm extended, driving broken cartilage into the skull and brain. Ambrose dropped and, with a loud thud, bumped his head on the shower wall. Shiryō pulled him up. He placed himself behind his body and swiftly finished him off with a sharp twist to the neck, one hand under the chin, the other balancing his head in a lift and twist motion. The banker fell into Shiryō's arms, completely limp. Shiryō deposited him gently on the shower's floor, the rain shower now the only ambient noise. The execution had taken only a few seconds.

He turned the shower off, still wearing his plastic gloves. The room was now immersed in silence. No one had entered. Shiryō walked to his locker and quickly half dried his body with a towel. He retrieved from his bag a self-standing, foldable plastic display sign that read CLOSED FOR TEMPORARY MAIN-TENANCE. It was in both English and Chinese, in black lettering over a yellow background. He placed it a couple of metres ahead of the cubicle in which Ambrose Wallace-Phillimore's lifeless body lay crumpled on the ceramic floor. Blood slowly trickled from its nasal passage.

The adrenaline still flowed in his bloodstream, but Shiryō was in control. He calmly dressed and packed his sports gear in his bag, also adding the towel he had just used. He could not take the risk of leaving obvious traces of DNA behind, even if these could not readily be matched to any police database. He replaced the wicker basket next to the changing room wall, where it had previously stood. He now wore his jeans and a hoodie, and also donned a pair of sunglasses and a baseball cap. He peeled his plastic gloves, put them in his pocket and exited the locker room. He walked at measured pace, without crossing anyone on his way to the reception area, and left the building as he had entered. Once on Hollywood Road, he walked down Lyndhurst Terrace and then up to the escalator. He followed the steps that ran parallel to the moving walkway, in direction of IFC Mall.

CHAPTER 37

THE 'ANONYMOUS' GROUP OF HACKERS had just officially declared a cyber-war on the Hong Kong police, through messages posted onto social networks in support of the protests. The force's computer servers and systems were down, completely overwhelmed, as they tried to cope with hundreds of thousands of requests per minute. As a result, database searches in connection with the bankers' cases had been temporarily suspended. That morning was therefore a perfect time for Suki to look into her theory and attempt to track down transactions on which Morgan Roberts and Swiss Securities might have worked together.

Ashok Patel, Morgan Roberts' head of equity syndicate, was currently pricing and allocating a deal in Jakarta. He was not expected to return to Hong Kong for at least another day. However, he had assigned a member of his team to assist with police enquiries. She introduced herself to Suki as Beatrice Fong. She was a petite locally born woman, whose family had acquired Canadian passports before the handover. She had long black hair and round metallic glasses that framed a pair of deep brown, intelligent eyes. With her high cheekbones, she reminded Suki of a cute squirrel. She wore a white blouse and an elegant light grey suit, with a pencil skirt that dropped just below her knees, in a style reminiscent of the 1950s. No rings adorned her fingers, but her wrist showcased an expensive Swiss platinum watch, with an open face.

'What is it with investment bankers and expensive watches?' thought Suki.

Beatrice explained she had earned a PhD in nuclear physics in the United States, before deciding that research was not for her. She had then chosen a career in investment banking. She had started in derivative sales at Morgan Roberts, before joining the equity syndicate team as a vice-president some two years before. She seemed extremely smart and immediately understood what Suki was trying to achieve. They met in a conference room that overlooked the bank's equity trading floor. Karen Wong, the firm's head of legal and compliance, also sat in. She did not talk, but took copious notes on her laptop. Traders and sales-people were constantly on the phone, or moving from one desk to another to discuss ideas or deliver sales tickets to be processed by the back office. It reminded Suki of a buzzing and busy nest of insects.

'If you're trying to find equity transactions in which specific banks have been involved, the best way would be the *Dealogic* database,' said Beatrice. 'We use it mostly to compile league tables, to show our firm in a good light versus our competitors, when we pitch for new business. But it also allows you to instantly obtain a lot of information about individual deals,' she added.

'How does it work exactly?' asked Suki.

'Basically, for any equity offering, details of the transaction are entered into the database by the provider, using information that's in the prospectus or regulatory filings. They're all publicly available. The senior banks involved also add to, or clarify the information. It's basically in everyone's interest for it to be accurate. Investment banks themselves are the main subscribers to the service and, quite frankly, we all use it.'

'I see. And what type of information does the database record?'

'Well, pretty much anything you could ask for, really. For example, the legal name of the issuer, the nature of the deal, the number of shares offered, or how many of these were new shares or existing shares sold down by shareholders. Other details include the price range and the offer price; the deal size; the launch, pricing and closing dates; which banks and other parties were involved; and so on.'

'Listen, you know what I'm after, how would you go about it if you were me?' Suki asked.

'The first thing to decide is how far back you want to go. The database covers a time span of perhaps twenty-five years, maybe even longer. So you probably want to narrow down searches to a more manageable timeframe.'

'That's a good point. Andrew Short joined your firm . . . six years ago from memory, and Pieter du Toit had worked at Swiss Securities for about the same length of time. So there's no point in going back beyond, say, 2011.'

'Okay, 2011 it is. Then, I suppose, that we should consider all types of transaction. Let's see what that search shows us before we narrow it down. But I can already tell you that we do a lot of deals. And Swiss Securities are also very active in

Asia, so I'm pretty sure we'll actually need to refine things further at some point.'

'Agreed. That makes sense.'

'We should also input in what capacities Morgan Roberts and Swiss Securities were involved in these transactions.'

'Do you mean seniority?'

'Yes, that's exactly what I mean. Are you familiar with the various roles a bank can have in an equity deal?'

'To be honest, not really,' admitted Suki.

'No worries! Very few people actually understand it outside our industry. Let me try to explain.'

'Thank you, Beatrice.'

'Oh – you can call me Bee! Everybody does. So, there's a bit of a hierarchy when it comes to the banks. Some of the senior houses can combine several roles, which complicates things even more. Generally speaking, the most senior role an underwriter can have is "global coordinator". It means that a bank is basically in charge of the execution of the entire deal. It will oversee all aspects of the work, from documentation, to valuation and marketing.'

'Got it,' said Suki.

'For the larger deals, you can have several brokers working together as joint global coordinators. It's actually the same principle for all the roles and titles. Next come the "bookrunners". Their role is largely the marketing of an offering.'

'So they don't get involved in documentation and other discussions?'

'Usually only if they are also global coordinators at the same time. In practice, all the global coordinators in a deal will also be bookrunners.'

'But the reverse is not necessarily true, right?'

'Exactly! Some bookrunners may be appointed in that capacity only. They won't really become active until the last phase of the execution process. But all the bookrunners have a key role, because they're the banks which decide how much stock each institutional investor receives.'

'So the banks that do not have a bookrunner title are at a disadvantage, then?'

'Absolutely! It's most unlikely that a portfolio manager would place an order for shares with a bank that isn't a bookrunner, since that bank would not be able to decide how many shares the investor receives at the end of the day.'

'Right.'

'More junior titles, such as lead manager, co-lead manager and co-manager, usually mean that the bank's role is restricted to the publication of pre-deal research reports, and to putting their name to the offer as an underwriter, for which they receive pre-agreed fees.'

'So, Bee, if someone was unhappy about a transaction and wanted to blame someone, those actually in charge of running the deal would be the global coordinators and bookrunners?'

'Definitely. Banks with more junior titles wouldn't really have much of an impact, to be honest.'

'I think I understand how it works, but it's quite complicated!'

'You get the hang of it after working on a couple of deals! Oh, one more thing. For IPOs only, there's another important role. It's for the banks that advise on stock exchange listing rules and help with negotiating the contents of the offer document with the securities regulator. In Hong Kong, they're called sponsor banks.'

'So they're distinct from global coordinators?'

'Actually, in practice their role is often similar. The main difference is that sponsoring is not a role that's related to underwriting. It's largely to do with due diligence and disclosure only.'

'So, a bank could be a sponsor, a global coordinator, and also bookrunner in an IPO?'

'Yep. They could even have other titles and roles as well but, to keep things simple, let's not go there right now. But, as an issuer, you wouldn't want to appoint too many sponsor firms, or indeed global coordinators, otherwise the execution process might get out of hand. Too many cooks in the kitchen, so to speak.'

'So, shall we look at deals using these three levels of seniority? With one search for sponsors, as well as the other senior roles; and the other just focusing on the global coordinator and bookrunner titles, to catch equity transactions other than IPOs,' suggested Suki.

'Easy.' Bee input the various parameters on a Lenovo laptop.

'Okay,' she said, 'over the period there were eighty-four deals across Asia in total.'

'That many?' said Suki disappointed, 'Bee, I think we need to put our thinking caps back on again.'

Her mobile phone suddenly rang. It was Ethan.

'Suki? We have another dead banker. And before you ask, yes, he was also a head of syndicate.'

CHAPTER 38

S UKI HAD JUST ARRIVED AT Sure Fitness, on Hollywood Road. Before leaving Morgan Roberts, she had heard that the computers of Beijing's liaison office in Hong Kong had been hacked. It was allegedly in retaliation for the government's decision to cancel talks that had been arranged, at long last, with the protesters. The withdrawal of the authorities had, in turn, been justified by calls from student leaders for a mass rally in Admiralty District. As in 2014, the number of demonstrators had fallen after a few weeks of chaos. For them, remotivating the troops had become a priority, but the tit-for-tat war of attrition continued on both sides. Meanwhile, a number of strategic locations around town continued to be blocked. Serious traffic jams were now common at peak hours. Increasingly frustrated sections of the population complained about losing business and not being able to go about their daily lives.

Constables had been positioned to restrict access to the gym's lobby. Suki flashed her warrant card and soon found Ethan on the third floor. He was busy talking to a visibly distraught receptionist.

'Ah, Suki,' he said.

'I came immediately, but I had to walk up the escalator from IFC. The traffic is horrendous, right now. Thank God, it isn't too hot today.'

'I know. And I fear it will get worse before it gets better. Anyway, follow me,' he commanded her.

They walked towards the men's changing room.

'The victim is an expat again. British. Ambrose Wallace-Phillimore. Head of equity syndicate at Eurocredit. He was found by a cleaner in one of the shower cubicles, around 2 pm. Completely naked, all crumpled on the floor. His face was lying in a small pool of blood.'

'Oh my God!' was all Suki could say.

'The doc is already here.'

A man in a thin white protection suit nodded, slightly waving his hand.

'It looks like no weapon was used,' he commented in a rather bored voice. 'His face was slammed very hard, probably fatally, although we'll have to wait for the autopsy to confirm this. His neck snapped, around the fourth cervical vertebra. It would have severed the spinal cord or, at the very least, disabled the respiratory function. It's where the nerves exit the cervical spine. He didn't stand a chance.'

Suki looked down at the body. It resembled a twisted doll, with sagging arms and legs, one of which seemed at an odd angle. Photographs had already been taken and the crime-scene team was now busy preparing to transport the corpse to the public mortuary.

'So, no one heard or saw anything?' finally asked Suki.

'No. It probably happened around one thirty, or thereabouts. Most of the club's members who train at lunchtime had already returned to their offices,' answered Ethan.

'And what about that sign over there, about the area being under maintenance?'

'That's the thing. Management are adamant it's not theirs. They said all the showers function perfectly well, which I've been able to confirm. So it was perhaps left behind by the killer, to ensure a clean getaway.'

'Clever.'

'Isn't it just? We're checking for fingerprints and DNA, although I doubt we'll find much that we can use.'

'And are there any cameras around?'

'It's what I was just discussing with the receptionist when you arrived,' said Ethan. 'The only cameras are at reception and outside the lifts on each floor. No CCTV in the individual training areas. This place is huge: the gym spans six floors. We've already taken the disks for analysis. Assuming it's him, hopefully our man shows up a bit more visibly this time.'

'Yeah, the gym's really big. I've actually visited a few times with friends, but it's expensive.'

They returned to the reception area.

'Oh, by the way,' added Suki, 'I may be on to something with my idea about equity deals led by the banks. There's a very large number of transactions to investigate but, with Eurocredit now as a third broker, we should be able to narrow this down quite a bit.'

Ethan questioned the receptionist again.

'I'm sorry to have to ask you so many questions, but I'd rather do this now, while everything is still fresh in your mind.'

'I understand,' said the cute, sporty, twenty-something. She had a slight Russian accent and wore a pink T-shirt with a Sure Fitness logo on the front. On it was clipped a name badge that read 'Natasha'.

'How does it work here? Do people have to check in when they arrive?' said Ethan.

'Oh yes. Everyone has a membership card, just like this one, with a bar code. You need to swipe it, here, like so. The reader basically shows if your membership is still current. See? The green light flashes. If not, we have to look into it manually. The card then allows access to the other floors, but you have to come here first.'

'And do you swipe it again when you leave, Natasha?'

'No. Only once.'

'So, you know when people have arrived, but you're not able to tell if, or when they have left, right?'

'Correct.'

'Then, would you have details of all the members who were in the gym from, say, 10 am? And is there any way of checking in without being a member?'

'I'll get you the list right now,' she said, after pressing a few buttons on her keyboard.

A printer whirred below the reception desk.

'Members pay through direct debit or credit card, and we also have their Hong Kong ID or passport details on file,' she added.

'There are various types of membership,' she continued, 'but they're usually for a few months at least, so it's generally not practical to pay cash. Normally people pay through bank transfers anyway. We also ask everyone to sign a disclaimer, so we record their IDs for insurance purposes.'

'I see,' said Ethan.

'And to answer your second question, some people come in for a trial session first, before they register for a membership, or not, as the case may be. But I've been here all day and there haven't been any of those so far. We only had members today.'

She retrieved a couple of pages from the printer below.

'There you go. So, since 10 am, we only had sixty-one visitors. Actually, it was pretty quiet today. We normally top twice that, or even more with the group classes. But, with the demonstrations and all, the numbers have dropped a fair bit. Hopefully it ends soon.'

She pointed out the various columns on the printed data.

'See, you have the time, the membership number, the full name, the Hong Kong ID or passport number, and a telephone number or email, depending on how people prefer to be contacted.'

'Thank you so much, Natasha. That's great,' said Ethan.

'So, unless our man is a member of staff, he should be on this list,' he added, to Suki.

She pondered and looked at him unconvinced.

'It really sounds a wee bit too easy, don't you think?' she finally said.

'I know.'

CHAPTER 39

1:21 pm, Wan Chai, Hong Kong, 14 October 2017

ANY DOUBTS THAT THE DEATHS of two heads of equity syndicate might have been anything other than a coincidence disappeared after the killing of Ambrose Wallace-Phillimore. The Securities and Futures Commission, the securities regulator in Hong Kong, and the Hong Kong Monetary Authority, the supervisory body for banks, took the unprecedented step of cautioning members of the financial industry. In an emergency closed meeting at the weekend, all the broking firms were informed that a killer was at large. Their equity capital markets staff, and those within syndicate desks more particularly, were advised to take extreme care. Even though Hong Kong was one of the safest cities among the world's major financial centres, it had not taken long for panic to spread through the ranks of its investment bankers. It had been stirred up by the media, with journalists only too happy to report on a lurid serial killer targeting bankers.

The commissioner of police, Mortimer Tse, attended the briefing by the SFC and HKMA. He was now under significant pressure from both the city's government and Beijing. Still, he, of all people, understood the difficulties associated with such a complex case, and especially at a time when a quarter of Hong Kong's police officers were focusing much of their effort on the political troubles. But what could be done was done. Some of the force would be redeployed towards the murder cases.

The list of the fitness club's attendees had been divided between Ethan himself and his team, comprised of Suki Lam, John Mok, Charles Au and Andrew Li. A couple of additional hands on deck provided assistance. The instructions from the powers-that-be had been to wrap things up within twenty-four hours, an objective that might be possible, since more than half of those on the list were female. It was now almost certain that the killer was male. The amount of brute force required to subdue du Toit underwater and kill Wallace-Phillimore by hand had left little doubt about it. Both had been tall, and particularly strong and healthy men. Efforts therefore focused on male club members.

'Ambrose Wallace-Phillimore was gay. He had recently split up with his partner,' said Ethan. 'However, we've already established that he was in London at the time. Plus, he was not a member of the gym,' he added.

The team was busy tracking the club members when Suki identified a possible issue. She was on the phone in the conference room that had been allocated to the team. She suddenly lifted her arm and called the room to attention.

'I've just been on the phone to this guy, Gary Lee. The thing is, while his name is on the list of visitors, he claims to have been in Taiwan at the time. In fact, he said he is still there right now, which should be easy enough to establish. Even more interesting, he said he had sold his membership, which still had seven months to run. It was a few days ago. The buyer was named John, apparently an Aussie, but of Asian ethnicity. He had contacted him through an ad placed on the AsiaExpat website. Unfortunately, he paid for the membership in cash.'

'That sounds like a major lead!' said Ethan.

'Now, according to the list we got from Sure Fitness, Gary Lee, or rather John, checked in at 11:16 am, yesterday. So we should be able to track his arrival on the recording from the third floor camera.'

Andrew Li, the team's tech specialist, fast-forwarded the recording until the timer reached 11:10 am. Then, for what felt like a few very long minutes, they watched the film unfold, on a large, wall-mounted television.

'No, that's a woman, let's see who comes next,' he commented aloud.

And then they saw him. He was an athletic looking man in his thirties, with a baseball cap and sunglasses. He was of medium height, with his head tilted down, just enough to hide some, but this time not all, of his face. He looked Asian, although it was difficult to tell for sure. He quickly swiped his membership card under the reader, before disappearing out of the frame.

'Ethan, I think it's the man from the bus recording in Turtle Cove Beach, and also from the dive shop,' said Suki.

'Andrew,' she added, 'can we take a still of him and put it alongside one from the bus video?'

Andrew fiddled with his computer for a few seconds. The pictures were both grainy. There was no way of telling for certain at first glance, but the odds were that they could indeed be looking at the same man.

'I'll use the face recognition software,' he said. 'Graphical representation should enable us to identify common structures within the images,' he added. 'The fact that he's looking down, and also that he's wearing a cap and glasses won't help, but hopefully there are enough FFPs, sorry, facial feature points, to obtain a decent statistical confidence level. It shouldn't take too long.'

'While Andrew's working, continue checking the other names on the list, just to make sure,' said Ethan. 'And, Suki, send the photo to Gary Lee, in Taiwan. Hopefully he has a smartphone or laptop. I want him to confirm this is the man he sold his membership to. The card might also have been stolen by a third party, so we need to be sure. Lastly, confirm with immigration that Gary Lee was indeed out of the country yesterday.'

'I'm on it,' said John.

About twenty-five minutes passed before Andrew announced that the two pictures matched to the tune of sixty-seven per cent. It wasn't a guarantee, but it was enough to dispel most of their doubts in the circumstances. Shortly thereafter, Gary Lee replied to Suki's message.

'He just came back to me. It's our man all right,' she said.

CHAPTER 40

9:37 am, Causeway Bay, Hong Kong, 16 October 2017

THE SUSPECT'S PICTURE had been widely disseminated within financial firms, as well as through the police website. Both the Chinese and English media had extensively printed it too. The *Apple Daily, Ming Pao, Hong Kong Daily News,* and *South China Morning Post,* among others, had run front-page articles, with titles such as IS THIS THE BANKER KILLER? The TV channels had also joined in, as had radio stations. They had also encouraged viewers and listeners to look at their respective websites for more information.

Some barricades in Central, Causeway Bay and even Admiralty, near the government's headquarters, where the bulk of the protesters were located, had been dismantled. Using chainsaws and power tools, the police had restored access to some of the city's major roads in a dawn operation. The number of demonstrators continued to dwindle during daytime hours. Meanwhile, the chief executive of Hong Kong was in hot water again, over an old story regarding payments he had received from an Australian firm, after his nomination as head of the government. His office had repeatedly denied any wrongdoing, but it looked like the case just would not go away. The Independent Commission Against Corruption, a body established under British rule to tackle bribery, had even looked into it following complaints of misconduct. But it had led nowhere.

Shiryō had been surprised at the publication of his photograph in the press. Or, to be more exact, at the speed with which it had made the headlines. By now, it was only logical that a clear connection would have been made between the three murders. The low-resolution pictures, however, were hardly a breakthrough. Shiryō was not unduly concerned. Over the last few hours, he had spent time significantly altering his appearance. He had dyed his hair grey, which had added a number of years to his appearance. He now also wore a fake beard and clear glasses with a round, metal frame. They made him virtually unrecognisable as the younger, sporty type who featured on the front pages of the city's dailies. Introducing himself as Australian, with a matching accent, to Gary Lee, the man from whom he had bought the fitness club membership, had further muddied the waters of what continued to prove a tricky investigation.

Now that some barricades around his serviced apartment had been removed, the number of police officers in the area would probably drop. Causeway Bay would gradually return to the frenetic commercial activity it was known for, further shrouding Shiryō in a blanket of anonymity. He would press ahead with his mission, he thought, as he left yet another Internet café. There, he had, for the third time, typed a coded word as a draft message, into his Gmail account.

CHAPTER 41

S UKI HAD RETURNED TO MORGAN ROBERTS to see Bee. Again, Karen Wong, from compliance, kept an ever-watchful eye over them. However, this time, Ashok Patel, the bank's regional head of equity capital markets, was also present.

'I'm sorry I couldn't be there when you last visited,' he said. 'I had to go to Jakarta, as Bee probably explained. In fact, it proved to be a complete waste of time! Anyway, I gather the two of you made some progress, so I thought I'd join in today. I obviously saw the news about Ambrose. What a dreadful way to die! I can't believe someone out there could be targeting us. We do compete like crazy but it's more of a tightly knit community than some would have you believe.'

'Did you know him well?' asked Suki.

'We never worked together for the same firms, but we came across each other quite a few times, either pitching, or executing deals. Andrew Short knew him even better, I'm sure. But that's water under the bridge, isn't it?' said Patel.

He looked at his reflection in the glass partition wall that separated the meeting room from the trading floor and subtly adjusted the knot of his blue Hermès tie. As he centred it between the wings of the cutaway collar of his white, custom-made Charvet shirt, Suki recalled Ethan's remarks about Patel's sartorial tastes and appearance. She had to admit he was quite dapper.

'Last time I came, Bea— sorry, Bee and I compiled lists of equity transactions, in which your firm and Swiss Securities had had leading roles. We should perhaps refine these further now by adding Eurocredit. It would be good to narrow these lists down anyway, since we have identified more than eighty offerings.'

'Indeed. It's no secret that we do a lot of deals. Over the last few years, we've really morphed from an advisory firm into a product-pushing outfit. We've become a huge transaction-processing machine. It's impressive.'

Karen Wong waved a hand in protest.

'Ashok, I'm not sure this has much to do with Miss Lam's enquiry,' she said.

'I guess I'm digressing. You're right, Karen. Bee, let's add Eurocredit to the *Dealogic* searches. What are we looking at? Sponsor, global coordinator and bookrunner roles, right?'

Bee nodded. She typed on her laptop's keyboard.

'There you are,' she said, after a short while. 'We went from eighty-four deals to seventeen, a much more manageable number. Now, where do we go from here?'

Ashok Patel looked at the new list that now appeared on the large wall screen slaved to the laptop.

'Let me see . . . hmm, I worked on all of these but, frankly, I can't recall any major issues with any of these transactions. How far back are we going . . . 2011? Obviously, we should do further searches for information relating to these corporates. We can also ask the relevant research analysts for clues. Just thinking aloud now, why don't we refine this further, and look at the share-price performance of these companies since the deals were completed? I mean, if someone was unhappy with one of them, it could well be that they had lost a lot of money in connection with the transaction. That might perhaps be a reason to seek revenge. For a deranged mind, obviously . . . oh, by the way, Bee,' he suddenly asked, 'are we also looking at units in REITs and business trusts?'

'Yes, we're keeping the search wide at this stage,' confirmed Bee. 'Let me include the offer price and current share-price data.'

'Good. Sorry,' he went on, 'as, I was saying, one or more investors might perhaps have lost quite a bit of money, and maybe on more than just one deal. We could look at the allocation books too. It's confidential information, however, so it would be for your eyes only. But all of these deals largely went to professional investors. Sometimes they lose, and sometimes they strike gold. It's just a fact of life, and they all know it. Alternatively, we could be dealing with a disgruntled share-holder. If a deal was priced cheaply, one might have been unhappy to have sold at a low level, if the share price subsequently shot up. Or it could have prevented them from selling down more shares at a later stage, if the price had sharply tanked. No one wants to be stuck with a complete dog for a long period of time. But, quite frankly, I would remember. And killing three ECM bankers for something as trivial as that. . . .'

Bee had processed the share-price information. On the screen were now three additional columns, one that showed the offer price for each of the seventeen transactions; another, the current price; and the third, the percentage difference. Nine transactions showed a positive return. Three had seen price increases of more than twenty per cent. Only two transactions had declined by that amount, one by a remarkable thirty-seven per cent.

'I'll tell you what,' said Patel, 'let's do some background searches, and we'll also talk to the analysts for those that have gone up or down by twenty per cent or more. There are only a handful of companies, so it should be pretty quick. Personally, I can't recall any major issues, but then again I'm not necessarily on top of how these businesses have fared since these offerings. The research analysts definitely would be. I fear we may be looking in the wrong direction, but we'll go through the motions. We should have a complete summary for you by . . . just after lunchtime?'

Bee made a face. She already knew she would be doing all the work.

CHAPTER 42

1:55 pm, Central, Hong Kong, 16 October 2017

BEE WAS BUSY COMPILING INTERNET searches and chatting to research analysts. These days, the latter could only be done, by corporate finance staff, under the supervision of the bank's Compliance Department. Meanwhile, Suki tucked into the plate of sandwiches that had been delivered to the meeting room, along with tea, coffee and soft drinks. Above a wall length of low, built-in cabinets, a heavy, engraved crystal paper-weight proclaimed the bank's creed: Clients First, Honesty, Dedication, Team Work and Respect for the Individual. Beyond the glass wall, the action continued uninterrupted on the trading floor. The firm had grouped all of its securities activities on a single podium, including equities, fixed income, foreign exchange and commodities. It made for a rather impressive sight, especially since the Hong Kong office was just one of the bank's regional offshoots. The firm's worldwide headquarters in New York would no doubt be truly spectacular.

Economists, research analysts, salespeople and traders were talking non-stop on their telephones to institutional clients and their counterparts at other houses. People sat at narrow desks, facing dual computer screens that were sometimes stacked three high. They constantly showed price changes, amid a sea of flashing red or green lights. On occasion, someone would come to deliver an announcement on a microphone, which then led to renewed frenetic activity.

Suki was certain she would not be able to last for more than a single day in such a working environment, even if the salary and bonus would amount to many times what she made in the police force. The money was good, but the work seemed repetitive and bore no relation whatsoever with what was happening in the outside world.

'The real world,' she thought.

The bankers seemed to work in a virtual space, like some sort of strange computer game, interacting only with their own kind. Suki could not help but think it was probably what had alienated financiers in the eyes of many people the world over. There had, of course, also been many scandals in recent years. In Hong Kong, these had included the mini-bond crisis. They were highly structured securities, whose terms were virtually impossible to comprehend, that had been sold mostly to unsophisticated mom-and-pop investors. Unsurprisingly, when issuers or their counterparties collapsed, many investors lost a large portion of their life savings. There was arrogance on the part of those working in the financial industry too. It probably came with the possession of large amounts of disposable income, and at too young an age. In addition, it remained an undeniably sexist world. Suki was attractive, and she knew it, but the way some of the male traders looked at her from beyond the glass wall was anything but subtle. Her crossing the trading floor would probably trigger invitations to multiple dates from these self-styled masters of the universe.

On one of the trading floor's walls, directly in front of her, was a giant flat screen, tuned on Bloomberg Television. Company results and interviews with portfolio managers alternated with breaking news that moved the markets. On it, Suki saw some of her police colleagues clearing street barricades, using hammers and pepper spray. After several weeks of protests, the government had decided that things must return to normal. The authorities did not want a repeat of the seventy-nine-day mayhem that had brought the city to a standstill in 2014. Democracy was off the agenda today. Hong Kong was becoming just another Chinese city, and that would be the end of it. Her mobile rang. It was Ethan.

'Suki? I thought I'd let you know the sales assistant at the dive shop you visited recognised our man from the Sure Fitness footage. We're definitely dealing with the same guy. Not that we really had much doubt.'

'So there we have it,' she answered, 'I can't even recall the last time we had a serial killer in Hong Kong! All we have to do now is find him. Oh, talking of which, I'm still at Morgan Roberts. We're looking into transactions that involved the banks where the three victims had worked. The people here are actually very helpful. I might have something for us shortly, even if the head of ECM isn't really expecting a breakthrough. He was personally involved in all of these offerings and couldn't recall anything out of the ordinary.'

'Let me know as soon as you hear back. We've also received a number of calls following the publication of the photographs. So far, just the usual thing, concerned citizens trying to play detective. You never know, though.'

'I'll have to call you back, the bankers have just returned. Hopefully with good news,' she said before hanging up.

Bee Fong, Ashok Patel and the ever-present minder from compliance made their way back towards the meeting room, walking across the trading floor in Suki's direction. Bee carried several large files. The ability of investment bankers to produce or recycle large volumes of paperwork in a short space of time never ceased to amaze Suki. Once they had returned to the room, Patel explained the work Bee had done over the last few hours.

'First of all, thank you for waiting,' he started, smooth as always. 'Bee has done a great job looking through the files of those companies on which we agreed to follow up. She's also spoken to the research analysts who follow these stocks.

'Now, the bottom line is we haven't really been able to find anything suspect, I'm afraid. In all cases, there seem to have been good, legitimate reasons why some of these stocks haven't performed. It was either due to macro events or company-specific developments. And it's also the same for those that have traded sharply up. In the latter cases, we've also established that the equity offerings were primary only anyway.'

'I'm sorry, primary?'

'Forgive me. What I mean is that there were no sell-downs of shares by existing shareholders. These deals took the form of capital raisings by the companies themselves. So it's not like a shareholder would have sold stock, and then missed out on a rally although, of course, they would have been diluted. In all such cases, the client was the corporate itself. We'll obviously leave these reports with you but, for now, I'm sorry there doesn't seem to be much worth pursuing. No scandals, no illegal deals. Nothing.'

Part IV

AIR

CHAPTER 43

WHILE MANY IN HONG KONG had hoped that the protests would quietly die down, violence erupted around Lung Wo Road, next to the government's offices. Police had, again, attempted to clear the area. Some of the demonstrators, including a member of the pro-democracy Civic Party, had been violently beaten up by members of the security forces and, to cap it all, in full view of the media's cameras. Some officers had been suspended, pending an investigation. The police had, so far, largely been praised for its restraint, in spite of a couple of isolated incidents, but its image had been significantly eroded as a result. What had, up to now, mostly been a peaceful movement was increasingly taking a turn for the worse.

Such were the thoughts on Rowena Ng's mind as she arrived on the sixth floor of the Four Seasons Hotel, one of Hong Kong's best. The entrance was located at the western end of IFC Mall in Central. She ignored the access to the spa and open-air swimming pool, which offered panoramic views over the harbour, and walked straight to the reception desk of Caprice. It was a two- (but previously three-) Michelin star French restaurant, where she was about to dine with clients and competitors from other investment banks. The dinner was in anticipation of a theatre-style roadshow presentation that would take place the following day, a few floors below. Instinctively, after the lift doors had opened, she had looked behind her shoulder. Everyone working in equity capital markets was nervous. She had known Andrew Short, Pieter du Toit and Ambrose Wallace-Phillimore well, and had worked with them on many occasions. While they had not been close friends, it was traumatic to have someone you knew brutally murdered. ECM was clearly not a brotherhood, but still a small community.

Rowena was unusually tall for a Chinese. She headed the equity syndicate desk for Asia at Hajimari Capital. She had worked in that capacity for four years, and had previously held various roles with J.P.Morgan and Citi, in both Hong Kong and London. Her clients tonight were the chairman, chief financial officer and director of investor relations respectively of China Easy Truck International Cayman (Holdings) Limited. Although incorporated offshore, it was a private enterprise based in Chengdu, a manufacturer of forklift trucks. Hajimari Capital was one of the lead banks for their initial public offering in Hong Kong, alongside two other firms. Her counterparts from Equity International and China Capital Securities were also at the dinner. It was the start of the roadshow, when management formally met with institutions. Simultaneously, shares would be sold to investors in a process known as bookbuilding. Orders for stock would be taken within an indicative price range that had already been determined.

The roadshow would follow the sun. The management team would travel to Singapore, and next to the UK and continental Europe. They would ultimately arrive in the US, where the offering would likely be priced and allocated to individual accounts. Rowena would meet them again in New York, but one of her colleagues would travel all the way with the presenting team, as would indeed representatives from the other major underwriters.

It was a terrible time to conduct an IPO. The markets were in free fall and investor demand seemed to have evaporated. There were a number of reasons for this. The endless crisis on Russia's borders, an overt war with terrorists in Iraq and Syria, a spreading Ebola epidemic, the moribund economy across the Eurozone and, now, renewed skirmishes in Hong Kong between pro- and anti-democracy protesters had all taken their toll on the markets. A sharp drop in oil and other commodity prices and continued uncertainties about where interest rates were headed had also contributed. The VIX, the so-called 'fear index' that measured market volatility, was at a two-year high.

The discussions to agree on a price range had been a nightmare. The management team had clung to unreasonably high expectations for the valuation of the company, in spite of the feedback received from the market at the pre-deal investor-education stage. Accordingly, the banks had been forced to start marketing the offer with an unusually wide range of almost thirty-five per cent. It sent the unfortunate message to investors that they did not really have a clue about where the transaction should be priced. Rowena was certain of one thing: the price would ultimately need to be set cheaply or the deal simply would not happen. The situation was compounded by the fact that there had been no advance orders for the shares by cornerstone investors. They were large and prestigious accounts, committed to buying a significant portion of an IPO at its offer price, but ahead of its formal launch. It enabled them to secure juicy allocations, always an issue when deals were significantly oversubscribed. Their presence often flagged a good deal to the wider universe of investors, in addition to de-risking the bookbuilding process for the banks, since a big chunk of the offer had already effectively been pre-sold. The absence of cornerstones had not gone unnoticed. Demand would likely be subdued and, if anything, some market participants would be looking to buy on weakness, after the start of trading rather than in the IPO itself. If the deal ever made it to listing that is.

Rowena shook hands with everyone and sat down, ready to brief her clients on market conditions. They would need reassurance and encouragement that they were doing well, on a personal level. Conversely, now would also be the time to start managing their expectations. Not that Mr Lu, the company's chairman, really cared. Sébastien, Caprice's French sommelier, soon approached the table, ready to suggest an aperitif or a glass of champagne for the guests to enjoy as they perused the menu. His attempts were abruptly rebuffed. Chairman Lu waved his hand in an arresting gesture.

'Bring us two, no, three bottles of Lafite!' he swiftly commanded, snapping his fingers, not caring about the vintage. He had not even looked at the wine list. The banks would pay the tab, but ultimately charge the company for the lot. The cost of the wine would be buried among other claims, as they computed the expense account. They might even add an additional US$10,000 or so, just for good luck.

Rowena sighed. She ordered a salad of violet artichokes, Colonnata pork ravioli, and Alba white truffle as a starter. She also chose Royale *langoustine à la plancha* and ravioli, mushrooms, watercress coulis and caviar for her main course. The evening had only just started and it likely would go on for a while. At least the food would be good and she would be spared the hours that might follow at a *karaoke* club in Wan Chai. As a female, such entertainment would be strictly off-limits for her.

At a nearby table, three giggling Japanese girls took pictures of their plates with their mobile phones, softly whispering how *kawaii* everything was. Within seconds, they posted food-porn photographs on social networks.

CHAPTER 44

10:01 pm, Causeway Bay, Hong Kong, 18 October 2017

J J HAD PROBABLY OVERDONE IT with drugs and alcohol that
evening. He was in a state of intense excitation. Dehydrated
and hooked on crystal meth, he had lost much of his sense of
reality. He had not showered for a few days and it badly showed,
and smelled. His apartment was, again, in a sorry condition.
The ashtrays were full and there were beer bottles everywhere,
as well as empty crisp packets and half-eaten items of junk food.
The window was wide open. The suitcase was still outside on
the balcony. He had not touched it.

Ayu was one of JJ's regulars. He had slapped her and
submitted her to countless humiliating practices many times,
but had always apologised afterwards and paid much more
than the going rate. And so, she always returned. She was a
tough girl from northern Sulawesi, on the Celebes Sea, a
Christian enclave within the world's most populous Muslim
country, Indonesia. She had seen her fair share of violent and
deranged men over the years, both at home and in Hong Kong,
where she was officially employed as a domestic helper. It was
a front for her activities as a prostitute, but it had fooled the

authorities for the best part of the last two years. It had probably also helped that a civil servant from the Immigration Department was quite taken with her. She had already saved a significant amount of money from her evening activities. She soon planned to return to Manado, where she would open a small bar, maybe even a restaurant.

Ayu adjusted her miniskirt and a T-shirt that proclaimed NO MONEY, NO HONEY, and knocked on the door to JJ's unit. She was particularly hard-edged and streetwise, but she immediately felt uneasy as he opened the door. JJ seemed to be even more disturbed than usual. The room stank of stale smoke and alcohol. Above all, it smelled of decay, as if a dead animal had been abandoned in the flat for a number of days. JJ had a strange fixed intensity in his eyes, unlike any she had seen before. He fetched a glass in the kitchen to pour her a drink. He did not even walk straight. She immediately took the opportunity to text her friend and roommate, Mita.

'Something's wrong. There's a strange smell. I'm afraid. I want to leave,' her message said.

JJ soon returned. He seemed completely lost, almost in some sort of trance.

'Baby, I really don't feel well, right now,' she told him. 'I need to go. I'll come back some other time, OK?'

JJ grinned and looked at her, his head tilted to one side. He was clearly annoyed now. Suddenly, without any warning, he jumped on her. He was astonishingly quick, his energy and reactiveness perhaps boosted by the methamphetamine. Ayu fell down and banged her elbow on the coffee table. The pain radiated throughout her arm, all the way up to her shoulder. He was now on top of her. He was much heavier than she was and she knew she could not escape. She screamed, but there was no one to help her. To her horror, she next saw the knife in his hand. It was one of those large models sold at military surpluses and hunting supply stores. It had a long fixed blade, made of heavy-duty stainless steel. On one side, it featured a saw-back serration. The opposite edge was razor sharp. The blade caught the reflection of one of the spotlights on the ceiling. It briefly blinded her. JJ tightened his grip on the hilt, his knuckles now white. He hesitated, for a second or two, and then repeatedly stabbed her in a savage fit of anger.

The blade delivered multiple injuries in rapid succession, slicing through her skin like butter. Some of JJ's hits merely lacerated tissue, as they tore through the pink T-shirt that stopped just above her belly button. Others, however, severed blood vessels, deep in her body. Much of the bleeding was internal. Severely in shock, Ayu soon passed out, as the loss of blood quickly led to the failure of her heart and lungs.

JJ stopped stabbing. He looked at her for a while, motionless but panting, a dribble of saliva slowly dripping from his mouth. He dropped the knife on the floor. Fascinated, he caressed her face and chest, slowly bathing his hands in the warm blood that oozed out of her wounds. A dark and smelly pool started to accumulate around her body, staining the beige carpet. He finally stood up and rubbed his hands on his face, applying a macabre war paint. He walked outside on the balcony and paused for a moment beside the suitcase. He looked at the moon above, expectantly. Now delirious, he stretched out his arms wide and started screaming like a wounded animal.

CHAPTER 45

11:02 pm, Causeway Bay, Hong Kong, 18 October 2017

ETHAN AND SUKI ARRIVED AT THE apartment just after 11 pm. A group of three police constables, who had been on patrol nearby, had gained access to the building through a neighbour and had knocked several times at the door of JJ's unit. When no answer came, they made a forced entry, their Smith & Wesson Model 10 revolvers drawn in front of them. JJ had not resisted arrest. The crime-scene team was already busy, combing the flat for clues. Cameras flashed a few times, as Ethan and Suki passed through the front door, protective plastic covers on their shoes. The place smelled of decay and death.

'We found a body in a locked suitcase, on the balcony. It was a young woman, naked. It looks like she'd been there for at least a week, maybe more. The smell was pretty strong. No wonder he kept her outside. At first glance, she was strangled,' said one of the constables.

'The second homicide,' he added, pointing in the general direction of the sofa, 'happened less than an hour ago. She was stabbed many times with that knife we found on the floor. The alert came from a security guard, on patrol in one of the buildings, on the other side of the street. He saw some of what happened and called 999. A colleague is taking his statement right now.'

There were red stains everywhere on the carpet. On the floor, the body of a petite, tanned girl was lying in a pool of blood. She was scantily clad, with a miniskirt and a ripped, low-cut tee shirt. She had multiple stab wounds.

'Any idea who they were?' asked Suki.

'They were both Southeast Asian, that much is clear. We still need to find out about the first one. I'd say perhaps a Filipina. The one he just killed was Indonesian. Her name was Ayu Kristanto. We found her papers in her handbag. She had a domestic helper visa, but most likely was also an occasional prostitute, based on some of the text messages on her mobile. Maybe the other girl was as well.'

'And who is he?' said Ethan, pointing to JJ, who was now seated on the floor. He looked tranquil and placid with a blissful smile, but his face was covered in dried blood.

'His name is Jasper Jersin. American. He's not very coherent. Rose & Rudd, the bank, made him redundant a few weeks ago. He had drunk quite a lot. We also found cocaine and crystal meth. He's obviously still under the influence.'

The flat was in a sorry state. Cleaners regularly attended to the units, so most of the disorder would have been quite recent.

'He even took a series of selfies with the Indonesian, after killing her. It's really crazy!' added one of the police officers.

'She had apparently just arrived. She texted someone called Mita, probably a friend, that something was wrong,' he added. 'I suppose you could say she saw it coming. But he killed her before she could react. There were a number of missed calls on her phone, from that Mita. We tried to call her back but there was no answer.'

Could this be the man who had killed three expatriate bankers? Suki doubted it very much. The other homicides had been well planned, and also professionally executed. These two looked amateurish in the extreme. The killer also bore little resemblance to what they knew about the murderer of the heads of syndicate. For one thing, Jersin was not Asian. And while he had until recently been an investment banker, the victims obviously were not. They were most likely looking at two distinct cases.

'At first glance, it looks like a rather clear-cut story. There's little doubt Jersin did it,' said Ethan. 'The open questions are whether he also strangled the girl in the suitcase and, if so, if he did it on his own. And why. Anyway, why don't I help the crime-scene team wrap things up here while you question the neighbours? Someone must have heard or perhaps even seen something,' he instructed Suki. 'Meanwhile, we'll take Mr Jersin into custody immediately,' he added.

Suki exited the flat. She knocked on the door of the adjacent unit.

Shiryō had heard the police sirens in the street down below. For a moment, he thought he might have been cornered but the officers had now been in the building for a good thirty minutes. They were obviously after someone else. Most probably, it was a domestic dispute. He had heard a commotion shortly after 10 pm. A woman had even screamed a few times, as had a man on the balcony. Shiryō was not too concerned. His cover was rock solid. He donned his round metal glasses and opened the door.

'Yes?' he said, in English.

'Good evening sir. I'm sorry to disturb you. My name is Suki Lam. I'm an inspector with the Hong Kong Police,' said Suki, flashing her warrant card.

'Oh? Good evening Inspector. What is the matter?'

'Can I first ask who you are, Sir? And also please see some form of identification?'

'Sure. My name is Edwin Sutanto,' said Shiryō with a slight Indonesian accent, slightly stroking his beard.

'I'm from Jakarta,' he added.

He fetched a passport in the breast pocket of his jacket and handed it out to Suki.

'I've been in Hong Kong for almost a month,' he continued, 'with a brief trip to Macau in between. I work for a mining company. Coal. I'm here to buy earth-moving equipment, from China. And also to secure lease financing from local banks.'

'I see,' said Suki, taking a good look at his face. The man looked like he was in his fifties.

'Did you grow the beard recently?' she asked, 'you're clean-shaven on your passport photograph.'

The ID snapshot looked vaguely familiar, although she could not tell why.

'Yes. I've only had it for a few weeks. I thought I'd take it easy, while I'm away from my family.'

She glanced at the gold ring, on the fourth finger of his left hand.

'I see. Did you notice anything unusual tonight?'

'Did something bad happen?'

'I'm afraid there's been a homicide. Your testimony would be most helpful.'

'A homicide! Oh my God! Unfortunately, I'm not sure I can be of much help. I don't know anyone in the building at all. I use this flat as a base, but I'm in meetings outside most of the time, and I also often go out for dinner. I returned around 9:30. It's true there was quite a lot of noise tonight. It was probably just after ten. I heard a woman scream, and then a man, only briefly. But at the time, I thought it might have been a movie on television. I did not see anything at all.'

'I understand. Thank you. Mr Sutanto. One more thing, do you know someone called Ayu Kristanto, an Indonesian woman?'

'It's an Indonesian name, all right. But no, I'm afraid I don't.'

'Can I please take down your contact details, in case we need to talk to you again?'

'Absolutely. Here's my name card. My mobile number is on it, or you can also call the residence's number. If I'm not around, just key in the unit number, 602, to leave a message. I'll make sure to call you back as soon as possible.'

'That would be great. Will you stay in Hong Kong for long?'

'I'll be in town probably for another week, two at most. But my plans might change, depending on developments back at the mine.'

'I see. Again, thank you. And please don't worry. Everything's under control as far as your neighbours are concerned. Good night.'

Suki left as he closed the door.

It had been sheer bad luck. She had seen his face and also closely scrutinised the photograph on his passport. Shiryō had no reason to believe the police had any particular interest in him at this stage, other than as a matter of routine enquiry. Still, he could not afford to take any risks.

CHAPTER 46

12 noon, Central, Hong Kong, 23 October 2017

SHIRYŌ HAD NOW FOLLOWED Rowena Ng for a few days. Lately, he had attended an IPO roadshow presentation, which she had hosted at the Four Seasons Hotel. He had simply turned up and handed a name card to the receptionist. It had introduced him as a senior fund manager. She had been unable to find his name of the list of attendees, but waved him through without any further issues. Shiryō was always amazed at what could be achieved in Hong Kong with a simple business card, or a rubber company chop. Such items conveyed an air of authority, of which he was only too happy to abuse.

There were about 150 people in the room. They were distributed among tables of ten or twelve guests, for a sit-down lunch. The starter had already been served, to minimise comings and goings by the waiters. The guests' attention had to remain firmly focused on the presentation by the company. The investors at his table introduced themselves without taking too much interest in him. They then sat down and immediately tucked into their lobster and mango salad. The sound of forks and knives echoed noisily in the ballroom, as they hit the porcelain plates. But Shiryō had not come for the food. After a short while, Rowena stood up and walked from the top table to a podium, where a speaker stand was placed. Confidently, she called for silence.

'Ladies and gentlemen, may I have your attention please. Thank you for attending this lunch today. My name is Rowena Ng and I'm the head of equity syndicate for Asia at Hajimari Capital. On behalf of China Capital Securities, Equity International and Hajimari Capital, as joint global coordinators and joint bookrunners of the IPO, I'm pleased to welcome you to this presentation by China Easy Truck International. . . .'

Shiryō was a good judge of character. He immediately observed she displayed absolutely no nervousness when addressing the large crowd. She was very calm under pressure and in a particularly unpredictable working environment. She was tall and assertive, and commanded both respect and consideration.

'May I first introduce Chairman Lu, who is joined today by Dr Wan, the chief financial officer of the company, and Mr Ren, director of investor relations. . . .'

As their names were called, each stood up to attention, one after the other, slightly bowing to the crowd, with comical effect. On their lapels were flowery rosettes, to better identify them as VIPs.

'The initial public offering of the company will be comprised of seven million shares. Of these, six million new shares will be issued by the company, with the balance sold by Chairman Lu,' continued Rowena, 'the proceeds will be primarily used to retire debt and for acquisitions across Asia, with a small portion for working capital and general corporate purposes. The offer also includes an over-allotment option totalling fifteen per cent of the IPO shares. . . .'

Shiryō's neighbours all stopped eating at that point, carefully listening to the key parameters of the deal. They were displayed on two large screens, placed on both sides of the head table.

'The indicative price range for the IPO has been set at HK$6 per share to HK$8.04 per share. Bookbuilding starts today. It will conclude on 31st October, when we expect to price the transaction. Listing will be on 3rd November. And now, without further ado, we'd like to show you a short clip about the company.'

At this juncture, amid a triumphant soundtrack, a three-minute film to the glory of China's premier forklift-truck manufacturer unfolded on the dual screens. A voiceover with a polished American accent narrated in the background, as some of the company's products were portrayed, lifting unsteady pallets across an impossibly large factory floor. The portfolio managers returned to their food, clearly bored. The lunch continued for almost an hour, as a question-and-answer session followed the presentation by management.

Shiryō shadowed Rowena after work, that same evening. She lived in Shek O, on the southeastern coast of Hong Kong Island. It was quite a long way from Exchange Square in Central, where Hajimari Capital's offices were located, in two of the highest floors of a still prime, but older building. At first, it astonished him that she rode a motorbike, a red Ducati Streetfighter 848, although it made perfect sense. The weather in Hong Kong, bar the odd showers and typhoons in the rainy season, was mostly fine. The traffic from Shek O to Central, and back, could often be congested, on what was mostly a narrow road. Riding a motorbike was simply the best way to beat the traffic jams at rush hour. Rowena Ng was married to an architect who often worked from home. She was ambitious and could also be aggressive. A portfolio manager at the event had gossiped she owed much of her fast-track career to an affair with the number two (he had, in fact, said 'the running dog') to one of the city's best-known tycoons. Rumour also had it that, behind her back, some within ECM circles knew her as 'PV'. It stood for 'the pit viper'.

Shiryō was taken by surprise at the sight of her motorbike. He was forced to abandon his surveillance, as she revved the engine and disappeared from view, the tyres squealing on the tar road. The following day, he came prepared. He had rented an inconspicuous but trusty Honda CB 400 and followed her from afar, taking great care not get noticed. She drove fast, very fast. Shiryō had trouble keeping up with her. She made systematic use of the Ducati Quick Shift system. It was a device normally used in racing, which allowed the driver to change gears without using the clutch, as the throttle remained open. At some point, she accelerated at 8,000 rpm up Wong Nai Chung Gap Road, towards the south side of Hong Kong Island, losing him for a few seconds. The cannon-style mufflers delivered the bike's unmistakable L-Twin sound, unleashing raw power. It suddenly dawned on him how he would strike. It would be deadly and there would be no comebacks.

CHAPTER 47

Shinjuku, Tokyo, 14 June 2011

S HIRYŌ HAD NOT BEEN THRILLED at the idea of targeting a woman, although he had long ago lost all sense of chivalry. The deal had come as a package, of which Rowena was an essential component. In fact, it was the second time he had been asked to kill an executive from Hajimari Capital. The assignment brought back memories, from what now seemed to him like an eternity ago.

It was one of Shiryō's first kills, following the death of the Japanese politician that had launched his new career. As often, a trusty third party, one Kaoru Hashimoto, a shady lawyer who worked for the great and good of Japan's considerable under-world, made the introduction. The issue was a straightforward marriage that had, quite literally, reached a dead end. Masaaki Sumino was a high-flying executive, who worked too much and was often away from Tokyo on business. Long overseas postings in New York and London had not helped, and his very pretty, but also very bored wife Miki, had, for some time, looked to put an end to the relationship. In desperation, she turned to her long-standing friend, Hashimoto-san, for advice.

Kaoru Hashimoto explained that a divorce would entail a long and costly procedure. Ultimately, there was little doubt about a positive outcome, but significant uncertainties remained about the terms of a possible settlement. It was likely that Sumino would not go down without a fight. Miki was not prepared to face months, or even years, of protracted negotiations in a family or district court. Hashimoto-san then suggested another possible solution. It was not one he could personally recommend, but Miki was firmly of the view that her husband had to be removed. It marked the end of Hashimoto's involvement in the matter and he did not accept any payment. The rest would be entirely down to her.

Shiryō was not as experienced or cautious back then. A few days later, he listened to the executive's wife, as she conveyed her predicament over coffee and cake at Almond, a well-known tea parlour with a pink façade, on Tokyo's Roppongi Crossing. She appeared genuinely distressed and her cute face convinced him to take on the contract. A price was agreed, a very reasonable six million yen, payable in cash and in advance.

Miki was quite wealthy in her own right. With many payments in Japan still made in cash, it was easy for her to assemble the sum without arousing suspicion. She paid Shiryō within a few days. It involved placing a thick unmarked envelope in a discreet pre-agreed location in Yoyogi Park.

Masaaki Sumino worked in Marunouchi, a district close to both the Imperial Palace and Tokyo Station, and also home to many of Japan's financial institutions. He started work early and returned home late, when he ever bothered to do so. He entertained clients and colleagues at least three times a week.

Shiryō followed him for a few days. He soon established he often drank whisky after work, at an exclusive hostess bar. The place catered to high-end executives on corporate accounts. It was located in a dimly lit and smoky basement of an otherwise anonymous building in Shinjuku. The range of drinks on offer was generous, and also very expensive. The music was rather good too, offering its inebriated but wealthy patrons the promise of a good time. Young hostesses laughed at their pitiful jokes, hiding their mouths and teeth with one of their hands, and generously refilled their glasses as the evening went by. On occasion, some of them even brought customers to a nearby hotel, for entertainment of another nature.

Access to the club was through a two-floor underground car park that also served the residential block above. It was not guarded and similarly not under the surveillance of security cameras, perhaps to better preserve the anonymity of its high profile clientele. Masaaki Sumino generally arrived after dinner, around 8 pm, staying until 11 pm, before driving his 7-series BMW back to his trophy home in Denenchofu.

One evening, Shiryō followed Sumino to the club, then waited, hidden behind a concrete pillar, for him to return to the car park. He was armed with a *tantō*, the shortest of all Japanese swords. Late in the Edo period, a craftsman named Oo Shigehide had forged its twenty-five-centimetre blade in Hizen, not far from Nagasaki. It was an antique weapon, but still lethal and as sharp as a razor.

Around 11:15 pm, Sumino appeared, looking tired. He walked around his car to open the front door, on the right, the driver's side in Japan. Shiryō grabbed him violently by the shoulder with his left hand. They faced each other for a fraction of a second. Shiryō then sliced deeply, only once, into Sumino's inner thigh, severing the femoral artery. He then stepped aside and avoided further contact with his victim.

Had the slash been made straight across the artery, Sumino's sphincter muscles might have contracted, in an attempt to close off the injury. Shiryō, however, had delivered a perfect cut, at a sharp, forty-five-degree angle. Blood immediately gushed out of the wound, creating an increasingly wet and dark stain on the trousers of Sumino's pinstripe suit. His face turned pale, as the shock set in. His hand frantically tried to stem the torrent of blood that rushed along his right leg, flooding his cashmere sock and polished slip-on shoe.

Shiryō silently looked on at the ever more desperate and pale Sumino. Not a word was exchanged. Within thirty seconds, the banker had lost consciousness. He collapsed heavily on the concrete floor. Blood continued to pour out, soaking his designer suit in a sticky pool. Finally, he died, in the dark Shinjuku car park.

CHAPTER 48

T HE PROTESTS HAD TURNED INCREASINGLY violent in Mong Kok. There, as in other areas, Hong Kong's High Court had now ordered the demonstrators off the streets. In another development, the authorities had finally agreed to hold talks with representatives of the students and Occupy Central movement. However, clumsy remarks by the city's leader that 'democracy could lead the poor to dominate the vote' were, in the views of many observers, likely to further fan the fire. The situation was as tense as ever.

Shiryō used the elevated walkway to walk from Alexandra House to IFC Mall. He turned right after the east-side entrance and continued until he reached the flagship Apple store. It was set over two floors, linked by an impressive glass spiral staircase. Outside, a number of touts were busy calling to passers-by. They sold, at inflated prices, new iPhones to day-trippers from the Mainland, where this latest model was not yet available. They counted thick wads of HK$1,000 bills in full view of the store's and mall's security staff. It was obvious what was going on, but no one seemed to care much. Parallel trading was just a fact of life in Hong Kong. Shiryō, however, was not interested in buying an iPhone.

He entered a nearby store that sold a variety of electronic gadgets, and zoomed in on a small quadricopter drone, made of carbon fibre and high-grade plastic. It could be remotely operated from an application downloaded on a smartphone. It measured approximately seventy-five by thirty centimetres, including a full hull shield. It could be steered from fifty metres away through a self-generated Wi-Fi network. It had on-board pressure sensors that assisted with in-flight stability. It could automatically correct and maintain a still position in the air, regardless of altitude, even when faced with winds of up to twenty kph. Most of the buyers used the mini drone to record videos with its built-in cameras. They would then upload them onto social networks. Others liked to stage indoor or outdoor battles, with other drone operators. The vendor assured him the lithium-ion polymer battery was already fully charged. It would allow up to forty minutes of flight time.

Shiryō paid cash for the toy and left the shop. He carried the cardboard box in which it was packed in a plastic bag. He took a series of escalators down to Central's MTR station, which could be directly accessed from the mall. He rode a train north for approximately twelve minutes and changed at Mong Kok, arriving at Diamond Hill Station after another six stops. There, he caught a No 92 bus, bound for Sai Kung, where he changed to a No 94, and finally alighted at Pak Tam Chung in the remote countryside. A number of hiking trails started there, but it would be largely devoid of ramblers on a weekday, and had the perfect terrain for testing the drone.

Shiryō chose an isolated spot, just off the main walking trail. He took an unlocked iPhone, which he had bought new, alongside a few others, months before in a small store in Thailand. He had never used it. He inserted a new, pre-paid voice and broadband SIM card into the handset. Even in such a forested area, the reception was surprisingly strong. He pressed the App Store icon and located and downloaded a free application. After a couple of minutes, he checked that the application was connected to the drone and started flight trials.

Operating the craft could not have been easier. It was genuinely intuitive. By gently tilting the smartphone, he could readily control the direction of the machine, which would also stabilise in the air when the controls were released. It could even perform barrel rolls and flip moves, just by hitting a button. Its onward and return course, speed and altitude could even be pre-programmed on a map, provided that the drone stayed within the phone's Wi-Fi range. It also featured a 'rescue mode' to spin the propellers in the event it became stuck up a tree branch. For a while, he practised take offs, landings, loops and other acrobatics. Shiryō had to admit it was clever, and also a lot of fun.

He did not meet anyone for the next twenty minutes. Once he was satisfied he could control the machine with ease, and in all situations, he landed the drone. He switched off the application and iPhone, and returned to Pak Tam Chung, where he caught a bus bound for Hong Kong Island. Within ninety minutes, he had placed the drone and smartphone away from prying eyes. As the night fell, he rode the Honda to Shek O. He carefully scanned the road along the way, memorising the terrain and assessing the best areas for an ambush. It took him the best part of fifty minutes, as traffic built up.

Once in Shek O, he parked his motorcycle in the beach car park. He walked the short distance to the Chinese-Thai restaurant, where he had a quick bite and drink. The weather had cooled noticeably over the last couple of weeks. It was now pleasant to sit outside and watch people and the world go by. There was a simple atmosphere around the Shek O roundabout, in sharp contrast to the nearby golf club, the city's most exclusive, where it took a decade or more to become a member. Memberships, when available, changed hands for at least a million US dollars.

Shiryō finished his dinner. He returned to the car park, unlocked his bike and revved the engine. He rode up Shek O Road, where some of Hong Kong's most exclusive houses were situated. They could not be bought and even renting one required the approval of a residents' committee. It was a convenient device to exclude outsiders from what was a *de facto* community of *tai pans* and senior executives, many working for the city's largest conglomerates. It was now dark. Shiryō accelerated around Cape d'Aguilar and drove downhill at full speed towards the bridge that jumped over the scenic Tai Tam Tuk Reservoir. The water level was low. As he crossed to the other side, the Honda's headlights revealed glimpses of the sand-coloured banks.

CHAPTER 49

THE PRO-DEMOCRACY MOVEMENT had become a part of every day's routine. The students and their supporters were stuck in a stalemate with the government, neither side prepared to offer concessions. The protesters were now talking of bringing their demands directly to Beijing, given the lack of progress about the whole affair with the authorities in the territory. As in 2014, the latter were clearly expecting the movement to die a slow death, but the opposition seemed more determined this time.

Hong Kong had also just come under the global spotlight again, after the spectacular arrest of Jasper Jersin for the murder of two alleged prostitutes. It had led to yet another media frenzy, in light of the particularly sordid circumstances of the case. At least, it had relieved some of the pressure on Ethan and his team to solve the bankers' murders. The homicides of what looked, at this stage, like sex workers, appeared to be completely unrelated to the others. Here, a banker was the killer, not a victim. A bloody knife had been found at the scene, and it looked more and more like a twisted story, involving the loss of a trading licence and drug-fuelled sex orgies.

Jersin was also said to have taken with his smartphone more than one hundred photographs of himself and at least one of the victims. The gruesome selfies had not been made public, but some tabloids had shot their own versions, using models to stage gory re-enactments.

Ethan was disappointed that Suki's lead had not resulted in a breakthrough. It was, after all, logical that a transaction involving the bankers' employers could ultimately be the reason behind these homicides. Serial killers often murdered their victims in the same way, as a sort of signature, but the only obvious pattern here was the bankers' occupation, as equity capital markets practitioners. The deals Suki had identified had not seemed out of the ordinary. The research analysts who covered these businesses had also not been aware of any suspicious circumstances. All the other avenues of enquiry had, by now, been exhausted. The murderer could also have since altered his appearance, further muddying the waters.

In the end, the probing of databases had proven a complete waste of time. The victims themselves did not appear to have been involved in any type of shady business. Obviously, their lifestyles as investment bankers bore no relation to what most people could experience, either in Hong Kong or elsewhere. They had disposable income the man in the street could only dream of, designer homes and, for some, flashy cars. They ate in the best restaurants, partied in private clubs, and regularly travelled for work and pleasure. In their world, a US$100 million transaction was small potatoes, a deal that would be handled by junior associates.

But jealousy was most certainly not what was behind these homicides. The murders had been too clean, too professional. There had to be a reason why these financiers had been targeted and why someone was systematically going after them. There had to be other links, something buried in their respective pasts, and which the police had so far failed to uncover.

CHAPTER 50

SHIRYŌ HAD POSITIONED HIMSELF high on a hill overlooking Cape d'Aguilar, on the last stretch of road to Shek O. A call to Rowena's office had brought confirmation that she was in Hong Kong that day. She would also be in town for the rest of the week. His position was perfect. A straight line on the road led to it. There, her motorbike would run at full speed. A deep cliff, planted with pine trees, bordered the sharp bend ahead. It rolled down to the sea, over a length of a few hundred metres. He had turned up early and parked his rented motorbike in a small trail. It led to a lighthouse, the oldest in Hong Kong, known as the Hok Tsui Beacon.

Shiryō readied his drone. Its polymer battery, like that of his iPhone, was fully charged. He used a piece of duct tape to attach a ninety-centimetre steel chain to the miniature aircraft. He had purchased it earlier in a hardware store in Wan Chai. Although the chain was solid, it was also light. It would not affect the drone's flight pattern. The duct tape was sufficiently strong to ensure the chain would not drop in mid-flight. However, once it became stuck somewhere, it would easily detach, allowing the quadricopter to continue its journey unimpeded. He checked his watch. It was 5 pm. There were probably still several hours before Rowena Ng would show up. It did not worry him. He was used to waiting. He took a bite from a biscuit and casually scanned the horizon with his monocular. He was well hidden by thick bush, even from the most careful of observers. The darkness would also soon render him completely invisible.

Rowena had had a terrible day. The IPO of the forklift truck manufacturer was going nowhere, as she had feared. Chairman Lu was still adamant the indicative price should not be lowered. The deal was heading straight into the wall. She already knew what would happen next. They would wait until the very last minute, confirm the transaction could not be covered by investor demand, pull it, and blame market conditions. Then would begin the hard work of convincing the issuer to re-launch the offering, with a smaller size and at a lower valuation. At that level, they would probably gather cornerstone support and the deal would ultimately be a success. But it would only happen in perhaps one or two months' time. Meanwhile, other investment banks would start circling the company like sharks. They would blame the failure of the listing on the global coordinators and seek to replace them or, at the very least, to be included in the syndicate alongside them. Same old.

It was now 8:30 pm. Rowena rode the lift to the underground garage. As she approached her bike, she did not notice the smartphone that was hidden, carefully wedged with sticky tape behind a water evacuation pipe. Unwittingly, she walked through the field scanned by its camera. Within seconds, Shiryō received an email on his iPhone. He opened it to see a relatively clear photograph of Rowena's face. It was a crude but efficient device. He now knew he probably had less than thirty minutes to wait before she would appear.

Rowena removed her Chanel coat and placed it in her backpack. She donned a leather jacket, above a pair of light cotton trousers. She similarly replaced her grey Christian Louboutin high heel shoes with a pair of trainers, the shoes joining the designer suit in her bag. She placed a shiny full-face black helmet on her head, revved the engine a few times, and roared out of the garage. She reached the Pacific Place mall and next turned into Queen's Road East, followed by Stubbs Road. She then veered towards the south of Hong Kong Island and onwards to Shek O. She was in a bad mood and drove particularly fast. The traffic was now fairly light. Most office workers had left hours earlier.

Shiryō heard an engine roar in the distance and scanned the road with his monocular. He soon confirmed it was a Harley-Davidson. He recognised the familiar two-tone exhaust sound, as it closed towards him. Some fifteen minutes later, the sound of yet another motorbike alerted him. This time, his target was in sight. Rowena accelerated as the straight stretch of road unfolded in front of her. Shiryō launched the drone, with its attached metal chain. It soon hovered above the road, level with the motorbike. The Ducati came towards it at full speed. There were no other vehicles.

Rowena approached the area where the road veered sharply to the left. Shiryō quickly positioned the drone some fifty centimetres above the road. He steered it to approach the motorbike from its left side. It would give him a clear view of what he was about to do. He now had to act very quickly. The drone would not be able to keep up with the speed generated by the 848cc engine. He violently banked the quadricopter as it came close the back wheel. The metal chain swung upwards. For a fraction of a second, it was almost parallel to the road and immediately wedged itself in the Ducati's transmission system. It instantly got caught and broke away from the drone, which Shiryō flew clear of the scene. He heard a very loud metallic sound. Rowena was fully taken by surprise. She immediately realised something was wrong, but there was nothing she could do.

The front of Ducati brutally lifted itself as the rear wheel jammed. For a millisecond, the motorbike seemed to float in the air, almost standing still on its rear. Then, it fell loudly on its side, with a metallic scratching noise. It rolled several times at high speed towards the cliff ahead, as the exhaust continued to unleash frightening grunting sounds. It hit the stone barrier that separated the road from the drop behind. Speed and the ensuing crash propelled it further into the air. It went over the barrier and straight to the bottom of the ravine, felling a number of trees in the process. Rowena was thrown from the motorcycle as it hit the retainer wall. She smashed into the masonry with a force of more than 35Gs. She stood no chance, even wearing her leather jacket and helmet. Her body now lay completely still on the asphalt. Down below, the engine had stopped, but the Ducati's front light was still on. It illuminated the area behind the wall. A halo of smoke and dust floated in the air.

Shiryō flew the drone back to his hiding place. He cut the power, dismantled it and placed it in his backpack. He climbed down the hill and scanned the road for cars and passers-by. No one was coming. He quietly walked towards Rowena and quickly confirmed she was dead. Her neck had snapped. The force of the impact had been particularly violent. There was still no incoming traffic, but Shiryō knew it would not last. The lights of the Ducati in the forest below would also soon attract curious onlookers. Rowena's body would then be spotted, likely within a matter of minutes.

He walked towards the lighthouse trail, recovered his Honda, started the engine, and drove off in the direction of Tai Tam. There was no traffic and it only took him about twenty-five minutes to arrive in Central. He parked his bike in the street and walked to the car park where Rowena had kept her Ducati. There, he recovered the smartphone. He would discard the SIM card later. Satisfied, he returned to the Honda. He drove at slow speed, observing all the rules of the road until he reached his destination.

CHAPTER 51

THE CALL HAD COME AROUND 11 pm. It was a quarter to midnight by the time Ethan and Suki arrived at the crash scene. An engineer who was driving back home to Shek O village after working late that evening had found Rowena's body, some ninety minutes before. The strange lights in the forest beyond the road and the debris and shiny glass that littered the road had prompted him to stop and investigate. He had immediately dialled 999 from his mobile. Within ten minutes, an officer driving a Honda VFR800P motorcycle had turned up. He had first secured the perimeter. He had assessed that nothing could be done for the victim and called on his radio for other traffic emergency vehicles. Rowena's identity was later confirmed, as her Hong Kong permanent resident ID card and name cards were found in her wallet. The report was processed at the police force's headquarters. In turn, Ethan was informed that the body of yet another investment banker had been discovered.

At first glance, it looked like a traffic accident. However, the death of a fourth head of equity syndicate within the space of just a few weeks was to be treated with suspicion. Three police cars with flashing lights were now at the scene. Access was restricted with traffic cones and police tape. Not that there were too many curious bystanders around. It was late, and as far from Central as it got on Hong Kong Island.

'It looks like that crash was really violent,' said Suki.

'Yes. She was probably driving very fast, no doubt about it. Then, for some reason, she hit the retainer wall,' observed Ethan.

Paving stones had even been dislodged from the wall, pointing to a particularly forceful accident.

'If there was no foul play, then she was surely killed by the force of the shock. By the looks of it, she had a bad fall and her neck snapped on impact. Her bike then tumbled and rolled down below,' said Suki.

She now carefully examined Rowena Ng's body, looking for details with a powerful Maglite torch.

'Assuming for a moment there's more to it than a simple traffic accident, it doesn't look like she was shot. Do you think it could have been caused by an obstacle, say a wire across the road?'

'I think that's unlikely. A wire would've been set for the driver to take the full impact. Her neck obviously gave. But there's no sign of any cut in the flesh. Her jacket is just scratched. At high speed, a wire would have pretty much decapitated her. Plus, it's a reasonably busy road, although clearly much more so during peak hours. You'd need to make pretty sure about who you wanted to hit. There's also quite a lot of logistics involved with setting up a wire across such a wide stretch of road.'

'And it would take time to recover too, I guess. Shall we go and see the bike, then?' asked Suki.

'Yep. But be careful. It's pretty steep down there.'

Behind the retainer wall, on a slippery slope, was a chaotic mess of branches, broken trees and pieces of what had once been a shiny Ducati. They found a broken mirror here, a slashed mudguard there. The front light of the bike was still on. The engine itself had probably died upon impact. The tank was badly dented. The acrid smell of oil, petrol and burnt rubber still floated in the air. Both wheels were severely deformed, although they were still attached to the signature trellis frame.

'I wonder how he did it,' said Suki, 'there was no oil slick on the road either.'

'You're already thinking about him!' ventured Ethan. 'Maybe she was knocked unconscious then? We'll need to look at her helmet carefully for any traces of impact.'

'I just can't believe it's a coincidence,' said Suki.

She examined the motorcycle, then suddenly pointed to the Ducati's transmission system, at the back of the 848 Testastretta 11° engine.

'See! It looks like a metal chain,' she said, 'it's completely wedged into the transmission.'

'Now, *that* is really weird,' said Ethan. 'I suppose that could explain it. You're driving at speed and, suddenly, your rear wheel jams. The bike spins out of control, tumbles, rolls. . . .'

'And if you're just about to pass a sharp bend. . . .' she added, without finishing the sentence. 'Not an accident, eh?' she finally said.

'Now that we've found this, it's unlikely. That chain clearly wasn't there before. Maybe it fell from the saddle and got caught down below? But why did it happen here? The road is smooth. I don't buy it. Look, a U-type lock is still attached to the bike.

I can't see why she would've needed a chain as well. And it's relatively thin. It's probably not even something you would use to lock a bike.'

'But how did it get stuck there?' asked Suki. 'If it was simply placed on the road, chances are the bike would just drive over it. And even if you were to elevate it, say, with a piece of cardboard as support, this chain is less than a metre long. The road is very wide here and the bike could easily have passed metres away from it.'

'I agree. But someone clearly managed to jam that bike's engine with it. Just how it got there, I've no idea.'

'So, he's done it again,' whispered Suki.

'Where did she work again?'

'The constable above said Hajimari Capital.'

'That's a new one,' he observed. 'Then I guess we'd better start looking into it, starting as early as possible tomorrow morning.'

CHAPTER 52

8:03 am, Central, Hong Kong, 27 October 2017

THE FOLLOWING MORNING, Suki had called Bee Fong again. As usual, she was up and about in her office, in the IFC Two tower. She was more than happy to help, although she had first needed to notify her Compliance Department. These days, it seemed, investment bankers could not do anything without an in-house lawyer to watch over their backs, as the threat of litigation and regulatory enquiries loomed. The all clear finally came, after half an hour. At Suki's request, Bee agreed to run another search on the *Dealogic* database.

However, much to their disappointment, she could find no equity offering for which the senior equity syndicate included Hajimari Capital, Morgan Roberts, Swiss Securities and Eurocredit. She had narrowed the timeframe down to four years to reflect Rowena Ng's last period of employment. What had looked like a promising lead had just become a major let-down. A somewhat distraught Suki had conveyed the news back to Ethan.

'What if I were to ask her to look at a longer period of time? But then, some of the bankers would have worked at other firms,' she said.

'Suki, it might be that he's after the individuals themselves, rather than the firms. Who knows? Anyway, go for it. I guess we have to try every possible avenue.'

'Yes, I suppose you're right.'

Suki was just about to call Bee to ask her to widen the search when her mobile rang. It was Bee again.

'I was pretty disappointed we couldn't find anything in the database. We were probably wrong to focus on transactions priced in the last four years,' she said.

'My thoughts exactly! Ethan and I were just talking about looking into prior years as well,' said Suki.

'No. That's not what I meant. My point is that if the bankers had indeed worked on a deal, but that the transaction had actually never completed, as a shareholder or as an issuer I would have been be pretty unhappy.'

'It makes sense, Bee, but. . . .'

'Listen! One thing you may not know is that the database also records details of deals that were pulled, suspended, or otherwise failed to complete, for whatever reasons.'

'Is that right?'

'Absolutely. So, I took the liberty of also conducting searches using those criteria, ignoring pricing and listing dates, as we had done up to now. Over the same period, I looked for all four houses in sponsor, global coordinator and bookrunner roles, for Asian equity deals that were launched, but *ultimately did not close,'* said Bee.

'And?' asked Suki expectantly. She felt like a child about to open a Christmas present.

'I've only found one offering that ticks all the boxes, Suki.'

'Bee, that's brilliant!' exclaimed Suki.

'The company was a conglomerate. China Strategic Group Limited, but everyone knows it as CSG. It was a rather chunky deal, a Hong Kong IPO, of over one billion US dollars. Well, the equivalent in Hong Kong dollars that is. The offering was launched in 2013, with Eurocredit, Hajimari Capital, Morgan Roberts and Swiss Securities as lead banks, in that order.'

'What do you mean?'

'Oh, it's just the way the names would have appeared on the cover of the offering circular. It was in alphabetical order. So it's likely that all the banks were on the same footing and, importantly, on the same economics. In other words, no firm was above the others in terms of seniority. Appearance is quite important, you know, it can convey messages to investors about who's actually in charge. A bank that's named out of order clearly has advantages, above and over the others.'

'Bee, tell me, were any other banks involved?'

'No, that was it. At senior level that is. There were three other houses in a junior, co-lead manager capacity, but they would have had very little visibility in terms of executing the deal. The four I mentioned would really have been the ones running the show all to themselves.'

'I see.'

'And, for Morgan Roberts, Andrew Short was, of course, the ECM banker in charge. I've just sent you the profile of the transaction by email, with details of the number of shares and offer structure. I wanted to talk to you first, obviously. I would have sent you a link to the electronic version of the prospectus, although back then on-line filing with the exchange was only voluntary and none was done at the time. The deal was pulled before the retail offer was launched. But I've just sent a copy of the preliminary offering circular to your office by messenger.

It's the version that was prepared for institutions, not for members of the public. Two different ones were printed, in English. But frankly what I just sent you would be ninety-five per cent similar to the other prospectuses. It's all to do with potential liabilities attached to the disclosure, don't worry about it. I hope it's OK. I reckon the document should include pretty much everything on CSG you might be interested in.'

'Fantastic! Very helpful.'

'I've also spoken to Ashok. He's marketing in Korea today. He actually conveys his many apologies. He remembers that deal rather well, now. He said he should have thought about it before. For some reason, it had slipped his mind. I guess we tend to remember successful IPOs more than the ones we prefer not to use in our pitches, if you know what I mean,' said Bee.

'Of course.'

'The bulk of the deal was by way of a sell-down by the chairman, who was also the controlling shareholder. That was rather unusual. In most IPOs, it's the other way around, i.e., the offer largely takes the form of new money raised by the company. The chairman's name was Simon Lo. I'm sure you've heard of him, he's pretty high profile, obviously. From what I could gather, he had widely unrealistic expectations in terms of valuation. It looks like he just would not listen. We thought at the time investor feedback would show him what could be achieved. But he took it all rather badly and abruptly called off marketing, after the first week of bookbuilding. Ashok said it was all rather disappointing. It could still have been a sizeable new listing.'

'Super! And, again, thank you, Bee. I'm sure we'll pay Mr Lo a visit soon. And Bee, please keep what you've just told me confidential, for your own sake and safety.'

Part V
FIRE

CHAPTER 53

11:45 am, Wan Chai, Hong Kong, 27 October 2017

THE CSG OFFERING CIRCULAR arrived by messenger at the police force's headquarters within a couple of hours, just as Bee had said. It was a very thick document of more than 700 pages, most of which seemed to be made up of the company's financial accounts, included in a never-ending appendix. To Suki, and she suspected to many people as well, it was largely unreadable. The vast majority of the members of the public who punted on IPOs only ever read the summary, if anything. She was sure that most of them probably did not even bother at all. Much of such documents was primarily written by legal advisers, for regulatory reasons, and essentially designed to counter litigation attempts. One would take forever to understand the business of the company in any level of detail. It was no wonder that investment banks and their advisers spent months, and even in some cases a year or more, knocking these circulars into shape.

In the front matter, some twenty-five pages of risk factors provided stark warnings to investors about everything that might potentially go wrong with the group and the deal. The results of operations and financial condition of CSG at the time, it seemed, had reflected certain extraordinary disposals of non-performing assets. The document also stated that the group might not be able to detect and prevent fraud, as well as other misconduct by its employees and third parties. Its business was also highly dependent on a limited number of members of senior management, headed by Simon Lo himself, and whose continued services might not be assured. A significant part of the business was also conducted in China. It had been conveyed to investors that protection available to them under the PRC legal system might be limited.

The business itself was extremely wide in scope. On the cover of the prospectus was a patchwork of images, meant to convey growth and success in a modern and ever-changing world. It included a jumbo jet, a high suspension bridge, construction workers, and even a good looking Chinese girl with a headset, impersonating a call-centre employee. CSG appeared to be involved in pretty much everything and any-thing, across both North and Southeast Asia, from air transport to shipping, and chains of supermarkets and fashion retailing. Reading through the strengths and strategy section, Suki saw that the bankers and lawyers had perhaps struggled to make sense of it all, and also to present the group as a coherent and focused entity. Profits had steadily increased but, as the risk factors had hinted at, there had been a number of one-off gains. They had perhaps distorted CSG's true financial performance. It had made money, but was growth sustainable in the long run?

'No wonder they had trouble gathering demand at a high price,' thought Suki.

The document included a comprehensive biography of Simon Lo, in the management section. Suki was vaguely familiar with him as he often graced the society pages of newspapers and glossy magazines. In them, he usually wore a dinner jacket and toasted the photographers of *The Peak* magazine or *Hong Kong Tatler* with a glass of bubbly at charity dinners and other events. His was a classic rags-to-riches story. He had landed in the crown colony of Hong Kong, itself still a relative backwater at the time, by crossing the South China Sea from the Mainland under cover of the night, from Shenzhen. It had been at the height of the Cultural Revolution, a time of major upheaval in China. He had made his first money producing cheap plastic gadgets, sold principally to a booming Western world, back in the days when Hong Kong was a manufacturing, rather than a services, hub.

He had then, as was the case for most tycoons in the city, invested in real estate. Prices could only go up at the time and, in some key locations, had skyrocketed. The rest was history. Simon Lo now sat on the boards of directors of more than eighteen companies. He was also honorary patron of half a dozen charities across the region. By all means, he was an insanely rich, powerful man; someone with status and connections, whom Ethan and Suki would need to approach with care. Such a man would have aggressive lawyers working for him on a retainer basis.

Ethan first discussed with the ACP how best to deal with the matter. He, in turn, thought it best to talk directly to Mortimer Tse in light of the high profile of this person of interest. After much pondering, Tse, visibly shaken, gave his green light. Simon Lo could be approached, but with firm instructions not to 'rock the boat' under any circumstances, unless irrefutable evidence of his involvement surfaced. Making a man like Simon Lo lose face for the wrong, or indeed, any reasons, might well signal the end of their own careers.

CHAPTER 54

O VER THE TELEPHONE, Simon Lo's assistant had indicated he would be available to meet with Ethan and Suki at his home, early the following evening, but only for fifteen minutes. He later had to attend a black-tie function at the Peninsula Hotel in Tsim Sha Tsui, where he was the guest of honour. It was out of the question that he turn up late to receive a prize. Traffic could be heavy around peak hour, even if his Rolls-Royce Phantom would make the short journey comfortable at the worst of times.

Lo lived in a 7,000 square foot mock Italian Renaissance mansion on upper Stubbs Road, one of the best addresses in the city. The property was located at the end of a private alley that branched out from the twisting road, perhaps appropriately enough not far from the Hong Kong Police Museum. The house was situated just below the fog line that often engulfed higher levels on the Peak. The panorama was breathtaking. At night, lights shimmered in the distance, as if to pay homage to the moneyed tycoons uphill.

Ethan and Suki arrived straight from police headquarters, in a marked police Toyota Camry. They had been spotted through a couple of cameras that overlooked an ornate front gate that opened as they approached on foot. A very tall and large man greeted them, just as they stepped in.

'Good evening, my name is Pha. I look after Mr Lo,' he said, matter-of-factly. 'We were expecting you. Please follow me.'

His demeanour was courteous, but neutral, on the verge of being cold. He had long hair, tied at the back in a ponytail, and was dressed conservatively, in a black suit, the jacket closed at the top by a Mao collar. He walked quickly, but his stance was mechanical, his fists almost clenched at the end of stiff and impossibly strong arms. He looked like a mountain of flesh and muscles, but there was nothing comical at all about his appearance.

Ethan and Suki silently walked behind him towards what was a decidedly impressive property. On its doorstep, Lo waited, a dog seated by his side in a heraldic pose. He wore a well-tailored black dinner jacket and smoked a cigar. He waved his right hand to welcome them, which created a small plume of blue smoke. The smell was sweet, with a hint of honey.

'Good evening, I see you've already met U Pha,' he said.

'The police inspectors, Ashin,' said the bodyguard, slightly bowing, before disappearing indoors.

'How do you do, I'm Chief Inspector Ethan Blake and this is Inspector Suki Lam.'

'I'm pleased to meet you too,' answered Lo in a friendly tone. 'Do you mind if we talk in the garden? I prefer not to smoke indoors. And it's a rather pleasant day today, isn't it?'

'Absolutely. That's a very good idea. And the view of the harbour is lovely from here, I might add. Just one question: Your servant, is he Burmese?' asked Ethan.

'Indeed. You're very observant, Mr Blake! U Pha is from Myanmar, as they now like to call it. I personally never quite understood the country's change of name. Have you ever visited it?'

'Sadly, I never had the pleasure,' answered Ethan.

'It's a shame, really. Lovely country. Anyway, U Pha previously served in their military police, the *Pyi Thu Yae Tup Pwe*. Some also call it the People's Police Force. I'm sure you've heard of them. He now almost never leaves my side. I absolutely trust him with my life. I'm convinced he would have no hesitation in giving his for mine, should the need ever arise. But, time is short, what can I do for you?'

'Quite,' said Ethan, looking at his watch. 'We understand that, in early 2013, you attempted to list your holding company, CSG, after mandating four investment banks. They were Eurocredit, Hajimari Capital, Morgan Roberts and Swiss Securities.'

'That's correct. It's a matter of public record.'

'You'll no doubt have heard of the recent homicides of investment bankers in Hong Kong, four of them in total. Each of them worked for one of these houses. It's what prompted our interest. We're particularly keen to hear the circumstances that led you to cancel the transaction, since our understanding is that the offering was ultimately never completed.'

'I was only aware of the death of three bankers, Chief Inspector. Has there been another one?'

'I'm afraid so, the night before last. Sadly, the regional head of equity syndicate at Hajimari Capital was the victim of a fatal traffic accident, on the road to Shek O. Confidentially however, we believe the circumstances to be suspicious. We're investigating.'

'I see. The banker would've been Rowena Ng, right?'

'Correct. Did you know her?'

'I suppose you could say I knew all of them rather well, at some point.'

'How so?'

'You see, they all came to see me as I was thinking of floating the business, softly bouncing the idea off the financial community. Soon there was no stopping them. They all claimed they could add value above and beyond what the other banks could do. They were hungry for the fees that would come with the transaction, of course. You know how these banker types are.'

'Actually, not as well you, I assure you. What happened next?' asked Ethan.

'They smelled money and started to visit me, every week at first and then every other day. Not just those firms, of course. I must have met someone from pretty much every single bank in town, at one time or another. I got calls at all hours, emails, text messages on my mobile ... one broker even managed to send me two letters from their CEO expressing interest, one week apart. Except that it was a different chief executive on each occasion! I've never seen an industry so dysfunctional in my entire life!'

Ethan silently nodded.

'Then they started hinting at attractive valuations for my shares to win the business, of course. It was pretty foolish on my part, but I believed them at first. I was personally heavily in debt back in those days, you see. For me, it was pretty much a matter of life and death. I had to sell some of those shares in order not to go under.'

'But the transaction was not to be,' hinted Ethan.

'Sadly it was not. I should've paid more attention when they couldn't secure a single cornerstone investor to anchor the deal. But, at the time, I thought that with my efforts, supporting marketing on the roadshow, institutions would come around. By the end of the first week of bookbuilding, it was pretty clear it was not going to happen. The higher numbers they had been touting around had all been forgotten by then. I should have seen it coming. All they were able to say, after kicking off marketing, was that I needed to consider doing a smaller offering, and at a much lower price.'

'An unfortunate, but I guess classic, case of bait and switch,' said Ethan.

'That's exactly what it was!' said Simon Lo. 'Bait and switch! But for their kind, it was just a game. If something doesn't work, they simply move on to the next deal. Meanwhile, they go on promising the moon, with the confidence and bragging rights their managing director title conveys. But for me, if I had not later secured lifelines from powerful friends in China, I would probably no longer be here talking to you. You're looking at a survivor.'

'Mr Lo, forgive me for asking, but I need to know of your whereabouts on the days the bankers were killed. I'm sure you understand.'

'I don't think I like what you might be implying, Mr Blake, but please call my office tomorrow. My assistant looks after my diary. She'll provide you with the details. I've been travelling rather a lot, recently.'

'Thank you, Mr Lo, we'll be sure to do so in the morning.'

'Now if you'll excuse me, I have a function to attend. Kowloon-side. It's getting late already. U Pha will walk you back to your car.'

As if by magic, U Pha reappeared at the door, ready to lead the way with his body-builder frame and robotic moves. Lo suddenly called up to Ethan, as they walked back towards the gate.

'Mr Blake?'

'Yes?' answered Ethan in the distance, after turning back.

'As I've just said, these bankers wasted a lot of my time, and rather a lot of my money. I was almost done for as a result. That doesn't mean I did it. And I certainly did not. You and Miss Lam are barking up the wrong tree, I'm afraid.'

'I see.'

Simon Lo blew a final curl of smoke and disappeared indoors.

CHAPTER 55

THE DRAFT MESSAGE in Shiryō's Gmail account included a single word, 'Sapphire'. The code was a request for an urgent meeting and it also meant that his client had a problem. Meetings were not something Shiryō readily agreed to. People trusted him to deliver. They paid handsomely, and in advance, for his services. The understanding was that the consequences would be dire for Shiryō if he ever failed to live up to expectations. It was something he readily accepted. Direct contact with principals, however, generally did not occur. He had often done so, in the early days, but he now knew better. Things were best handled through others. They did not need to know what he looked like. The odd telephone conversation might help seal a deal, but meeting face to face was best left for emergencies. And now, Simon Lo had just made such a request.

Shiryō had executed all four contracts, as instructed. He speculated that Lo either wanted another hit performed, or that the police were probing his involvement in the bankers' deaths. The latter was probably not much of an issue. He knew Lo had planned to be out of Hong Kong over the previous weeks.

There was no evidence to link him to any of the homicides. If Lo did not panic, which was always a possibility, things would be fine.

Shiryō entered a hotel in Central. He ordered a coffee in the lobby lounge. He finished his beverage, paid and walked to the reception, where he asked to place a local telephone call. The receptionist was only too happy to oblige, directing him to a nearby telephone. Shiryō called Simon Lo's office and asked to be put through to the tycoon. His personal assistant answered instead, as he had expected.

'Good morning! I'm calling Mr Lo about the sale of a blue sapphire, which we previously discussed. If his diary allows, would you please be so kind as to tell him I'd be most happy to meet, at two o'clock today, in the Clipper Lounge at the Mandarin Oriental Hotel. I've little flexibility on this occasion, unfortunately. But if the arrangement is not to his satisfaction, he knows how best to make contact with me.'

'I'll relay the message to him, thank you. And who shall I say called?'

'Just mention the sapphire, please. He'll understand.'

Shiryō was certain Simon Lo would turn up, given the implied urgency of his message. It left a few hours to kill, which he spent leisurely walking around the district. On the island, most of the sites occupied by the students and other protesters had now been vacated, although a large area near the government's offices was still blocked to traffic. A sea of tents and barricades was a clear sign that the struggle for democracy was still the order of the day. There were increasing rumours that the authorities might soon act to clear the streets that remained outside their control. Episode two of the so-called Umbrella Revolution also continued to generate huge traffic jams across the business area. It was a situation that taxi and minibus drivers found increasingly unacceptable. As in 2014, lawsuits had now even been filed, citing the economic impact created by the obstructions.

At 1:45 pm, Shiryō entered the Mandarin Oriental Hotel. He spent time in the ground-floor shop, browsing through some of the magazines and books, and then sat in the lobby facing the harbour. Less than ten minutes later, Simon Lo walked in. Oblivious to Shiryō's presence, he arrived from the Connaught Road entrance, where U Pha had dropped him in his gunmetal grey Rolls-Royce. It carried the vanity plate SIMON. He did not appear to have been tailed by anyone, but Shiryō was not ready to take any chances. Lo next walked up the stairs to the Clipper Lounge café.

Shiryō walked past the reception desk and rode the lift to the first floor. He entered the Chinnery, a dark wood-panelled bar named after an eighteenth-century painter, and ordered a Perrier. The place was now quiet. It was, however, usually packed for lunch, when it offered classic English fare of bangers and mash, pies and Indian curries. After business hours, it would welcome executives working in Central again, for a pint, or a dram of one of the more than a hundred whiskies displayed behind the leather-bound counter.

After a few minutes, Shiryō asked to place an internal phone call. He was immediately connected to the Clipper Lounge.

'Good afternoon! I was meant to meet with Mr Simon Lo. I believe he should now be seated, expecting me at one of your tables. I unfortunately won't be able to make it. May I speak to him to convey my apologies in person, please?'

'Certainly, Sir, who shall I say is calling?'

'My name is James Sapphire.'

Simon Lo was so well known in Hong Kong that the waiter walked to him without hesitation. He passed on the message, handing out a cordless telephone to him.

'Yes?' said the tycoon.

'Be on the Star Ferry to TST at 2:45 pm, on the upper deck. Come alone.'

Shiryō hung up, paid for his drink, and left the hotel on foot, through the Connaught Road exit. He turned left and, some thirty metres further, walked up the stairs at Chater House. It was an office building, whose tenants included J.P.Morgan. A few floors above its lobby lounge was a connection to an elevated walkway, which led to the Central piers. Almost simultaneously, a pensive Simon Lo left the Mandarin Oriental through the same door. He stepped into the back of his car through the rear-hinged coach door. He sat on the full grain, Consort Red leather lounge seat in the privacy of the rear passenger compartment and instructed U Pha to drive the short distance to the Star Ferry pier.

CHAPTER 56

ETHAN AND SUKI CONTACTED Simon Lo's office in the morning. His assistant had already prepared the information they requested. As Lo had mentioned the previous day, he had travelled rather a lot in the previous weeks. In fact, he had been out of town on the dates on which each homicide had been committed. More specifically, he was away in Singapore on the night of Andrew Short's demise, as well as in Shanghai when Pieter du Toit's body was lifted out of Turtle Cove. He was in Beijing when Ambrose Wallace-Phillimore was killed, and in Shenzhen, just across the border from Hong Kong, when Rowena Ng's motorbike plunged into a ravine near Shek O. It was almost too perfect.

Of course, someone else could still have acted on his instructions, but proving it would be a whole new kettle of fish. Subsequent enquiries showed that U Pha had also been away, although in Singapore and Shenzhen only, at the same time as his employer. It was inconclusive. Maybe Simon Lo simply felt safe enough without the bodyguard at his side when he visited the corridors of power in Beijing and Shanghai?

Ethan asked Andrew Li to check the GPS locations of U Pha's mobile at the time of the homicides of Pieter du Toit and Ambrose Wallace-Phillimore. A couple of friendly calls with telecom operators in Hong Kong provided the information within less than a quarter of an hour. Again, it led nowhere: in each case, the phone's location was confirmed to have been that of Lo's mansion on Stubbs Road. U Pha, however, could well have left his phone there, with a view to deceiving any enquiries. Proving he had been at Turtle Cove would be impossible. There was no record of him on the list of witnesses who had been interrogated by the Marine Police; nor had he appeared on the list of visitors at the fitness centre on Hollywood Road, nor on the video recordings there. It seemed to rule out his involvement. In any event, it was not like U Pha could easily go unnoticed, with his juggernaut of a body frame. And he certainly did not match any of the photographs they had of a possible suspect. It had to be someone else. U Pha might perhaps have been involved, but he had clearly not killed the bankers by himself.

Ethan could hardly justify putting Simon Lo under surveillance under the circumstances, but he asked Andrew to start tracing U Pha's mobile. At least, they would know what he did from now on. It was a relatively straightforward, if not entirely legal, process. Wherever U Pha went, Ethan and his team would know, with an accuracy of a few metres.

Ethan, however, did not dare remotely activate the microphone on U Pha's phone. He was already bending the rules, but wiretapping would require a sign-off from a judge, or from authorising officers appointed by his head of department, the ACP, which he knew he would never obtain. He did not wish to push his luck, especially when dealing with such a powerful figure as Simon Lo.

Right now, it looked like U Pha stood just outside the Star Ferry pier, in Central. Unfortunately, there was no way of knowing what he was doing there.

CHAPTER 57

2:47 pm, Victoria Harbour, Hong Kong, 1 November 2017

SIMON LO HAD FOLLOWED Shiryō's instructions. He sat alone on the upper deck of *Twinkling Star*. It was one of the eight ferries operated by the Star Ferry Company along two franchise routes between Central, Tsim Sha Tsui and Wan Chai. Even though the Hong Kong and Whampoa Shipyard had built her in 1964, she was still in service. She could carry up to 576 passengers at a time, from one side of Victoria Harbour to the other. Her ride offered one of the best views in the world, all for less than three Hong Kong dollars.

That afternoon, though, *Twinkling Star* was hardly full. Simon Lo had a whole row of seats to himself. To ensure a comfortable sailing, he had positioned the swinging backrest so that he could face the Kowloon peninsula. He took in the sweeping views, from the Ocean Terminal mall on the port side to the Inter-Continental Hotel to starboard.

It had been quite some time since Simon Lo had travelled on a cross-harbour ferry. Nowadays, he more often than not shuttled to the 'dark side', as many expats had dubbed Kowloon, in his chauffeured-driven car.

The short ride reminded him of his younger days, the light breeze and salty marine air carrying memories of years past. Everything had been easier then, it seemed. He had already been rich under the British, but he had made the bulk of his fortune after Hong Kong had returned to the motherland. The Chinese had held no grudges at his youthful escape to the crown colony. They now needed powerful allies to navigate the waters of capitalism, all without losing their communist soul. Simon Lo was even one of the 1,200 happy few who elected the chief executive, the *de facto* ruler of Hong Kong.

The term of the current leader had formally expired in July but it had, for now at least, been extended, pending a decision on the manner in which the next elections would be conducted. On pro-democracy social networks, the incumbent's nickname was '689', on account of the actual number of votes he had received, a far cry from universal suffrage.

In the distance, a CMA CGM container ship slowly glided towards the east, careful to stay in the deeper channel that was assigned to commercial traffic. The Peninsula Hotel gradually appeared behind the rows of twenty-foot intermodal boxes. Simon Lo was reflecting that he should cross the harbour this way more often when he heard a voice whispering behind him.

'Don't turn around. I asked you to come alone. What is the Hulk doing in the front section?'

'Good afternoon! We haven't formally met and I don't know your name but, whoever you are, your reputation precedes you. I'm not a man to take chances, as you will appreciate,' said Lo.

'And neither am I. Your arrival at the pier in that shiny Rolls-Royce, with SIMON on the number plate, was hardly discreet.'

'This is Hong Kong, old boy! People know who I am, from the chairman of the stock exchange to the latest immigrant from across the border. Even those three *tai tais,* on the first row. I heard them talking about me earlier. There's hardly anything I can do to change that.'

'We had a deal. The four contracts have now been fulfilled. What more do you want?'

'I also said no comebacks. Two police inspectors came knocking at my door yesterday.'

'They can't possibly have anything concrete against you. You were out of the country on all occasions. There's nothing to link you to any of the homicides, and we never even met until today. Don't panic, keep your head down, and you'll be fine.'

'It's easy for you to say. I thought they came after me rather quickly, after you took care of Rowena Ng. Congratulations on that one, by the way. She was a nasty little bitch and she deserved everything she got. I'm still slightly confused about how you managed to pull it off, however, as I believe the police are. Anyway, it seems to me they've already found out why the bankers were targeted.'

'Your failed IPO is hardly a secret. Linking the four banks to it would be child's play, for anyone who knew where to look. But it's a dead end.'

'I'm sure this quote from Sun Tzu will ring a bell: "If you know yourself but not the enemy, for every victory gained you will also suffer a defeat". Right now, we know nothing of what they know. And it bothers me rather a lot,' concluded Lo.

'Please don't lecture me on the art of war. I've been to hell and back many times over. I've seen and done things you couldn't even imagine in your worst nightmares. So, let me ask again: what more do you want?'

'I want you to abduct that inspector, Suki Lam, for me. I need to find out what the police know.'

'You're out of your mind! That's out of bounds. You couldn't possibly let her go after she talks, assuming she has anything to say in the first place. When she turns up missing and then dead, you'll be the first one they'll go after. And, believe me, they'll keep digging until they find out who did it. Right now, with your alibis, they can hardly justify investigating you further. Hear me, Simon: let it be.'

'That's for me to worry about, old boy. U Pha can take care of her, once she's in my custody. Just bring her to me. I'll add us$100,000 to the million you've already received. No one ever says no to Simon Lo.'

As Lo became increasingly agitated. U Pha had gradually come closer to investigate if anything was wrong, although he was still at a reasonable distance. Waving him off, Lo indicated for him to return to the front section of the boat.

'What you need is in this,' said Lo, sliding an envelope behind him.

'Now that you've dragged me all the way to Kowloon, make it us$200,000. Payable in advance and in full, to this account in Labuan,' said Shiryō.

He discreetly palmed the envelope and, at the same time, passed Lo a small piece of paper.

'Once I've received the money, I'll contact you again,' he said. 'Think of somewhere remote, and above all quiet, for me to bring her to you. Not your house on the Peak.'

'I already know where.'

'By the way, this is the last thing I'll do for you.'

'You never know, you never know, old boy,' countered Lo.

The tycoon suddenly placed his elbow on the backrest and swung around. The ferry was just about to dock in Tsim Sha Tsui but the killer had already gone.

CHAPTER 58

SHIRYŌ NEEDED TO FIND OUT more about Inspector Suki Lam. He got to work, as he waited for Lo to credit the agreed amount to his Malaysian bank account. What Lo had given him included a photocopy of her name card. It stated that she worked in the Department of Crime and Security at the Hong Kong Police Force's headquarters in Arsenal House. There was also a photograph, most probably a still frame of footage by one of the surveillance cameras at Lo's mansion on the Peak. The picture, which was a headshot only, was fairly clear. Shiryō guessed she would be in her mid-twenties. She was also attractive. Her hair was worn up, in a ponytail, and her eyes looked directly at the camera, which she would have noticed above the gate at the tycoon's home.

Lam was a common surname in Hong Kong. However, Shiryō was unable to find any person of that name with the first name Suki in the directory inquiries section of the website of PCCW, the city's fixed line operator. In any event, it looked like Suki Lam was off directory, or it could perhaps also be the case that she was actually listed under her full Chinese name, which he did not know. He would need to try something else to discover where she lived.

Shiryō had already returned his Honda to the rental company. He chose to walk past Arsenal House around late morning. There were high expectations the surrounding area would be cleared of protesters at any time, following a court order to be enforced by bailiffs. But the adjacent streets were still blocked to traffic, as they had been for the best part of a month. The deviation sent any incoming cars into a maze of one-way streets in Wan Chai. At rush hour, anyone driving there would be stuck solid in traffic jams for an hour or more. It was something one expected to happen in Jakarta or in Bangkok, but not in Hong Kong.

Shiryō reasoned that conducting surveillance just outside police headquarters would expose him too much. All the streets there were under the constant watch of CCTV cameras and he could hardly explain the reason for standing still, opposite one of the gates that led into the complex. That would surely attract attention. In addition, the police headquarters housed four different buildings. He would miss Suki Lam altogether if he stood at the wrong corner.

Instead, he deduced that she, like a good portion of Hong Kong's population, might probably take the MTR to travel to work and back to her home. Arsenal House was equidistant from the Admiralty and Wan Chai stations. However, if she lived in Kowloon or in the New Territories, which was likely given her pay grade, it would be more logical for her to board a train at Admiralty. In such a case, the closest exits would be E1 and E2, both on Rodney Street. A quick check confirmed that they were closed because of public works and also, probably, because of the protests.

The next option would be exit D, just outside United Centre, where the Transport Department was located. Around it was a constant flow of pedestrians, on their way to renew their car licences. The area was busy. It suited him perfectly. Conveniently, a number of fast food outlets were also in the vicinity. He could easily buy a sandwich or a coffee while waiting for her to appear. In addition, a number of bus stops were also close by, so he might still come across her if she travelled home using that means of transportation.

Of course, there was always the possibility that she lived in the western or eastern parts of Hong Kong Island. If so, she might perhaps catch a train at Wan Chai Station instead. She might even drive to work, although Shiryō doubted she would be allocated a parking space, given her junior rank. Public car parks were notoriously expensive in Hong Kong. It had to be public transport. If he missed her, he would try another exit or station. It probably would not take more than a few days for him to find out, and Shiryō was nothing if not patient. He decided to return around 4:45 pm. He mingled with the flow of office workers on their way to buy lunch and walked towards Lockhart Road to grab a bite himself. He waited there until late afternoon.

Just before 5 pm, he was back, sipping coffee bought at a nearby McDonald's. He also read a newspaper and changed places from time to time, alternately wearing a baseball cap or a jumper to slightly modify his appearance. At 7:20 pm, he finally saw her, walking at a brisk pace. She wore civilian clothes, a pair of blue jeans with some sort of thin grey twin-set, and a pair of hiking shoes. She also carried a small document bag and a clear plastic drink bottle. In it, green leaves bounced in the liquid, in tune with her steps.

As she walked the stairs down to the Admiralty MTR station, he started shadowing her from a reasonable distance. As he had suspected, she followed the signs for the north-bound Tsuen Wan line, towards Kowloon. Shiryō passed through the turnstiles and soon joined her on the platform, hiding among the many commuters on their way back home at what was still rush hour.

The platform screen doors opened and she went in. There is no separation between MTR cars in Hong Kong, so as to accommodate the maximum number of passengers. Shiryō boarded the train four doors away from Suki, all the while retaining visual contact. She clearly did not expect to be followed and did not pay any attention to him. She listened to music on her earbuds and played with her smartphone. The train stopped a couple of times, at Tsim Sha Tsui, and Jordan. At Yau Ma Tei Station, she alighted and walked to exit A1. Shiryō followed her down Pitt Street and past Portland Street. At the next corner, she turned right into Shanghai Street.

CHAPTER 59

8:00 pm, Yau Ma Tei, Kowloon, 2 November 2017

S HANGHAI STREET IS PERHAPS best known for its array of shops
that sell cooking utensils and merchandise. They include
bamboo baskets, to steam *dim sum* dumplings, and Japanese
knives of all shapes and sizes.

It was a market for professionals. It was located in a lively
area and, at the same time, still a bit of an oddity, a remnant
of old Hong Kong. The traditional districts were experiencing
rapid gentrification all over the city. Increasingly, chains of
stores that sold jewellery and watches, or even pharmacies,
where Mainlanders could stock up on medication guaranteed
to be genuine, were replacing mom-and-pop stationery outlets
or wet markets.

Shiryō walked some twenty metres behind Suki. She passed
a small entrance, its stairs leading up to a *tong lau,* dating from
the 1950s. Its lobby was dimly lit by a pink fluorescent tube,
which he knew was a coded signal that advertised the discreet
services of a prostitute to passers-by. Suki turned right into a
low-rise, walk-up apartment block. It was sandwiched between
a real estate agency and a 7-Eleven convenience store. Shiryō

positioned himself on the opposite side of the street and waited. After a couple of minutes, the lights went on, on the fifth floor. She was still young. Hers was probably a small, single-person rented accommodation. He thought it likely she lived alone.

Shiryō checked into a small Internet café in an adjacent street. Simon Lo had already wired the US$200,000 to his account in Labuan. He logged into his Gmail account. There was a draft message, which gave an address in Aberdeen. Shiryō memorised it and erased the message. He replaced it with another draft message that simply read 'Monday night'. He returned to the MTR station and went home.

The following Monday, around 5 pm, he took a small, dark-coloured bottle from his wash bag. He pocketed it, along with a cotton handkerchief. The bottle contained halothane, a colourless liquid that was marketed under the name Fluothane. It was widely used around the world as a potent general inhalational anaesthetic. It was much safer than chloroform or diethyl ether. It had a moderate induction and recovery time, but Shiryō knew from experience that it could knock someone unconscious for a few hours. It would be enough for what he had in mind.

He returned to Yau Ma Tei, walking randomly around the neighbourhood to confirm he had not been followed. He soon spotted someone parking an inconspicuous, grey Toyota Corolla E90. The car was probably more than twenty years old, although still functional. He would not need it for more than a short drive in any event, and it suited his purpose perfectly. It looked like it belonged to a commuter returning home. Its owner disappeared in an old building. The car was conveniently parked in a fairly quiet area. It did not appear to be alarmed, although he could see that it had an automatic lock.

Shiryō checked that no one was observing him. He now wore plastic gloves. He inserted a thin wooden door-wedge between the upper part of the door and the body of the car. He tapped on the thick end of the wedge until he had created a space of about half a centimetre. He then inserted a metal rod he'd made from a hanger. He guided the rod down, towards the door's lock button and pulled it open with the hook he'd made at the end of the rod. He had unlocked the door within less than twenty seconds. Not a soul had seen him break into the vehicle.

Once inside the Toyota, he sat in the driver's seat and removed the plastic cover from the steering column, revealing the wiring access connector. From the bundle of coloured wires, he quickly identified those leading to the battery, ignition, and starter. He stripped a couple of centimetres of the brown plastic insulation from the battery wires, twisted them, and connected them to the ignition wires. He stripped the starter wires from their yellow plastic cover and sparked them against the wires he had just connected to start the car. He revved the engine a few times and removed the starter wires. It had all been very easy.

The engine was now on, but Shiryō still needed to break the steering lock. He popped open the cover of the metal keyhole with a small pocketknife. It released a simple spring, which allowed him to easily break the lock. Moments later, he drove away in the old Toyota. He went around the block and parked it just outside where Suki Lam lived. He then killed the engine by unfastening the battery wires.

He left the car, entered the building and walked up to the sixth floor. There, he sat on the steps and quietly waited for Suki to return home.

CHAPTER 60

IT HAD BEEN ANOTHER FRUSTRATING day at the office and Suki was tired. The investigation into the bankers' deaths was still not making much headway. Even though it had all seemed so coincidental, it had been established that Simon Lo had been out of town when each of the murders had been perpetrated. At this juncture, there were just no other leads to follow. Still, she continued to believe they had been digging in the right direction, but the powers-that-be were adamant that Lo should be left undisturbed, unless and until clear evidence incriminating him surfaced.

The police had now cleared the area around CITIC Tower, which was on the waterfront, adjacent to the Central Government Offices. It had happened rather peacefully. However, removing protesters from the Mong Kok site was proving to be something else altogether. An incredible ten per cent of the entire police force had been dispatched to support the work of the bailiffs. Then, in another development, a group of young people had managed at night to break into the Legislative Council building, the city's parliament. The episode had been particularly violent. They had broken windows with baseball bats and thrown metal barriers into the edifice. It had culminated in a pitched battle with members of the Police Tactical Unit, all under the cameras of the world's media. In its second phase, the movement for democracy was smaller in scale, but the increase in violence was perceptible.

Suki walked to Admiralty Station and boarded the train to return home. She could not help but notice the increasing number of Mainlanders who visited the city, in spite of the recent disturbances. Aside from their Mandarin speech, many were instantly recognisable by their bulky wheeled suitcases. Some among them used their luggage to sneak goods across the border. In 2013, jail sentences had even been decreed for anyone exporting more than 1.8 kilogrammes of powdered formula milk from the city, in a bid to curb a frenzied underground trade. Fakes were everywhere in China and many mothers there just would not rely on what was available locally to feed their infants. Food safety was still a major issue, following a series of scandals, from milk tainted with melamine, to glutinous rice *zongzi* dumplings made to appear shiny with a coat of gutter oil. The latest case had involved frozen berries produced in Chinese factories, which had turned out to be infected with Hepatitis A.

Next to Suki, a group of daytrippers from Guangdong province were involved in a heated discussion, comparing the respective merits of their smartphones and branded handbags. Their voices were loud, the accents unmistakable. Clearly, one needed to be heard to stand out in a country of almost 1.4 billion.

Suki left the MTR at Yau Ma Tei Station and walked west. Along the way, she shopped for food at a couple of nearby stores and for an evening newspaper at the 7-Eleven. She checked her mailbox before slowly climbing the stairs to her apartment. She inserted her key into the door lock and was entering her flat when she heard a voice behind her:

'Siu je. . . .'

The expression for 'Miss' was correct, but pronounced with a strange accent. The tonal Cantonese language was notoriously difficult to master and she could instantly tell it had not been spoken by a native. Before she could turn around, she felt someone restrain her from behind and apply a wet cloth to her nose and mouth. The smell was medicinal, although not all that unpleasant. She immediately realised her attacker was trying to knock her unconscious.

As part of her induction with the police, Suki had been trained in martial arts. She struggled hard to break away from her assailant, but she was no match for him. She let go of her shopping bag. A couple of bright red pomegranates rolled under a chair in the minuscule entry hall. The man's grip was incredibly strong and her senses were ever more dulled by the powerful anaesthetic. She desperately tried to roll her head and neck from side to side to escape from his grasp, but to no avail. One of his hands firmly maintained the wet cloth on her airway. Within fifteen seconds, she collapsed in his arms.

Halothane did not induce much muscle relaxation and Shiryō could feel she was still tense from all her struggling efforts. He swiftly closed the door to the apartment behind him. With a quick check, he confirmed no one else was in the property. He suddenly heard a plaintive cry coming from the kitchen. There, he found a tiny grey kitten. It looked frightened, hidden behind the corner of the refrigerator. Shiryō went down on one knee and gently stroked the head of the tabby with his forefinger. He found a bottle of milk in the fridge and replenished its bowl on the floor. Before long, the creature was lapping it up while emitting a gentle purr.

Shiryō then returned his attention to Suki. He took her mobile handset from her pocket and placed it on the chair in the corridor. He did not want the signal to be traced to him and, in any event, she would have no use for it where she was going. He searched her and checked that she carried nothing that could facilitate an escape. Satisfied, he placed her left arm around his neck. Firmly supporting her body, he carried her down the five flights of stairs. She was not particularly heavy. He made good progress when, having just passed the second floor, he heard the unmistakable noise of someone walking up below them. He quickly pressed Suki's body along the wall and covered her with his own, as if in a sensual embrace. An old woman passed them by. He could not understand the words, but it was obvious she was cursing them. Cantonese is well known for its countless, colourful swearwords. Hong Kong was still a relatively conservative society and making out was not something one did in front of the neighbours. Suki's reputation would take a major dent, if she returned to her Shanghai Street apartment that is. It would be down to Simon Lo, but Shiryō very much doubted she ever would.

Once in the street, he checked again that no one was watching them. He carefully sat her on the passenger seat of the Toyota and secured her body against the backrest with the safety belt. He walked around the front of the car to the driver's side on the right, and sparked the engine. He then set off towards the western tunnel under the harbour to Hong Kong Island. The car would not beat any speed records, but it would serve its purpose.

CHAPTER 61

I T WAS THE COLD MORE THAN anything else that awoke her. It was completely dark. Suki checked the luminous dial on her watch and saw it was almost one o'clock. She assumed one in the morning. She could not have been unconscious for more than a few hours, not with a crude inhalational anaesthetic. The whole thing had happened so fast. She remembered someone calling her and the violent struggle on her doorstep. She also recalled the wet cloth on her nose and mouth and then, nothing. She had not had any time to see the face of her assailant, although he was clearly very strong. But she did not sense he had been particularly large, or even overweight.

'Not U Pha, then,' she thought.

She suspected it might have been the man whose face had been caught on camera at the fitness club, as well as on the bus at Turtle Cove. But there was no way of knowing, not yet anyway. But why kidnap her? Killing her, right there and then, would have been much easier. Maybe the man wanted to make her suffer. At that thought, she fought back a panic attack. It did not make much sense. The bankers' deaths had all been quick, almost painless.

Slowly, her eyes got used to the darkness. It looked like she was in some sort of cell, perhaps forty to fifty square feet in size. The walls were bare and made of large, cemented concrete blocks. The floor was covered in metallic sheets, while the ceiling seemed to have some sort of plastic cover. Ahead, a metal gate with bars closed the room. She could not reach it. Her right hand had been handcuffed to a metal ring mounted on the back wall. There was nothing available that she could use to pick the lock. Besides, it was easier said than done, she remembered from her police course, especially with one hand only.

She saw that beyond the gate was a corridor. The place was a bit damp, but worse it was freezing cold. It was as if the air conditioning had gone on overdrive. She shivered in her shirt, jeans, and very thin pullover. She would surely catch a bad cold and maybe even worse, if her confinement lasted for a while. With her free hand, she checked her pockets. She could not find her mobile. Her keys had also been taken away, as had her wallet. At least she still had her shoes on.

She had never been in such a situation before. She was afraid, of course, although it was as yet unclear what would be requested of her, or of others. Her breath was short again, her mind suddenly all over the place. She soon came up with all sorts of theories. Was she to be exchanged for a ransom? But who would pay it? She hardly had any family left. Those who remained were not close relatives anyway, and certainly not wealthy either. An attempt to ransom the police would also be a first. It had to be something else.

Clearly, her abduction had to be related to the enquiry into the bankers' deaths. Turning up with Ethan at Simon Lo's mansion had perhaps triggered alarm bells. The tycoon might even now be in a panic. If indeed he was responsible for these homicides, perhaps he intended to use her as a bargaining chip? But then, there would be no way he could stay in Hong Kong, not after something like that. Most probably he wanted to find out what the police had already discovered about his involvement, she reasoned. Frankly, it did not amount to much. But, in such a case, it would be impossible for him to release her. She would know too much. Either way, she was in deep trouble. She also had a stomping headache, probably due to the anaesthetic. She was thirsty, and very hungry too.

She looked at her watch again. Only forty-five minutes had passed and it was still bitterly cold. She next wondered where she was. It was probably some sort of industrial building, she thought, one with refrigerated facilities. A meatpacking plant perhaps? There were many warehouses of this kind in areas like Kwun Tong and Aberdeen. But was she even still in Hong Kong? Perhaps she had instead been smuggled to the Mainland, or to Macau? It was unlikely, she finally reasoned. It would have taken more time to take her there, and it would have been risky crossing the border. At least, she was certain she was not on a boat. The walls were made of solid concrete. She had a bit of vertigo, but it did not feel anything like a vessel rolling or bobbing on water.

Except for the distant engine noise, the place was completely silent. There was certainly no point in calling for help. Whoever had taken her would have made sure the place was deserted. She was sure someone would come in the morning. Meanwhile, she had better try to catch up on her sleep, if that was possible in such an uncomfortable position. In the morning, she would need to be strong again. By then, Ethan and the others would have noticed her absence and would start looking for her. She just had to bide her time and she would be fine. There were still a few hours before daybreak. All of a sudden, she felt very tired.

She slowly started to fall unconscious again. Sliding in and out of a dream, she thought of her kitten, Ding Ding Tong, named after the traditional dragon's beard candy. She hoped he was all right. With a sigh, she wrapped herself with one hand around her knees for warmth, her right arm still secured to the cement wall. Then, all of a sudden, she was asleep.

CHAPTER 62

8:02 am, Aberdeen, Hong Kong, 7 November 2017

B EYOND THE METAL GATE, a ray of light in the corridor brought Suki back to consciousness. Suddenly, more light flooded the area nearer her cell, blurring her sight. After a few seconds her vision became clearer. She checked her watch: it was just after 8 am. At least she had managed to sleep for a decent amount of time. But it was still bitterly cold. She heard footsteps on the metal floor, probably more than one person. Soon, one of them was at the door. The man pulled it open, after struggling for a few seconds with what looked like a huge padlock. It did not take long for her to recognise his huge frame: it was U Pha.

He opened the door wide and threw in a small bottle of mineral water, a blanket, and a couple of cereal bars on the floor towards her. He retreated towards the gate and waited. At all times, he had kept his eyes on her. Another man entered and stood with his arms crossed next to the Burmese bodyguard. While U Pha was bareheaded, a thin black balaclava covered his face. His physique was much slimmer than U Pha's. She instantly reasoned he might be the man who had assaulted her the previous evening. Maybe he had also carried out the bankers' homicides. The last person to enter was Simon Lo. U Pha wore his usual Mao-collar jacket. The man with the mask was dressed in casual clothes, in dark jeans with a pullover. Simon Lo, however, stood in front of her in a well-cut, charcoal pinstripe suit and burgundy tie, looking very much the dapper tycoon. He considered her for a couple of seconds, his head slightly tilted to one side.

'Good morning, my dear! I must apologise for last night's rough treatment. You're probably wondering where you're being held, and why. I'll come to all that in a moment.'

'You must be out of your mind abducting a police officer. My colleagues will soon start looking for me. It's only a question of hours before they come and arrest you,' answered Suki.

'That, I doubt very much,' countered Lo. 'You see, there shouldn't really be anything to link me to those bankers' deaths, as I'm sure you've already found. But you'll tell me more shortly, no doubt. I was away on business when our friend, on my left here, took care of them for me. He did a splendid job too, I might add.'

'So you hired an assassin,' she said, 'who is he?'

'Ah,' said Lo, 'no names, no identity. Our friend here is a ghost, some even call him the spirit of death.'

The killer remained silent. Suki took a sip of water and chewed one of the cereal bars. She then wrapped herself in the blanket. The warmth was a blessing. She needed to store up on energy, whatever came next.

'First things, first,' said Simon Lo, 'you're probably wondering why it's so cold here. And it's only fair that I should answer you. We're in an industrial building I own, in Tin Wan, at the far end of Aberdeen. It's currently being refurbished into a wine storage facility, strictly high-end stuff. We're not open yet, but the temperature must be stable before we can receive our clients' collections. It's set on thirteen degrees Celsius, all year round. We'll soon also have a fail-proof, redundant electricity supply. The humidity's constant too, there's no harmful external light, and the place is vibration free. Simply put, the perfect conditions for seamless ageing. Please allow me to apologise for one thing: we should have supplied you with a blanket and something to drink last night. That was an oversight.'

'And for how long do you intend to keep me here?'

Lo ignored her question and continued his monologue.

'Many of Hong Kong's great and good have already signed up, as have a variety of wine merchants, even those tight-ass Brits. Now, it's a bit early still, but I'll gladly share a bottle with you later, as you and I develop a dialogue. Maybe I should float my wine business on the stock exchange, what do you think? Only this time, I'll pick my bankers a little more carefully.'

'Why did you have them killed?'

'My dear, I think you already know the answer to that question. On a scale of one to ten, they promised me twelve, and ended up trying to make me agree to three,' he said, moving his hand from up to down to illustrate the point. 'That was completely unacceptable, of course. They knew I was under pressure and thought they could try some fun and games.'

Lo paused for a while for greater effect, and then added, 'As your colleague Mr Blake rightly said the other day, it was pure bait and switch! They were just a bunch of overpaid liars. Kids in suits, who play poker with people's livelihoods, and for a fat fee to boot! I was even younger than them when I swam across to Hong Kong, to escape the Red Guards. Did they really think I was going to cave in and submit to their ridiculous little blackmail? It took me a while to get back on my feet. For a moment, I even thought I was finished. But I never forgot. Ultimately, they had to pay the price.'

'Now that you've told me, there's no way you'll let me go. What will you do?'

'You're absolutely right, my dear. I knew you were a smart one. As far as you're concerned, things are very binary indeed. Eventually, you'll need to die. But, it can either happen soon, or later. It can also be painless, as I hope for your sake it will be, or excruciatingly painful. You can chose. All I want to know is what you and your colleagues have discovered about me, and those dead bankers. Once you've told me what I want to know, we can all move on. But, until then. . . .' He paused for a while and continued, 'I must apologise again, but I obviously can't take any chances. You already know that.'

The man was clearly mad. Suki felt a burst of energy. Adrenaline rushed through her system at the sudden realisation that she might perhaps soon die. But the longer she held up, the longer she would live, and the higher the chance Ethan and his team might find her alive. She had no choice but to play for time.

'Why would I answer you? You're going to kill me anyway.'

'Yes, you'll die,' said Lo with a weary voice, 'but you might not like what U Pha might do to you before that happens. I have no doubts about his considerable skills, and he's also most eager to demonstrate his abilities. Now, why don't we all let things sink in and leave you to think for a little while? We must go now, but U Pha will return very soon. That's a promise.'

CHAPTER 63

7:59 am, Wan Chai, Hong Kong, 7 November 2017

S UKI USUALLY TURNED UP very early at the office, so Ethan thought it unusual not to see her as he arrived at his desk, at 8 am. Still, she might have gone to bed late, or simply been held up on her way in. Public transport in Hong Kong was very reliable but, occasionally, incidents happened, sometimes even in spectacular fashion. The chaos brought about by the demonstrations might perhaps also be to blame. She usually alighted at Admiralty's MTR station, around which some of the protesters were still assembled. It was probably all there was to it, even if he did not recall anything being reported on the morning news. He always listened to the radio on his way to the office. He made himself a double espresso and caught up on news and the progress of ongoing enquiries. But, as the time neared 9 am, he started wondering why she had not yet made it to Arsenal House.

She would have telephoned by now if she were calling in sick. After another fifteen minutes had passed, he determined he had better find out what was the matter. No one answered on her mobile line. It diverted to a recorded voice mail message after a few rings. The same happened after he had called her land line. He left messages on both numbers, with instructions for her to return his calls. He also asked each of his other team members, in case they had heard from her. No one knew where she was. There had been no news since the previous afternoon.

Around 9:45 am, he grew increasingly concerned. Charles Au, one of the inspectors working for him, was not overly busy that morning. He was swiftly dispatched to her apartment in Yau Ma Tei. Even though Hong Kong residents rarely entertained at home, they had all visited the place for birthday drinks a few months earlier. Charles knew exactly where she lived. To beat the traffic, he travelled by MTR and was at her door within thirty minutes. He climbed the five floors to her flat and rang the bell once, and then a second time. There was no sign of any break-in. Charles called her mobile again. He could distinctly hear the phone ringing inside her apartment. Maybe she had forgotten to take it with her that day, unlikely as it might sound.

Charles called Ethan to report his findings. He was given the authority to enter Suki's flat. Charles always carried a small kit, comprised of a professional grade pick and a tension wrench. He inserted the tension wrench in the lower portion of the keyhole. He used it to apply torque to the cylinder, both clockwise and anticlockwise. He felt the firmness of the stop and held the wrench in place with his left thumb and forefinger. Next, with his right hand, he inserted the pick in the upper part of the keyhole and felt the individual pins with the tip of the instrument. He pushed them up and used the tension wrench to increase the torque. Once all the pins were up, safely rested out of the cylinder, he slowly turned the tension wrench to unlock the door.

He pushed the door open with his foot and cautiously entered the flat. He now held his SIG Sauer semi-automatic service pistol in front of him with both hands. There was no manual safety on the SIG. The automatic firing pin would enable him to immediately use his weapon, if needed. He moved from room to room, his arms extended, the gun at the ready. Charles quickly cleared each room of the small apartment in rapid succession.

He found Suki's smartphone on a chair, still operational but with the battery almost completely drained. Below the chair, fruit had rolled onto the floor. He also saw two shopping bags, with more food and a magazine. There were no traces indicating a fight although he found on the floor, hidden behind the open door, the small pendant she liked to wear around her neck. It was a small jade Buddha. The chain was broken. In the kitchen, plaintive meows caught his attention. A cute kitten was hiding in a corner. It could not have been more than a couple of months old. He stroked the cat gently. Next, he called Ethan again, holding the purring tabby on his lap.

'Boss. I'm in. She's not at home. But it looks like she might have left in a hurry. Yesterday's groceries were still in the corridor. Some had rolled onto the floor too. And I found her mobile, the battery was almost dead.'

'Was the bed slept in?'

'Negative. It looks like she's been away since late yesterday. There was an evening paper in one of the shopping bags. Oh, and I also found her necklace, the one with the jade Buddha. The chain was broken, on the floor. Not good. And there's a faint smell too, I can't put a name on it. Boss, it looks like she may have been taken.'

'Check with the neighbours first and report back to head-quarters. I'll send some people over immediately.'

Most of Suki's neighbours were out at that time of day, but an old lady on the second floor confirmed she had seen her the previous evening. It must have been around 8 pm. From what she said, Suki had been misbehaving in the staircase with a man. It was not something to be proud of, she had added, and very much unlike her too. The man was older, Asian, with a beard, although she did not get to see his face well. Maybe it was the man on the grainy photograph Charles showed her next, but she could not be completely sure.

A couple of constables soon arrived. Charles left the apartment and the kitten in their care. As he was walked back down to the street, he felt a twinge of jealousy. Even though he fancied himself as rather handsome, Suki had rejected his timid advances on several occasions. As far as he knew, she was still single.

CHAPTER 64

10:00 am, Aberdeen, Hong Kong, 7 November 2017

THE 2,000-SQUARE-FOOT ROOM was designed to look like the vaulted cellar of a French château, even if it was, in truth, part of a modern cold-storage facility. Wooden racks of various sizes and shapes lined the walls. Some fitted individual bottles, while others could accommodate larger formats, magnums mostly, but also jeroboams. It was meant as a showpiece tasting room, to entice wealthy collectors to deposit their wine under Simon Lo's custody. A few wooden barrels and candles added to the clubby atmosphere. The low-intensity lighting, allied to the constant temperature and hygrometry, created an optimal ageing environment. In the centre of the room, Simon Lo sat at ease, his legs crossed, beside an antique table. He flashed a smile and welcomed Shiryō.

'Please sit down. I want to thank you again for everything you did for me. You delivered at every turn, and well beyond my expectations.'

'Drop the pitch, Simon. It was business and nothing else. But, as I told you a few days ago, you and I are now done. I sincerely hope you know what you're doing. It probably won't be long before her colleagues start looking for her. Don't complain later I didn't warn you. For my own part, it's time I left,' said Shiryō.

'Yes, yes,' countered Lo, mildly irritated. 'It's a shame, though, that we should end our collaboration. A man of your talents will, of course, not remain unemployed for long. Still, I'm sure you could've had a bright future in Hong Kong.'

'And I'm glad we're finally seeing eye to eye. So, if you will now excuse me. . . .'

'Please stay a little while longer!' commanded Lo. 'And before you go, I hope you'll join me for a parting drink.'

Lo stood and fetched an ornate glass decanter that stood by a green glass bottle with a square black and gold label. Two large wine glasses had already been poured.

'It's a 2010 Château Palmer,' he said. 'Amazingly, it's only a third growth but, to my mind anyway, it deserves a much higher ranking. Did you know Robert Parker gave it a 98-plus? It's a rather lovely Margaux. Frankly, it's so young it's almost a crime to drink it now, but I had it decanted two hours ago, so that it could breathe. It's sensationally rich, with complex camphor, barbecue smoke, cassis and blackberry aromas,' he added, holding both glasses by the stems, offering one to Shiryō.

'Thank you, but I never drink before dinner time. It's a rule.'

'Now, old boy, you're adding insult to injury! That, I will not allow. Besides, rules are meant to be broken.'

'Very well,' answered Shiryō, sensing he might perhaps have vexed Lo more than he had intended. He reluctantly took the glass.

'A farewell drink, then.'

'With my heartfelt thanks,' said Lo, toasting Shiryō.

He next took a sip of the wine. Obligingly, Shiryō did the same, with a polite gesture, one hand holding the stem, the other slightly cupped underneath the base of the glass.

'I suppose you'll now return to Japan?' asked Lo amiably.

'There. Or elsewhere, who knows?'

'Of course, I understand you'd prefer not to say. Much better that way.'

'That wine is lovely, Simon. Thank you,' said Shiryō politely.

In truth, he had detected a faint salty flavour. The wine was clearly not faulty, but perhaps the glass had not been stored, or even washed properly. It was always a possibility in what was, ultimately, nothing more than a beautified industrial facility.

'Don't mention it,' replied the tycoon.

They spent a few minutes exchanging pleasantries. But, as he drank more, Shiryō increasingly felt his senses dulled by a dizzy, nauseous feeling. As it progressed, it started to trigger alarm bells. He tried to steady himself, firmly holding on to the side of the table with one of his hands. Soon, there was no escaping it: he was becoming increasingly disorientated. The room slowly started spinning around him. Lo had drugged him and he had fallen into the trap like a rookie.

'What . . . have you . . . done to me?' he asked, hesitantly.

'It's amazing isn't it? Gamma-butyrlactone, they call it; GBL. What a horrible word! It's almost impossible to pronounce, I wonder where they find these. Anyway, it's closely related to GHB, which I'm sure you also know as a date-rape drug. But, in this case, a much smaller dose is required. I've never had any use for it myself, but I'm told it does wonders. It's colourless, odourless, largely tasteless and very hard to detect when mixed with a drink. I'm told there might just be a faint, salty taste, if you're extremely finicky, that is. Did you actually get that? Best of all, it acts very quickly, and the effect is considerably enhanced when diluted in alcohol.'

Shiryō struggled to stay awake. Simon Lo's voice was first widely amplified and next, barely audible. He even had difficulty breathing. He could sense he would soon pass out.

'You . . . you,' was all he could articulate.

'Quiet, now! You should be out for action for a few hours. I can't afford any loose ends, you see. And you now know way too much. But, fear not, I'll be back later to take care of you, personally. It's not something I'd leave to U Pha. He can deal with the girl all right, but you and I will part like men, face to face. It's a real shame you must go. I really am indebted to you!'

Shiryō's vision was almost completely blurred. His eyelids felt heavy. In a last ditch effort, he tried to stand on his feet to resist what was coming, but his body was in no shape to support even his own weight. He painfully banged the table and fell to the ground like a limp mass. As he collapsed, he dropped the hand-blown Riedel glass. It first shattered on the table, what remained of the wine splashing everywhere, before breaking into smaller pieces on the floor. The last thing he thought he saw was Simon Lo toasting him again, his other hand slowly waving a final goodbye. Within seconds, he had completely blacked out.

CHAPTER 65

12:01 pm, Wan Chai, Hong Kong, 7 November 2017

ETHAN HAD BEEN PREPARED for many things, but Suki being abducted had most definitely not been one of them. According to Charles, it looked like she had been taken the previous night. The necklace, which he had found on the floor, likely pointed to some sort of struggle in her apartment. She might have been ambushed and then quietly whisked away by a man, of whom all they knew was that he was Asian, with a beard, and in his mid-thirties. The description was pretty thin; and she could be anywhere by now.

Suki had been diligent in updating Ethan with her lines of enquiry. Perhaps she had secretly pursued another lead of her own and fallen into a trap? It clearly had to be related to something she worked on. The main case she had been assigned to was that of the bankers' homicides. Suki had also accompanied him when he had visited Simon Lo, although he, rather than she, had done much of the talking, there and then. What they knew about the man she had last been seen with, in the staircase of her building, was very much unlike Simon Lo, let alone his bodyguard, U Pha. So there was obviously someone else, perhaps contracted to undertake Lo's dirty work? It could explain a lot of things. Lo had a motive for killing the bankers, even if the investigation team had been unable to find anything that could incriminate him personally. If they could prove a link between him and the kidnapper, it might change everything.

Ethan's brain was in overdrive, processing all hypotheses, however far-fetched they might be. Maybe Simon Lo had been startled by their visit and had decided to abduct Suki, but why? Blackmail was unlikely. An attempt at finding out what evidence, if any, the police already had against him sounded more plausible. Either way, it was irrational behaviour. But, if true, it also meant Suki was in mortal danger. Once Lo had obtained whatever information he was after, getting rid of Suki would be top of his agenda. Ethan asked Andrew Li to locate Lo's bodyguard.

Andrew fiddled with the tracking application for a short while.

'The GPS points to a building in Tin Wan, Aberdeen. By the looks of it, he's been there for the last few hours, since fairly early this morning, actually. He came directly from Lo's home.'

Ethan instructed John Mak to get in touch with the surveillance team posted outside Simon Lo's house, on upper Stubbs Road. There was no one tailing him, that could not be justified yet, but arrivals at, and departures from his home were still being monitored. John placed a brief telephone call and informed Ethan that Simon Lo had left early that morning, driven by U Pha in a black Toyota Alphard. He had only just returned, but without his bodyguard.

'Now that's interesting,' observed Ethan, 'why would he use a relatively inconspicuous car, rather than his Rolls-Royce, to travel to Aberdeen, leave U Pha there and return on his own after a few hours? Are we sure he was alone on the return trip?'

'No one else was seen in the car. Obviously, someone may well have been lying on the back seat, or perhaps even in the boot, but the latter is pretty tight in an Alphard. And from what you said U Pha is not exactly kid-size either. He probably would have been spotted. But we have no way of knowing what goes on beyond the residence's gates.'

'What do we know about this building in Tin Wan?' asked Ethan.

Andrew tinkered again with his computer for a few more minutes. He conducted several online searches and soon informed Ethan it was an industrial warehouse. All of its thirty floors belonged to Simon Lo, although most had been rented out to third parties. One such tenant was a high-end wine storage business, a company that ultimately also belonged to Lo. It comprised six podiums of 25,000 square feet each. It was still being fitted out, but set to open within weeks. It had been the subject of considerable press coverage and even touted as the ultimate facility of its kind in Hong Kong.

It was likely that the place would be fairly deserted, subject only to builders and workmen applying finishing touches before it became operational. Moreover, it was not far from Simon Lo's offices and residence, in Central and the Mid Levels, respectively. In short, thought Ethan, perhaps the ideal location to hold someone captive without attracting unwanted attention.

'It makes sense he would check on the works prior to opening, but I'm still intrigued by our friend U Pha staying put there. Lo told me U Pha almost never left his side. They would only have parted for a good reason. I think we should pay a visit to this place in Tin Wan. But, John, please let us know immediately if Lo appears to be heading back that way.'

CHAPTER 66

2:15 pm, Aberdeen, Hong Kong, 7 November 2017

STILL LIGHTHEADED, SHIRYŌ silently cursed himself. He had delivered Suki to Simon Lo, but now found himself in her very own predicament. Like her, his right wrist was handcuffed to a metal ring, solidly sealed in the back wall of a wine cellar. How ironic! U Pha was nowhere to be seen, but still probably in the vicinity. Lo would likely return in the evening to finish him off. A quick look at his watch told him the time was 2:15 pm. He had been knocked unconscious for no longer than a couple of hours. Even though he still felt fuzzy, in survival mode he immediately started scanning the cell for anything that might help him to escape. But first, he had to get rid of the handcuffs.

The floor was metallic, he had observed earlier, probably to channel cold air throughout the building. He soon noticed that the skirting where it met the concrete wall on his left had been badly sealed. Over a small area, it had already given way. There was a small gap, not wider than half a centimetre, which he could now feel with his fingers. The layer of metal was very thin there. He reasoned that if he managed to break off a small piece, he might use it as a shim to unlock the cuffs.

He slowly pulled the metal sheet with his thumb and forefinger. Soon, he had a piece that was perhaps five centimetres long and one wide, protruding from the floor. He had badly cut two of his fingers in the process but that was unimportant. He then slowly bent the piece of metal backwards and forwards a number of times, until it finally snapped. Within fifteen minutes, he had a flat piece of stainless steel that was thin enough to fit in the locking mechanism of the handcuffs.

With his free hand, he wedged his home-made tool between the locking mechanism and the teeth of the cuff. It took a bit of effort, but he managed it after a few tries. He slowly pushed in the shim, to further tighten the grip by one notch. The next step involved carefully pushing the shim back. The cuff clicked and opened.

'Child's play,' he thought.

Now he had to get out of the cellar. The walls were made of cemented concrete blocks that separated the individual units. The ceiling was covered in thick plastic sheets, perhaps for added insulation. Affixed to the ceiling were a pipe and an automatic sprinkler. Close to the door was a naked bulb, connected to a sensor: the light would automatically switch on when someone approached the gate from outside. In a corner, an electric wire, concealed in plastic tubing, ran from the ceiling to the floor, parallel to the metallic door. It disappeared just above the plastic skirting between the metallic floor and the grey cement walls.

Shiryō stepped onto a bar in the metal gate to reach the low ceiling and was soon able to dismantle first one, and then two of the plastic panels. They were both rectangular in shape and each about half a metre square. They were held in place with loose plastic retainers. Unfastening them had been easy.

He suddenly heard a voice he recognised in the cellar next to his, to the left.

'Hey? Can you hear me? This is Suki Lam from the Hong Kong Police.'

'Suki, you're still here! Do you remember me from last night?'

'Oh, my God! You?' she said. 'What are you doing here?'

'Let's just say Simon and I are no longer colleagues,' he answered.

'What do you mean? Are you locked in here too?'

'I am, but only for now. I've managed to un-cuff myself. Can you see my fingers?' he asked

Shiryō ran his arm along the wall, outside the metal gate. His hand reached the entrance to Suki's cell.

'Yes! My God! How did you manage to break free? These handcuffs are killing me.'

Shiryō did not answer this time.

'Tell me, do you still have some of that water they gave you in the morning? If so, could you slide the bottle in direction of my fingers.'

'I've drank about half of it. But why should I help you? You're the one who brought me here in the first place.'

'Listen, Suki,' he said, 'whether you like it or not, right now, I'm the only chance you might have of making it outside alive. I personally have nothing against you. All I know is that Chewbacca will be back here soon. If we ever are to escape from this place, we'll need to get rid of him first. They're planning to kill both of us, believe me. So, now, can you please send that bottle my way, I have a plan. But take your time! Since you're still stuck to that wall, you'll only have one go at this.'

Suki was in two minds. The man was a killer and answerable for at least four homicides, Simon Lo had admitted as much. On the other hand, her immediate priority was to survive. There would always be a time to catch him later. Besides, cooperating might be a good way to learn more about him, and it might even help when it finally came to arresting him. His voice was definitely familiar, but she still could not remember where, and when she might have heard it last.

'Okay. Move your fingers so that I can see them,' she said. 'I'll slide the bottle towards them. Be ready to catch it, I'd rather throw it with more force than is needed, than have it fall short. On the count of three, now: one . . . two . . . three!'

She threw the bottle across the cellar floor, but it stopped a few centimetres from Shiryō's fingers.

'Move your fingers slightly to the left if you can, you're pretty close,' she said.

'I can't go any further,' he replied. 'Do you still have your shoes on? Try to nudge the bottle in my direction by knocking it with one of them.'

Suki did as he had instructed. She untied one of her hiking shoes. With only one hand, it took a little longer than usual. She then tied her laces together to recover the shoe if her first attempt did not work, and threw it across the cellar. The bottle finally landed in Shiryō's hand.

'What are you planning to do with it, anyway?' she asked. 'And also, how do I call you? Since we're in the same boat now, we might as well get to know each other.'

'No names, Suki,' he said. 'And, to answer your other question, I'm going to fry that son of a bitch.'

CHAPTER 67

S HIRYŌ CAREFULLY CHECKED THE panels he had detached from the ceiling. They were solid plastic without any metal components. Perfect. He slid one of the panels below the bottom of the gate that closed his cellar and, with a strong circular motion, sent it gliding into Suki's own cell.

'The floor's made of metal, so you may want to crawl onto this,' he said. 'And keep your whole body on the plastic until I tell you it's safe. If your remaining shoe has a plastic sole, you may perhaps also want to sit on it, for added protection. And try not to hold on to those handcuffs too tightly.'

Suki caught the edge of the panel with her toes and laboriously dragged it towards her. After bringing it close to where she was seated, she did as he had just instructed.

Shiryō tore part of his shirt and dipped it in the water. He used it to wipe the floor clean where he had torn the piece of metal earlier. He erased traces of blood he had shed and also wiped the hard surfaces he had touched with his bare hands.

Shiryō positioned the other sheet of thick plastic on the metal floor, in front of the cellar gate and simply stepped on it. He also wore shoes with rubber soles. With the palm of his hand, he tapped forcefully several times on the plastic tubing that ran from the ceiling along the wall. He quickly dismantled it and exposed the plastic-coated electric wires. He pulled and tore the wires, revealing their copper inner core. He took care not to touch any of the wires, which were now live, and slowly emptied the bottle of water onto the floor, just outside the gate. The trap was set. Next, he called out loudly for U Pha.

The Burmese bodyguard was in the tasting room. It was conveniently located next to the lift lobby. It enabled him to control access to the entire floor and to turn away any unwanted visitors. The works were largely completed. The likelihood of a contractor turning up uninvited was probably slim, but it still remained a possibility. In the distance, he heard a voice shouting his name. The Japanese had woken up, sooner than he had expected. He clearly was not happy, which was understandable. Reluctantly, U Pha left his seat. He might as well take the opportunity to check on them both. U Pha was very large, but surprisingly agile for a man of his size. His job required peak physical condition, and he trained every day with weights in Simon Lo's well-equipped private gym.

He approached the cells from the right and first walked to Suki. The plastic panel on which she sat was grey in colour, as was the metal floor. She was still wrapped in the blanket and he did not notice anything untoward.

'Hey Inspector,' he said, 'are you now ready for a little chat?'

'I suppose I don't really have a choice. But I'll only talk to Simon Lo, not to you.'

'I see. Reasonable at last! I'll make sure to pass on the good news. He's at home on Stubbs Road, right now.'

U Pha slowly moved to the next cell, where Shiryō was held.

'You called room service?' he asked ironically.

He immediately realised Shiryō was no longer cuffed to the wall. He now looked straight at the Japanese, just across the metal gate, not more than fifteen centimetres away. Something was clearly wrong. He quickly scanned the cell for clues, but failed to notice he now stood in a small pool of water. As U Pha placed his hands on the doorway for a better look, Shiryō tugged on the plastic insulation to pull the wires towards the metal bars. When the live wires touched the metal, a bright arc appeared. The current instantly passed through U Pha's body, the effect compounded by the metallic floor and the puddle of water.

Within a fraction of a second, his muscles went into spasm. The skin of his hands blistered and became very red. His hair and skin started to burn, creating horrible scarring all over his face. His body further stiffened, as the electrical current quickly burned off increasing amounts of the chemicals present in his muscles. His body bounced forward and backward a few times, as if in a macabre dance. The contractions finally became so strong that his heart simply stopped beating. For a few seconds he remained motionless, before collapsing onto the floor like a beached whale. His body emitted a few dying sparks, as well as a powerful smell of burnt flesh and hair.

Shiryō had immediately curved his body into a ball to protect himself from burns. With a quick brush of the hand, he pushed the coated part of the wires away from the gate, breaking the circuit. He made sure they could not accidentally touch the gate again and waited for a minute, still standing on the plastic panel. He checked that the gate was no longer charged before calling to Suki.

'Are you OK?'

'I'm fine,' she answered. 'But what happened out there?'

'I electrocuted him. He's dead. He won't bother us any more.'

Shiryō felt U Pha's pockets. He soon discovered a set of keys, one of which fitted the padlock on his cell. He unlocked it and slid the door open, stepping above U Pha's body. He quickly walked past Suki's cell. It was now dark. The lights had gone off. But she still managed to see some of his face, only for a fraction of a second. She immediately connected the face to his voice, and now also remembered his name. Edwin Sutanto, the Indonesian next-door neighbour to Jasper Jersin. But right now, Suki thought it best to keep quiet about it.

'Hey!' she shouted, as he walked down the corridor, 'are you going to leave me here?'

'Someone will come soon,' he said, 'but where I'm going, I need to be on my own. And I must get there fast.'

CHAPTER 68

2:36 pm, Central, Hong Kong, 7 November 2017

A T LONG LAST, THE AREAS around CITIC Tower and Mong Kok had finally been cleared of protesters, but a portion of the Admiralty District still remained occupied. There were now only a few students left camping on the streets at night. But significant roadblocks to cordon off their location still sent cars, taxis and buses into a frantic merry-go-round. For some reason, the traffic jams seemed to be getting worse. No wonder a recent opinion poll had found that eighty per cent of the population was, at this stage, unequivocally in favour of a pause in the movement. For now, it also meant that Ethan and Charles were stuck solid in traffic, outside the Cheung Kong Center. It was one of the tallest towers in Central and home to several investment banks, as well as the city's securities regulator. It also housed the headquarters of a conglomerate controlled by the richest man in Hong Kong. The company had given its name to the building. Buses and cars progressed at a snail's pace all around their police vehicle. There was little they could do, even with a siren or blue light, until they reached Pedder Street. Then, they would finally be able to speed up on the highway towards Kennedy Town. They would drive in a loop around the west of Hong Kong Island towards Aberdeen, where Tin Wan was located.

It took them the best part of an hour before their Mazda 626 reached the industrial building. The car bore unmistakable police markings. They did not even have to flash their warrant cards to the security guard manning the barrier at street level. They turned right inside the car park and followed the ramp that led to the first floor, where they alighted. They walked to the reception and lift lobby. Andrew Li had said that the wine-storage facility occupied six entire floors, from the tenth level to the seventeenth. The thirteenth and fourteenth floors had been omitted, in an attempt to appease Western and Chinese superstition, respectively. They rushed into the service lift and rode to the seventeenth level. They planned to progressively walk down to the tenth floor, as they searched for any traces of Suki.

The seventeenth floor was still a bit of a building site, as were some of the other levels, and the electricity was playing up, the man in the building's control room had warned them. The access was unlocked, but they saw that all the major construction works had already been carried out. What remained to be completed was largely of a cosmetic nature. Armoured doors still had to be affixed and connected. For now, their panels simply rested on one of the walls. Magnetic cards and face-recognition devices would ultimately enable Simon Lo's clients to fetch their wine at any time of the day, or night.

'It looks a bit over the top for a wine storage,' observed Charles.

'Yes. But I'm sure some collections are worth millions, better to be safe than sorry,' said Ethan. 'You wouldn't believe what some of these people can buy.'

'Oh I know,' said Charles, 'I read about Henry Tang's auction.'

The city's former chief secretary, the government's second in command, was rumoured to have owned, at some point, tens of thousands of bottles of Burgundy. A sale of 810 lots of these by Christie's had netted him more than US$6 million in 2013.

Each of the 25,000-square-foot podiums was laid out around a central light well. They started walking clockwise around it. Entire corridors had been divided into individual cellars of various sizes, from forty square feet up to almost twenty times that size, each closed by a metal gate.

'It's freezing in here,' said Ethan, rubbing his hands in a vain attempt at warming them.

After a couple of minutes, they were back to their starting point. Suki was not on the seventeenth floor. They walked down one level and continued their search. She was also nowhere to be found on the sixteenth floor. The layout of the fifteenth floor, however, was different. It was obviously destined to act as the reception for the entire facility. Adjacent to the lift lobby, they found a huge cellar, about 2,000 square feet in size. It was fitted out with wooden wine racks of various sizes. Wine barrels, against which one could lean to sample a bottle or two with friends, and candles completed the traditional effect. But what was most remarkable was that the candles were all actually lit. It obviously signalled a human presence. Unlike on the other two floors, they could not switch the lights on. Encouraged by the sight of the candles, Ethan called Suki's name out loud, in an attempt to locate her. It did not take long for him to get an answer.

'I'm here! Over here!' she shouted.

Since there was no electricity, they patrolled the corridor, finding their way with a powerful Maglite torch. The fifteenth floor was still cool, but noticeably warmer than the other two levels they had already explored. They had now also drawn their service pistols. At first, all they found were empty cellars but, after the first turn of the corridor, they could tell they were getting closer, as Suki's calls became louder.

Their torch beams revealed a body on the floor. Ethan instantly recognised the distinctive mountain of muscle. U Pha's body was badly scarred and also had a strange, spiky hairdressing. There was an acrid smell of burnt flesh and hair in the air. Facing him, a metal gate was ajar. To the right, in the cellar next to it, and whose own door was still closed, they finally found Suki. She was wrapped in a blanket, all curled up towards the back wall.

'Thank God we found you!' said Ethan. 'Are you OK? What happened here?'

'I'm fine. I was freezing, but the cooling system went off as the electricity died. It's a bit better now,' she answered, with a nervous laugh.

'Simon Lo had hired an assassin,' she added, haltingly. 'He killed the bankers on Lo's instructions. I'm not sure what exactly happened but, after kidnapping me, Lo ended up locking him in the cellar next to mine. I guess they must have had trust issues.'

Charles fiddled with the padlock on the cellar door.

'Charles, I think the keys should be somewhere on the floor,' she said. 'I saw him throwing them there before he left.'

Charles soon found the key and opened the door.

'He was the man from the photographs, all right. He's deadly. He was handcuffed to the wall, as I am, but he managed to break free. I don't know how exactly. Next, he fiddled with the electricity system and electrocuted U Pha. It all happened very fast, it was incredible,' she added, visibly shaken. 'He gave me this plastic panel, which he broke off from the ceiling, to insulate me from the electric shock. He never tried to hurt me. Ethan, can you uncuff me?' she asked. 'My muscles are so sore!'

The handcuffs were standard police issue and she was soon freed. For a minute or two, she vigorously massaged her wrist and stretched her legs.

'My God, that feels so good! Anyway, he's gone now, but I managed to see his face. I know that man. I saw him before. He lives next door to Jasper Jersin, in the C Residence. I even spoke to him when I questioned the neighbours, the other night. His name is Edwin Sutanto. He's Indonesian. I'm sure he's gone after Simon Lo. U Pha said he was at home. We should head there right now and also put the house under watch.'

'Relax now,' said Ethan, 'we already have some people watching Lo's house. Charles, call them right now, warn them. But I don't want them to enter the property. Sutanto is obviously very dangerous. We must also call for reinforcements. Just ask them to let us know immediately if he turns up. I also want the C Residence in Causeway Bay put under surveillance. Put the SDU on high alert, ready to intervene. Knowing what he's capable of, it could all end up in a bloodbath. Suki, how long ago did he leave?'

She quickly looked at her watch.

'I'd say an hour or so, maybe more. He should already be at Lo's by now.'

'Do you know if he's armed?'

She thought for a few seconds, trying to remember.

'I don't think he is. I didn't see any weapon and I don't think U Pha had a gun either. Then again, I was stuck to that wall, so I couldn't see much from where I was.'

'You stop worrying, now. We'll get you to a clinic.'

'No way! I'm perfectly fine,' she protested. 'And I'm coming with you. I want to get that bastard.'

Ethan looked at her. She was brave, but she had gone through a lot already. On the other hand, only she knew what Sutanto looked like. It could prove invaluable if they were to get their man. Reluctantly, he agreed to her request.

'Charles, since you're on the phone already,' he added, 'request a crime-scene team to process the mess here, and please wait for them. Suki and I are going to Simon Lo's house. We'll meet the Tactical Unit there.'

CHAPTER 69

T HE TAXI DROVE PAST Simon Lo's house on Stubbs Road. Shiryō immediately identified a couple of police officers posted opposite the front gate. They seemed to be just monitoring the comings and goings of visitors. Shiryō calculated he had still a little time to act and instructed the driver to stop just outside the next building. He alighted a few hundred metres down the road, after a sharp turn. He was now out of the view of the constables. The house, one of only a few on that stretch of Stubbs Road, was surrounded by thick vegetation. Shiryō walked over the parapet that bordered the road and silently crawled into the jungle towards the mansion. His dark clothing blended with the undergrowth, acting as camouflage. The slope was steep and slippery. He could not walk very fast on the treacherous terrain. After a few minutes, he came in view of a thick fence that restricted access to the grounds of Simon Lo's property.

There were no cameras that he could immediately see, but some could well be hidden in the branches above. Razor wire at the top of the fence blocked access to the garden. Construction workers had dumped some debris nearby. Improvising, he found a thick tarpaulin to provide some degree of protection from the sharp blades. He gripped the wire fence, which was not electrified, and climbed. He was soon at the top. He threw a doubled-up, folded piece of tarpaulin over the razor wire and slid over it, sustaining only minor damage in the process. He silently dropped to the ground on the other side. Crouched, he listened for any signs of activity. A dog was barking in the distance, but he could not tell if it was within Lo's property.

He slowly progressed, hidden by the dense foliage, in the direction of what looked like an immaculately manicured garden. Within seconds, he saw a solitary Great Dane running at full speed towards him. The size of the dog was impressive. It had clearly been trained to spot and grab hold of intruders. Its jaws flashed a set of vicious teeth and it went straight for Shiryō's upper body. The Japanese dodged the bite and dove sideways, sliding on the bare earth. The dog, carried by its momentum, missed him. As it turned back on its tracks to attack again, it had lost much of its speed and impetus. Shiryō snatched its thick leather collar and seized its right hind leg. He wrestled the restrained hound with the full weight of his own body, and soon controlled the jaw, firmly maintaining it in a closed position. With his other hand, he sharply twisted it up, and then back, severing the cervical vertebrae, instantly killing the animal. Thankfully, it had all happened very quickly and quietly. It was unlikely to have caught the attention of the police officers on the road outside or, indeed, of anyone within the house or in the garden.

Shiryō stopped for a while, catching his breath. His hands had scratches from the dog's claws, but otherwise he was fine. He dragged the animal's limp body for a few metres and hid it under the bushes. He then walked towards the mansion, under cover of the tree line that surrounded the garden. There was a peaceful landscaped pond with *koi* carp, surrounded by a well-tended lawn. Beyond it was a rose garden. In the distance, behind the expanse of the garden, Central's skyscrapers provided a dramatic backdrop. He approached the house from its side and reached a covered garage. It was large enough to accommodate four cars. The door was not locked. He carefully peeked inside for any signs of human presence, but it was empty. He entered the low-rise building. Inside was a black Toyota Alphard. He also recognised Lo's Rolls-Royce. Both vehicles were unlocked.

At the far end of the garage was a wide workbench, with a variety of tools. Shiryō donned a pair of 3M plastic gloves, which he took from a pack of twenty, to avoid leaving any fingerprints. He then selected a bunch of large cable ties, a can of WD-40 spray lubricant, wire-mesh pads, a bottle of ammonia-based domestic cleaner and a roll of heavy-duty duct tape.

He next found a battery-operated nail punch, which was shaped like a pneumatic gun. It was a powerful, professional machine. It could sink large flathead nails to a length of 100 millimetres into the hardest of surfaces. He checked that the battery pack was charged. The nail magazine was also full. He placed his bounty in a medium-size canvas tote bag he had found at the back of the Alphard. He pulled his balaclava from his back pocket and adjusted it on his forehead. He quietly left the garage, bag in hand, and walked to the house.

The front door was also unlocked. He first found himself in a large marble lobby. It was flanked by two Chinese altar tables on which were displayed a collection of Burmese silver bowls, from which protruded colourful stems of orchids. No alarm had been triggered. As U Pha had indicated at the wine storage facility, Simon Lo was most probably at home. At the far end of the lobby, he saw what looked like a small service area. It housed the control system for the surveillance cameras that were strategically placed around the property. What they recorded was not watched live, but the footage could later be accessed as evidence in the event of a break-in. Shiryō was familiar with the system. He disconnected it and took one of the DVDs. He would destroy it later. There was no remote backup. Whatever had been logged over the last hour would no longer be available.

The next room, to his left, was the kitchen. It was massive, twice as large as the size of an average Hong Kong apartment. It included an array of flashy appliances. Shiryō saw four double-size wine cabinets with oak drawers. Clearly, Simon Lo liked to show off. A quick glance at the labels also confirmed his fondness for Bordeaux's finest and rare German Trockenbeerenauslese dessert wines.

Of more immediate concern to Shiryō were Imelda and Divina, Lo's two Filipino maids. They wore black uniforms and were busy prepping food for the evening meal. They both froze as soon as they became aware of his presence. The balaclava clearly indicated intentions that were far from friendly. The threat was further confirmed as they spotted the nail gun in his hand. In a low voice, Shiryō questioned them. They confirmed that Simon Lo was currently the only other person in the house. He instructed them to lie face down, flat on the floor. He secured their wrists behind their backs with the cable ties. The plastic was thick and they could not remove them unassisted. All the same, he doubled them, just in case. Lastly he gagged them both, with swatches of duct tape.

Satisfied that they would be unable to escape or call for help, Shiryō continued to explore the ground floor. He silently crossed a dining room that could accommodate twenty-four guests, and a sitting room. Both were decorated in classical style. Lo was a fixture at auctions, where he purchased more than his fair share of antique furniture and artifacts. Sculptures, pottery, delicate porcelain bowls and rare paintings decorated the various rooms. Beyond the sitting room was what looked like the tycoon's office, decorated in English club style complete with bookshelves, fox-hunting paintings and antique marine charts. Quietly seated behind an impressive mahogany desk, his face partly lit by an Anglepoise bankers' lamp, was none other than Simon Lo.

CHAPTER 70

I T TOOK SIMON LO a few seconds to register that Shiryō was observing him from the adjacent room.

'You?' he articulated, his eyes wide open in disbelief.

'Yes, me,' answered Shiryō. 'I'm afraid U Pha is dead. It wasn't pleasant to watch, believe me. I also killed your dog, Sniper,' he added.

He threw the small medallion that bore the canine's name onto Simon Lo's desk, where it rolled a few times, like a coin tossed for a game of heads or tails. Lo was livid.

'I . . . I agree I over-reacted. Clearly, I underestimated you. But I'm sure we could come to some sort of arrangement . . . listen,' he pleaded.

'That . . . I doubt very much,' said Shiryō, sharply interrupting him.

Still talking, Simon Lo carefully moved one of his hands out of view. If he could distract Shiryō for even a few seconds, he thought he might perhaps slide the desk's central drawer open. In it was a Beretta 92 semi-automatic pistol. It was fully loaded and ready to use. It was a massive gamble but, if he were quick enough, he might shoot a couple of rounds in Shiryō's direction.

Shiryō, however, had already spotted the tycoon's move. He grabbed Simon Lo's right hand and slammed it flat on the desk. He next punched an eighty-millimetre nail through Lo's hand with the pneumatic nail gun. The coated steel nail was designed to penetrate concrete. It slammed through the metacarpal bones with a thud, solidly securing the limb to the desk's top panel. Simon Lo screamed. The pain was excruciating. Methodically, Shiryō nailed Lo's other hand to the desk. Blood started to trickle from Lo's palms onto the leather top finish, the stain slowly expanding. Lo now sweated profusely. He panted heavily, in a full-blown panic attack, and was ready to pass out at any time.

'Please ... please stop this. I'll ... do anything ... look ... the safe behind me is open ... there's close to a million dollars ... in US bills. Take it all, but please don't kill me. ... '

Shiryō opened the drawer and recovered the Beretta. He was familiar with the firearm. It was an old model: production had ended in 1983. He liked the hard-chromed barrel and the open-slide design. It ensured smooth feeding and ejection for the 9 mm Parabellum ammunition. In Japan, it had been used by some of the police's special investigation teams. Next to the gun was a silencer, which he now screwed onto the barrel.

'Oh, I will take the money, of course,' said Shiryō.

He knelt to slide open the safe's door. Just as Simon Lo had said, it housed neat bundles of brand new US$100 bills. Shiryō picked up and emptied a monogrammed Goyard holdall that lay on the floor, next to the desk. On its side was a painted red and white stripe, above which were the initials SL. He would need to discard it later but, for now, it would do. To the tycoon's apparent satisfaction, he emptied the contents of the safe in the travel bag.

'See ... just take the money ... and leave me. It was just business, you understand. . . .'

Shiryō now faced him, from the other side of the desk, aiming the gun straight at his face.

'I fully understand. And as you just said, it was only business. Unfortunately, Simon, you had to make it personal,' he snapped.

He shot a single bullet into the centre of Simon Lo's forehead. The silencer muted most of the blast but there was still a ballistic crack. The ejection of the cartridge and the sound of a new round being loaded onto the gun's chamber further broke the silence. Lo's head jerked back as the bullet penetrated his skull, travelling at a velocity of more than 380 metres per second. The round shattered the frontal bone and reduced much of the tycoon's brain to a pulp. After a quick recoil motion, his head slowly slid down, as if to acknowledge what had just happened. His chin sagged, before ceasing to move altogether. Shiryō dropped the Beretta on the desk, and left the room. He walked towards the kitchen, still carrying the Goyard and canvas bags.

He helped the two maids onto their feet and instructed them to walk up to the first floor and lie down in one of the rooms without moving, for at least an hour.

He now needed to create a diversion to ensure a safe escape. From the canvas bag, he took the wire mesh. He stretched it slightly and placed it into one of the kitchen's high-end microwave ovens. He added the can of WD-40, discarding the red plastic cap. In one of the cupboards, he found a plastic container with a slide-on cap, which the maids would have used to mix salad sauces. He emptied the ammonia-based liquid cleaner in it and filled up the container to the brim. He slapped on the cover and it soon joined the other items in the microwave. He set the appliance on full power for an hour, but with a delay of two minutes, and pressed the start button. As the timer began to count down, he left the house and ran towards the tree line.

CHAPTER 71

4:11 pm, Central Mid Levels, Hong Kong, 7 November 2017

S HIRYŌ HAD ALREADY REACHED the razor-wire fence when the microwave oven turned on. Within seconds, the dielectric heating process ignited the wire mesh, projecting tiny sparks everywhere. After thirty seconds, the liquid cleaner and the contents of the WD-40 can had expanded significantly. The lubricant was principally made up of petroleum distillates. As it violently vaporised, bursting out of its red-hot container, it mixed with the boiling ammonia, combining into a highly explosive mixture.

By now, the hot wire mesh had created an electric arc. It instantly ignited the flammable concoction. The oven exploded with a deafening noise, exposing the designer kitchen to a violent shock blast and fireball. The windows were pulverised. Simon Lo's showy wine cabinets now lay in ruins. Hundreds of bottles had been reduced to broken glass and a sticky mass of rubber-like hot liquid. A thick black smoke engulfed the flaming kitchen. As it made its way across the house, it triggered the sensors of a hidden network of water sprinklers, adding to the clutter and confusion.

Shiryō heard the explosion just as he scaled the top of the fence. With a satisfied grin, he removed his plastic gloves and balaclava and walked down the slope in a northerly direction. Soon, he reached a steep, but paved, green trail. He followed it towards the harbour. He passed a panting elderly woman. She was climbing up the slope, with visible effort. Lower down, he saw an old Chinese man carrying a small bird in a wooden cage for its afternoon stroll. He did not meet anyone else along the trail, which he followed all the way to Kennedy Road. He crossed the road and took the steps down to Queen's Road East on the other side. There, he discarded the gloves, balaclava and CCTV disk in separate rubbish bins. He then hailed a taxi outside the Hopewell Centre, still carrying the Goyard and canvas bags.

The explosion had caught the attention of the police officers on guard duty. They failed to elicit a response after first ringing the doorbell. They next attempted to reach the occupants on the property's landline, but to no avail. The heavy smoke that followed the explosion left little doubt about what was happening, and they immediately called the Fire Services Department. One of the constables climbed over the heavy metal gate. He had just finished unlocking it when Ethan and Suki arrived in a marked police vehicle, siren screaming. Seconds later, they were joined by a van from the Tactical Unit.

'What's happening here?' asked Ethan, as he stepped out of the car, fearing the worst.

'We just heard a loud explosion,' explained one of the officers. 'As you can see, fire has also broken out. The FD's on the way. We couldn't get a response from anyone inside the house, so I climbed over to open the gate.'

Ethan now walked along the driveway, followed by Suki. They had both donned blue bulletproof vests.

'Ouch! I'm afraid we're too late,' she observed.

'It looks that way,' he said. 'What a mess! That guy's a one-man army,' he added, almost admiringly.

Part of what had once been an imposing home now bore all the hallmarks of a war zone. There was broken glass everywhere. Window frames had been propelled into the garden by the violence of the explosion. Flames and thick smoke escaped from gaping holes. For now, they prevented access to that part of the house where the kitchen had once stood.

'Let's go around, to the other side. The fire appears to be confined to this area. The firefighters are on the way anyway,' suggested Ethan.

'Do you think he could have booby-trapped other entry points?' asked an anxious Suki.

'I doubt he would have had the time. Most certainly, it was a quick job. The fire must have been a diversion,' he answered, as they reached the back of the house.

They saw a large sitting room through a sliding window. It was located away from the area that was now on fire. It was bathed by a thick shower falling from sprinklers, discreetly mounted inside a false ceiling. The window was locked.

'Step back,' he said, 'I'll break the window. I don't think it'll create a draught. We're very much at the other end of the property here, and there's water everywhere inside, anyway.'

Ethan picked up a large paving stone. It was wedged against one of the external walls to keep a long water hose neatly coiled. The window broke, in a shattering of glass, just as Ethan lowered himself in the opposite direction, further protecting his eyes with his forearm. Two scouts from the Police Tactical Unit went in first. Ethan and Suki followed them, stepping over the hollow metal frame.

With guns drawn they carefully explored the maze of rooms. In addition to the ground floor, there were also two upper levels, spread over several thousand square feet. They soon stumbled on Simon Lo, in what appeared to be his office. He was seated at his writing desk. His hands were strangely affixed to it, his head tilted down. There was a red hole in the middle of his forehead. He had obviously been shot at point blank range. On the desk lay what was likely the murder weapon, a shiny Beretta 92 pistol with a silencer still attached to the barrel. Water poured from above, almost directly on top of his head. It was like a scene from a horror movie.

'Oh My God!' said Suki, 'have you seen his hands?'

'Yes . . . back in Aberdeen, you said they had a disagreement. Looking at Lo now, I guess that was an understatement. Let's try to turn off these sprinklers, and then to have a look in the other rooms?'

Ethan and Suki heard a loud siren in the distance. The firefighters had arrived. They would soon put out the blaze. It was diminishing in intensity in any event, as the sprinklers gradually doused some of the flames. They continued to explore the rest of the ground floor. As before, heavily armed officers preceded them, the laser beams of their automatic weapons systematically sweeping all angles. All the rooms were empty. They next walked up to the first floor. There, they soon found the two Filipino maids.

They were in shock. Hearing the explosion, they had crawled crying under a bed, in one of the upstairs bedrooms. They were otherwise unharmed. They quickly confirmed the house was empty, except for Simon Lo, of whose demise they were evidently unaware. Ethan sent a Tactical Unit party to clear the top floor. Once the maids had recovered their senses, he interviewed them further, but they were unable to provide more information. He next called the SDU team and a request to storm Sutanto's serviced apartment in the C Residence.

The death of Simon Lo was always going to be big news. The matter would need to be handled with care. Ethan immediately telephoned the ACP to report on the situation. They both knew they probably had twenty minutes, at most, before journalists, photographers and television crews besieged the house. Everyone in Hong Kong knew who lived there. A statement would need to be issued. Outside, the firefighters' thick hoses drenched the main wing of the house with tons of water. Passing through it, a late afternoon ray of sunshine created a small rainbow.

CHAPTER 72

NIGHT BARELY FELL as the Special Duties Unit, Ethan's old detachment, prepared to break into Sutanto's flat. In the event, they never had to storm the premises. An initial enquiry with the management office quickly established he had already checked out. It was soon confirmed as a physical inspection of the unit was carried out. Instructions were immediately given for it to be sealed, but the C Residence's cleaners had already been at work, inadvertently erasing any fingerprints and generally making a mess of whatever other traces he might have left behind. It was doubtful that combing the scene for clues would uncover anything useful. Sutanto had cut his stay sort, leaving on the day following the arrest of Jasper Jersin. Un-surprisingly, he had not provided any information about where he might be going next. The man had now vanished.

All the border checkpoints were instructed to look out for him. An international warrant for his arrest was issued through Interpol. Fortunately, a copy of his passport had been retained on file by the management office of the C Residence. At long last, the police had a clear picture of the man. The Indonesian authorities confirmed that Sutanto had left the country some months before, to fly to Hong Kong. The Indonesian consulate in Kuala Lumpur had issued the passport in 2014. It was then realised that some of the supporting documents submitted at the time had, in fact, been extremely good fakes. In other words, Edwin Sutanto was not the killer's real name.

The credit card he had given to book his accommodation was traced to an account in Jakarta. It now stood empty. The money had been wired to another account in the Solomon Islands, and then onwards to another offshore location, where the trail went cold. The good news, for now anyway, was that he might still be in the territory. There were no records of him having left Hong Kong, at least under his assumed name.

Within a few days, the full extent of Simon Lo's involvement in the saga was revealed to the media. It was front-page news and both the Chinese and English language press had a field day, after weeks dominated by coverage of the pro-democracy protests.

As had already been the case in 2014, the various factions within the students and their supporters remained bitterly divided. They could not agree on the way ahead, a situation which the government quickly took advantage of to justify an increasingly repressive stance. Soon, the last roadblocks and barricades were lifted, and what remained of the sit-ins and tents disappeared. The second stage Umbrella Revolution had effectively come to an abrupt end.

The Goddess of Democracy and other pieces of street artwork created during the movement became collectable items, as famously had, in an earlier time, those of the protests in France in May 1968. The long-awaited election of Hong Kong's leader soon followed, pursuant to the rigid framework initially outlined by Beijing. Nothing whatsoever had changed. China's take on Hong Kong's Basic Law had prevailed: everyone entitled was able to vote, but a panel controlled by the Communist Party would screen all the candidates. A Hong Kong businessman with close ties to Beijing soon got elected with a moderate voter turnout. His election was immediately hailed by Beijing as a great victory for democracy and universal suffrage.

Investment bankers had lost much of their aura since the onset of the last financial crisis. However, for many, in a city obsessed with money, it was simply beyond belief that a tycoon could order the murder of brokers who had failed to agree with him. A regional lobby group for the banks saw an opportunity. It argued with a certain success that working in the industry presented clear and real dangers, on top of the ever more present risks of liabilities that came with executing Chinese IPOs. As an indirect consequence of the killings, the Securities and Futures Commission, the city's financial regulator, was informally instructed to show leniency and understanding in selected cases of misconduct.

'Heads they win, Tails you lose,' wrote a well-known maverick columnist in the *South China Morning Post*, in reaction to the financial sector's newfound lease of life.

Simon Lo had no children. The bulk of his estate passed to a nephew, John Tang, who had made his own mark in real estate, building high-end shopping malls in Taiwan. He managed to make himself popular by issuing an unreserved public apology on behalf of his family. There were also rumours of compensation paid to the bankers' families, amounting in total to well over US$20 million, although it was never confirmed.

One of his first decisions, as new corporate *tai pan* and leader of the family clan, was to demolish his uncle's house.

On it was soon built a low-rise, luxury apartment block, designed by the French architect Jean Nouvel. He proved unable to resist the commission, to compete head on against the Opus residence, built earlier by Frank Gehry only a few hundred metres down the road. Soon, the price per square foot of a flat in the new building, which had been christened 'L'Oeuvre', reached a high never before seen in Hong Kong. Initially for rent only, the 4,000 square foot apartments with panoramic views of the harbour quickly sold at auction in ensuing years, netting John Tang several billion Hong Kong dollars in the process.

Jasper Jersin was sentenced to life imprisonment, and jailed at the Shek Pik maximum-security prison, on the southwestern coast of Lantau Island. There, he wrote his memoirs, which got snapped up by a savvy publisher. The book became a bestseller and was translated into thirteen languages. Jersin married his lawyer a few years later, while still in custody.

Bee Fong, Morgan Roberts' vice-president, whose mastery of the *Dealogic* database had been instrumental in unmasking Simon Lo, was swiftly promoted to become head of Asia equity syndicate. In fact, the vacuum created by the sudden demise of four heads of syndicate that year led to an unprecedented merry-go-round among the various banks. Candidates for the vacant roles got poached, and then replaced by other hires, across the entire region.

Ashok Patel, to whom Bee reported, got headhunted. The dapper investment banker joined another blue-blooded us banking firm, after a leisurely gardening leave. He spent a good portion of his break selecting fabrics and undergoing fittings for custom-made suits in Savile Row, in London, and via Fatebenefratelli, in Milan. The lure of a partnership, and a package of six million US dollars, guaranteed over two years, proved hard to resist, even if much of it took the form of stock options with claw-back clauses attached. He soon got transferred to New York in a global role.

While Edwin Sutanto himself could not be immediately apprehended as part of the investigation, Simon Lo was as big a catch as they got in Hong Kong. Within months, Ethan Blake got promoted to the rank of superintendent, to head one of three divisions in the Organised Crime and Triad Bureau. Suki Lam, for her own part, was awarded the Medal for Bravery (Silver), for gallantry of an extremely high order. She continued to serve at the Crime Unit headquarters, later re-joining Ethan as a senior inspector.

CHAPTER 73

11:03 am, Chungking Mansions, Kowloon, 9 November 2017

SHIRYŌ HAD ESCAPED unharmed from Simon Lo's villa on Stubbs Road, but his immediate priority was now to leave Hong Kong. He had little doubt the Edwin Sutanto identity had been blown. By now, it was most likely that Suki Lam would have remembered it from their brief encounter at the C Residence. Checking out had been a good move, and he had been able to lie low for a while, but now he had to become someone else. It meant not just acquiring a new passport, but also one that could be matched, upon leaving the country, with a record of entry. Travelling on a Hong Kong document would require him to also produce a Hong Kong ID card. In turn, it would involve a fingerprint match. There was no way he could get around it. The solution was simple: he had to pass for a tourist instead.

Shiryō's contacts within Asia's underworld were extensive, and he knew just where to go. Early in the morning, he crossed the harbour on the Star Ferry and alighted in Tsim Sha Tsui. He walked the short distance from the ferry terminal to Nathan Road.

Five minutes later he entered Chungking Mansions. The building, built in 1961, comprised five blocks identified simply as A, B, C, D and E, and spread over seventeen floors. Initially, it had been a residential complex, but it had evolved over the years to include hotels, restaurants and a variety of shops. More than 4,000 people now lived or worked there at any one time. It was particularly well known among backpackers. Its guesthouses offered almost 2,000 beds, mostly of the lowest category.

Chungking Mansions was also famous for its unsanitary conditions and haphazard electrical wiring. Some twenty years before, a tourist had died in a fire and, a few years later, an electrical explosion had cemented its infamous reputation as a firetrap. The corridors were also home to a brisk drug trade and housed illegal immigrants from all nationalities.

Shiryō entered the main arcade. He found his way to Block B and rode the lift that served levels with even numbers to the sixteenth floor. As the doors opened, an intoxicating smell of curry and exotic spices assaulted his senses. A members' only bar, which catered to patrons from the Indian sub-continent, played Bollywood music at full volume. A number of them were noisily involved in an argument about something he could not understand. Shiryō walked passed them and, after a few turns, reached a green door, on which a small plaque read LOTUS TRAVEL AGENCY.

He knocked twice and let himself in. A tune of catchy zouk music played in the background, on a ghetto blaster. There were three occupants inside. One was a man in his thirties. The others were two girls, not much older than their late teens. All were black Africans. The girls had dreadlocks and one of them flirtatiously played with her colourful bin-bins, a set of beads she wore on an elastic string at the waist, above her pants. In

Senegal, the rustling of the beads as the women walked is said to strike men dumb with desire. The man looked up and addressed Shiryō.

'Qu'est ce que tu cherches ici, mon frère?' he asked with a heavy African accent.

'Bonjour,' said Shiryō, 'but I'd rather speak English, if you don't mind.'

'Yes we can! No problem, brother. What d'ya want?'

'Dominique in Tokyo said you might be able to help me.'

'I see,' answered the African gravely. *'Les filles, allez faire un petit tour,'* he added, for the women's benefit.

The girls stood up and lazily headed for the door, the considerable buttocks of one of them drawing the men's eyes as she walked out of the room. Once they had gone, the man spoke again.

'My name's Karim. What do you need? A gun, drugs, papers?'

'Karim, I need a passport, with a recent and valid Hong Kong entry stamp. It's better if it's from a country that doesn't require a visa. I'll only use it once, to leave the city. But it *has* to be genuine. I don't want any trouble at immigration.'

'It'll cost you.'

'Money's no object.'

'I might have something for you,' said Karim after reflecting for a moment. 'From time to time, tourists who travel on a budget run into trouble, and out of money,' he said.

His voice was slow. It sounded like a bedtime story.

'I pay them well for their passports, to help people like you,' he continued. 'They also agree to a delay, at least one or two weeks, before they report the loss to the police and their consulate. But, by then, no one really cares any more.'

'The photograph and age must be a reasonable match but, if the passport was issued several years ago, it's probably better.'

'Not a problem,' said Karim, 'I should be able to get you a British passport. Or maybe one from Canada or New Zealand. Actually, one from Oz might be even better, if you prefer an older one. Most countries changed the validity to five years some years back, but Australia still goes for ten years. I'll see what I can find. There are plenty of Asians from Commonwealth countries who flock to Hong Kong, before travelling to the rest of the region. . . .'

'It sounds perfect. How soon could you get something for me?'

'Come back this evening, with one hundred thousand Hong Kong dollars. And the price is *not negotiable,*' he added, insisting on the last two words.

'Even for friends of Dominique?'

Karim let out a loud laugh, flashing a set of immaculate white teeth.

'Man, you're a friend! That price already includes a discount,' he added, now deadly serious.

'There's something else I need,' continued Shiryō, 'an ICC, an international certificate of competence. It's an international boat licence. From the UK is probably best, for a forty-five-foot sailing yacht. Just like this. It's a colour photocopy, but I've blanked out the name. You don't need to know who I am. It has to be in the same name as the passport. Unlike the passport, I don't care if it's a fake, but it must look like the real thing.'

'Now, that might take a while longer to procure.'

'As I said, money's not an issue.'

'In that case let's say 125 K for the lot, brother. Come tonight, after ten o'clock. Together, we'll create a photograph for that one, to match the face on your new passport. I've got everything I need close by. I'm thinking it might perhaps be best to laminate the boat permit too. We can make it look like it's well worn, that way it will stand up better to scrutiny.'

CHAPTER 74

S HIRYŌ VISITED THE District Marine Office, on the third
floor of the Harbour Building on Pier Road, in Central.
There, he cleared immigration without a hitch. Karim had
been true to his word and had secured a well-thumbed passport
in the name of Michael Williams, from Australia. The photo
was that of a younger Asian man, but not unlike Shiryō a few
years before. Williams had arrived in Hong Kong in mid-
October. No questions were asked.

Shiryō also produced a general declaration, on a document
called Form MO 618A, together with the certificate of registry
for the boat he was about to sail, and a sailing notice. This
provided details of the vessel, of its life-saving equipment,
particulars of his intended voyage (Shiryō had written the
marina on the island of Phuket, in Thailand, as his destination), and communication equipment. He paid a fee of HK$58
for the issue of a port clearance. It would be valid for seventy-
two hours. The boat was registered in the name of a company
incorporated in the Cayman Islands, but all the paperwork was
in order, as was his British ICC licence, in its stained laminated

cover. Its owner was obviously a seasoned sailor. With his salt-and-pepper moustache and tanned face, Shiryō even had the looks of one.

'Have a great crossing!' said the immigration officer with a smile as he stamped his passport, adding a friendly 'Cheerio!' for good measure as he left.

Shiryō took a taxi to Hebe Haven, a yacht marina on the road to the Sai Kung country park. A number of sailing boats, speedboats, motor launches and junks were moored across what was a vast expanse of water, their masts and hulls gently bobbing in sync with the wavelets. The name of the place was well chosen. The anchorage was a tranquil refuge for mariners, away from the hectic city centre.

Shiryō hopped onto a small *sampan*. He instructed the captain to take him to a white Xc45 yacht, anchored on a swinging mooring, in the middle of the marina. She was a luxury vessel designed for long-distance cruising. As the *sampan* approached, carefully steering around other boats, the name of the yacht was revealed: *Strike Price*. A Hong Kong flag at the stern flapped gaily in the wind. She was the boat he had acquired several months earlier from Andrew Short.

The hull's deep sections provided good interior volume for accommodation. Shiryō had already spent three weeks there, since checking out of the C Residence. He would sail alone, a skill he had honed extensively at the naval academy at Etajima. A high keel weight ensured good stability. Twin wheels graced the wide aft cockpit.

Shiryō tipped the captain of the *sampan* and stepped on board. In the cabin, hidden in one of the cupboards, was a leather bag. It contained the cash taken from Simon Lo's home safe. He had provisions for a few days in the main saloon. The fuel and water tanks had already been filled. Without losing any time, he started the engine. He checked overboard at the stern to confirm seawater was cooling the 75 HP engine. He slowly cast off towards the open sea, powered by the three-bladed folding propeller.

Once the shelter of the marina was almost cleared, he untied the fenders and stored them in one of the four cockpit lockers. He removed the sail ties from the sixty-one-square-metre mainsail and tied them to one of the wraparound wire railings. He turned the boat head to wind and, after a quick look aloft to confirm all was clear, hoisted the mainsail as he eased the mainsheet. He hoisted most of it by hand, before taking the halyard to the winch to tighten it up. He secured the halyard to its cleat, coiled up its tail and eased off the topping lift. He later set the genoa, turned the engine off and adjusted his heading after a quick glance at the compass on the central instrument console.

The weather forecast was favourable, the typhoon season now over. There would hardly even be any need to tack along the route. Within three days, and an approximate distance of 480 nautical miles, he would anchor off San Fernando in the Philippines.

Glossary

aikido: a Japanese martial art that involves throws and joint locks.

amah: a female domestic helper who lives at her employers' home, often from the Philippines or Indonesia.

Apple Daily: a popular tabloid-style newspaper published in Hong Kong.

Ashin: an honorific title in Burmese, equivalent to 'Lord'.

cha: tea, in Chinese (and Japanese).

dai pai dong: an open-air food stall.

dojo: a studio where martial arts are practised.

DRC: Domaine de la Romanée-Conti, one of the most expensive wines in Burgundy.

ECM: Equity capital markets.

gaijin: a foreigner, in Japanese.

gweilo: a foreigner, in Cantonese and, initially, a derogatory word equivalent to 'foreign devil'.

Hakka: Han Chinese people from southern China, but with a distinctive language and traditions.

hamon: the visual result of the tempering process on the blade of a Japanese sword.

iaido: a Japanese martial art that involves fighting with traditional swords.

ichi, ni, san: one, two, three, in Japanese.

katana: a long Japanese sword.

kawaii: cute, in Japanese.

kendo: a Japanese martial art that involves combat with a long bamboo sword.

MTR: the Mass Transit Railway, Hong Kong's mostly underground metro.

nuguigami: paper made of soft, sensitive pulp tissue used to wipe Japanese swords.

PM: portfolio manager.

ramen: Japanese noodles, an increasingly popular dish in Hong Kong.

sampan: a small, flat-bottomed Chinese wooden boat.

sensei: a teacher, or master, in Japanese.

tai pan: a high profile executive and usually the head of a major trading company. Literally, 'big shot' in Cantonese.

tai tai: the Hong Kong equivalent of 'ladies who lunch'.

tamahagane: high-quality steel made of iron sand, used to forge Japanese sword blades.

tong lau: a low-rise tenement building in Hong Kong, built in the first half of the twentieth century.

triad: Chinese secret society, originally revolutionary, now criminal.

yakuza: the Japanese equivalent of the Italian *mafia*.

About the author

Philippe Espinasse spent almost two decades working as a senior investment banker in the US, Europe and Asia. He lives in Hong Kong, where he now writes and works as an independent consultant. He is also Honorary Lecturer in the Faculty of Law of the University of Hong Kong.

He has published several non-fiction books and has contributed articles to a variety of newspapers and magazines, including the *Wall Street Journal*, the *South China Morning Post*, the *Nikkei Asian Review*, the *China Economic Review* and the BBC News website. He also pens the 'Clawback' column on Asian equity capital markets for Euromoney's *GlobalCapital*.

Hard Underwriting is his first novel.

www.ingramcontent.com/pod-product-compliance
Lightning Source LLC
Chambersburg PA
CBHW032143190626
46814CB00005BA/1815